LOVE-ALL

James Leasor

James Leasor Publishing

elocution teachers could make it, but chill as wind blowing through cypress trees in a snow-covered cemetery. They could erase his harsh Marseilles accent; but no one could rub out his depth of power and ruthlessness.

'Let him go now,' Diaz said briefly. 'But pick him up later, when he's found what or who he's looking for. Over and out.'

He moved a second switch with his toe and the voice of the man on the rooftop spoke from the speaker. 'Receiving you. Our subject is now approaching the building. We will bring him in afterwards. Out.'

Diaz flicked up the switch before another watcher, sitting in the back of a cruising taxi, or, at least, what appeared to be a cruising taxi, three hundred yards ahead of the man walking up the promenade, could add his comments. But then, what could a hired hand say that could conceivably interest him? They were paid to carry out his orders, any orders, not to query them.

The man being watched was actually quite young, but he walked slowly, because it was hot and his feet were sore, and he felt almost unbearably tired, and so appeared to be in middle age.

His shirt was dirty and open at the collar. Several button threads had broken and he had no one to sew the buttons on again, and neither the wish nor the ability to sew them on himself. He wore sandals and faded jeans, ragged at the ends, and held up with string through the belt loops. His skin was curiously pale, almost luminous around the eyes, and sallow and sunken on his cheeks, and streaked with sweat. His hair hung down to his shoulders, greasy and dark as voles' tails, completely covering his ears. Around his neck he had a string of metal beads, with lucky charms that he fingered as he walked; a crucifix, a swastika, a horseshoe, a tiny, bent Maltese cross.

The sun hit him like a fist, reflecting the white pavement so he seemed to be walking into an endless, cruel vortex of heat and light and pain. He should have brought a hat, but then he'd never expected to have to walk so far.

His mouth was furred inside like a thrown-away kettle, and spittle had dried white and salty at the edges of his lips. He carried a scrap of paper in his hand on which the air hostess had written an address. As he passed each of the new blocks of flats facing the sea, he stopped momentarily to read its name; El Houmid, El Rashid, Le Roi House. Sometimes, the name was written with a huge red flourish in neon, like the signature of an electronic giant; other buildings had huge anodized numbers or signs in the unintelligible curlicues of Arabic script.

The farther he walked, the slower he moved. He would have given a lot for a drink, but really what had he got to give, apart from his time and his effort, to find this man, to tell him he'd like the price of a haircut?

After all, he was a sort of relation, wasn't he? He knew he was, but his mind refused to recall either his relationship or his name. The bastard would give him something, wouldn't he?

He wondered what would be the least he would get, so that anything more could come as an unexpected bonus. Blessed is he who expecteth nothing, for he is never disappointed. Maybe he would give him an iced drink, foaming over the top of a long glass, frosted by its own coldness. Maybe he would have a bath or a shower.

These were probabilities, almost certainties. Money, though, or an air ticket? These were improbable possibilities, for as a general rule, his own sometimes painful experience had proved that the richer people were, the meaner they became.

Most people he called on, claiming a tenuous mutual acquaintance or some equally slight link, by which to introduce himself, sent him on his way as quickly as they could.

They didn't like him around with his long hair and bitten fingernails and filthy clothes. One dour-faced Scotswoman in Colombo had actually told him he smelled. She was quite right; he did. His lips cracked in a half-smile at the memory.

This man would probably be no exception, but then insults were the price he accepted in return for money or some gift in kind; and this fellow was rich all right. Surely he'd pay him something, even if only to move on? Where he went did not really matter, so long as it was out of this beating, blinding, cauterizing sun.

The methedrine he'd been on for the past few months pumped round his veins with every labouring beat of his heart. He had a temperature, but then he'd probably had one for hours. Maybe he needed more methedrine - or less?

He'd never been in Beirut before, and he would probably never return. It had been pure chance that made the pretty airline hostess in Morocco hock him one of her own concession tickets in return for the morphine ampules he was carrying for someone else. He always seemed to meet people like her; it was as though he perpetually travelled through cities pulsating with warmth and crowds, while he remained marooned from them by his own overwhelming loneliness. He seemed to be desperately running away from something or someone; maybe from himself or the thought of the future, the shadowy recollections of his boyhood. Where was he going? And how long would the journey take?

'Herbert,' she'd said above the stereophonic din in the discotheque, 'you will do this one thing for me, won't you?' And she had told him about the man, even said he was some kind of relation. But maybe that was only to make him more eager to go and see him.

Now the thought of the good things that must stem from their meeting flushed all else from his mind, so that he had reached the building he wanted, and was walking past it, before he realized that the name over the futuristic canopy sheltering the American cars, iridescent red and green and blue, with their tinted windscreens and white-walled tyres and double radio aerials, was the name she had written on his piece of paper.

So. This was the place. Now for the flat, number 1792. He could remember that well enough; the date of the French Revolution. Floor seventeen, flat two. The nine was just a dummy digit to make the building seem more important than it was. Some people did that with their names and added an extra initial for the same reason: Harry S. Truman, for example.

His mind was clearing now, if he could reason like this. Maybe the drug was starting its secondary stage of euphoric goodwill?

He smiled happily, in this world but not not quite of it, and screwed the paper up into a ball. He would have put it in his trouser pocket, because he had been brought up to be tidy, when he remembered that his pockets had rotted away, so he pushed the ball of paper inside a belt loop.

His father had been tidy; neat and precise, like his hand-writing. His mother had been far more casual. It was odd to consider what the mutual attraction between them had ever been, but then why did a smooth cold magnet attract glittering iron filings? The attraction hadn't lasted, anyhow, for she had gone off with another man, not even leaving a note, and his father had gassed himself, and Herbert and his elder sister had been boarded out with relations.

He was in the hall of the building now, all grey marble and blue mosaic tiles, and large rubber plants with stems as thick as a man's wrist. It felt very, very cool. The inevitable piped music and the concealed hum of an air-conditioner were the only sounds. The difference in temperature from the sun outside was so sharp that Herbert shivered.

A commissionaire came out of a tiny office, and looked at him inquiringly. He wore a grey uniform. His cap had left a reddish mark around his forehead. He stood, fingering his prayer beads. Of course. It was Friday, the holy day for Muslims. That's why so few people were about; they were in the mosques.

friends. You had to know such a lot nowadays. That's why he took drugs. Just a little. Well, not much. He could stop when he wanted, of course. Only he didn't want. He needed something to give him a start; that little extra lift to make him equal with the rest, with the cleverer people. Maybe like this fellow, for instance?

'I'm just guessing,' the man said. 'My name's Carter - Jed Carter.'

Herbert held out his hand. The skin felt scaly and dry to Carter's touch. So the kid was switched on, as he'd thought. Mainlining. Poor sod. You could only go so far along that track, for death was waiting impatiently at the end of the line.

'Herbert Ellis.'

'Glad to meet you, Herby.'

Carter's hand engulfed his. Herbert winced at his grip and also at the contraction of his name; it was as though they knew each other well already. His father would not have approved of that too-easy familiarity. He didn't, either.

'Been here long?'

'Few minutes.'

'Cigarette?'

'No, thanks.'

Herbert shook his head and then wished he hadn't. He closed his eyes again to try and stop the colours flashing and flaming like a furnace gone mad in his mind.

He must find a drink somehow, and then another fix, or perhaps he shouldn't have any more? It was difficult to know on his own. Usually, he had someone stronger willed around to tell him, to suggest another shot, sometimes to give him one.

Carter lit an Egyptian cigarette, flicked the match with his nail neatly into the nearest round tub of sand. He watched the younger man through a faint haze of blue smoke.

'Did you ask for him downstairs?'

'Not for him personally. Doorman just told me to come up.'

'Well, it's no good hanging around if he's not in. The police in Beirut don't like it. Got a law against it, even. If there's a crowd of more than three, then everyone's got to keep moving.'

'I didn't know that,' said Herbert.

'You do now,' said Carter. 'Been here long?'

'Yesterday. I was in Morocco. Came on from India. Delhi. From Darjeeling.'

He was proud of the distance he covered, all without work; borrowing money, sometimes stealing it, or living off his sister.

'Ah,' said Carter, a wealth of understanding in his voice. He knew all about the constant traffic in hippies and other human flotsam to and from this former hill station. Marijuana and many of the softer drugs were so easy and cheap to buy from the caravans of carpet-sellers, who brought them in from Tibet.

Some Indian authorities were rather amused, in a quiet, totally unofficial, condescending sort of way, at the odd-looking representatives of the once-superior Western world who crowded their cafes, sipping tea cooled by goat's milk, willing to pick up a few rupees posing for photographs with rich tourists as part of the indigenous local surroundings.

Other Indians cultivated them. They made a lot of money from these drop-outs who had conveniently dropped out on the far side of the world - and then went home to smuggle drugs.

Carter wondered how well Herbert knew the man they had both apparently come to see. He wondered whether the man was also making money out of Herbert. He wondered a number of things.

The red 'down' arrow flickered above the lift entrance, and the doors opened.

'Let's go while it's here,' Carter said suddenly, making up his mind.

The doors sighed shut behind them, and they sank swiftly through seventeen floors to sugar-coated waves of George Gershwin and Manning Sherwin.

Beyond the plate-glass front doors in the entrance hall the bay blazed like splintered blue glass. A speedboat carved a huge white arc of foam through the sea, towing two skiers; one of them was waving. There was more traffic on the road now; the mosques must be emptying.

'I'll ask whether he's expected back,' said Carter. He called 'Shop' once or twice, but no one answered. Maybe the commissionaire was off duty, drinking green tea and puffing his narghiles, the Lebanese equivalent of the Indian hubble-bubble. If so, there was no point in hanging around.

'Where are you off to, then?' Carter asked Herbert.

The young man shrugged his shoulders listlessly. He had no one to see now. He dreaded going back into the heat, only to walk without an aim under the burning sun. He felt cool and safe in the womb-like marble cavern of the entrance hall. From outside, where the pavement lay bright and hard and hostile, the braying of the taxi horns cut into his brain like blunt knives.

'I've nowhere to go,' he said dully, for this was the truth; nowhere in the world.

'Come back to my hotel,' said Carter. 'We can have a cold beer together, and maybe a fix, if that's what you're after. What are you on?'

'Methedrine.'

"Very hard, eh? That may be a bit more difficult, but I'll see.'

They walked out together. Carter cut down the length of his stride to match the slower pace of his companion. Cars fled past them in an unending stream of noise and colour. Then one, slower than the rest, pulled in just in front of them. The rear door opened.

The commissionaire Herbert had spoken to looked out at them.

'Did you find seventeen ninety-two?' he asked Herbert in English.

'He's not in.'

'He'll be back, I think, in the afternoon. At this time he often goes to see friends.'

'Why didn't you say that before?'

"You did not ask. And, of course, I don't know, but I think. It is his habit at this hour on most days.'

'Are you going anywhere near the Avenue General Fouad?' asked Carter.

'Within five hundred metres.'

'Give us a lift then, will you? It's hard work walking in this heat.'

'It is my pleasure.'

They climbed into the back of the Mercedes, with its white, pleated curtain draped carefully across the rear window to keep out the worst of the heat, and transparent plastic covers over its cracked upholstery.

Another man was driving - a tubby man wearing dark glasses and a red fez. A string of ivory beads rattled round the rear-view mirror, above a plastic plaque of St Christopher on the dash. These fellows were taking no chances, thought Carter. They paid their religious dues like insurance premiums, on both sides of the street.

'You are visitors, yes?' asked the commissionaire.

'Just passing through,' said Carter. 'We come in peace and we go in peace.'

'Amen,' said the commissionaire. 'What a world it would be if all was peace.'

They digested this unlikely possibility for a couple of gear changes, and then Carter said, 'Shouldn't we have taken that right fork?'

'The driver knows a quicker way,' replied the commissionaire.

'He is my brother-in-law,' he added, as though this had some serious bearing on the matter.

They slowed for a line of camels, each carefully holding the tail of the one in front in its mouth, and then for a crowd of children pulling an old blind woman on a wooden trolley. Her face, framed in a black shawl, was lined as a tortoise neck, her sightless eyes peeled almonds in a parchment-covered skull.

'We're going away from the Avenue,' said Carter again, more sharply. 'I don't know this place well, but I do know that. What's happening? Has your brother-in-law gone mad?'

The driver's foot trod on the accelerator as heavily as if it were a beetle. The car bucked as more power poured through to the back wheels.

'We're missing the traffic,' explained the commissionaire, aggrieved. 'Relax. Enjoy the journey. We do not hurry here so much as you in the West.'

Carter sank back in his seat, as though he'd given up worrying about their destination.

They ran down into an intersection, where traffic lights flickered from green through amber to red. As they stopped behind one of the big, blue and silver air-conditioned Nairn buses that cross the desert to Damascus, Carter suddenly pulled back the door handle and opened his door.

'Thanks for the ride,' he said abruptly. 'But I must leave you. My mother told me never to go out with strangers.'

'But wait, you're wrong,' called the commissionaire, his homely face puckered with surprise at this extraordinary behaviour. 'We are not strangers. We are friends.'

But Carter was out by then, and running, his hair streaming behind him, like a Holman Hunt painting suddenly come to life.

He dodged between shoppers in the souk, up an alley lined with tinsmiths' stalls, and was gone.

'The English,' said the commissionaire in amazement, looking back at Herbert. 'You are often very strange. Do you want to go, too?'

'I'll stay,' Herbert said thickly.

His heart was labouring as though he'd been running up-hill for a long time; too long. He leaned back against the welcome coolness of the plastic seat cover, thankful just to be still, and out of the sun.

The car accelerated when the lights changed, and a wave of nausea swept over him as it rolled on a corner. He shut his eyes and clenched both hands to try and fight back the vomit that grew sour in his throat. He failed, but managed to reach a window and wind it down, and voided out into the street. Gobbits of green and yellow clung to the side of the car; sweat poured from his face, but he felt better, and leaned back against the seat, heart beating more slowly.

'Filthy English bastard,' said the commissionaire, looking at him with disgust. 'My car was cleaned yesterday. You are no better than a pig.'

'I'm sorry,' said Herbert, and he genuinely was. After all, this man had given him a lift, and was being kind to him, and so few people were kind. Tears of shame and self-pity pricked his eyelids like pin-points. He must have another fix. If he didn't, the next stage would be remorse and gloom, and then those terrible dreams when the floor became liquid, and the walls closed in on him and hands with fifty fingers tore his throat to pieces.

The car stopped.

'Get out,' said the commissionaire, roughly, all kindness gone.

Herbert struggled through the door. He almost fell on the pavement, and had to lean against the car, feeling the hot reassuring metal against the thin stuff of his shirt.

The driver looked at him, and he saw contempt and un-expected hatred in the man's eyes. He staggered back across the pavement, nearly knocking over a woman wearing a black veil that completely screened her face. He apologized, and his voice sounded shrill and nervous; people were looking at him.

'Come with me,' the commissionaire ordered.

'A drink,' said Herbert weakly. 'I must have a drink. I'll be better then.'

The man gripped him by the wrist so tightly that he cried out, wondering suddenly whether all this could be real, or whether it was only a fragment of the recurring nightmares he always suffered when the effects of methedrine wore off.

They went through a doorway, held open by a shadowy servant, into a hall, tiled in black and white marble squares like a gigantic chessboard, then up a flight of stairs lined with castor oil plants in stone pots and cacti with green fleshy leaves, thick as a drowned man's fingers.

Gilded angels and statues watched him with stone eyes, but were they real, or would he soon awake, with pounding heart and dry mouth, tongue swollen and leathery, his vision blurred, his skin aflame with fever?

'Stop!' he cried. 'Stop!'

But his lips could not form the word properly, so it was only a moan. He opened his eyes and leaned weakly on the commissionaire's shoulder, because he had to stand against something or he would fall, and as he leaned he remembered what he should have told the man who hadn't been at home in flat seventeen ninety-two. 'Can I have the money for a haircut?'

But why - and did he really need one? The thought clouded his mind, as though it was important, more important than anything else in his world.

When he opened his eyes, he was in a much larger room, with basketwork furniture and a trolley on big brass-spoked wheels, heavy with bottles, and a gold bucket of ice cubes. He would have given anything to have had one of those cubes melting in his mouth or pressed against his burning face, but as he moved to pick one up, the commissionaire pulled him back roughly.

Another, older man was sitting in a basket chair, watching him, legs crossed, a new cigar in his hand. His face was empty of all expression, showing neither disgust, distaste, nor even interest. Herbert might have been a shadow on a screen, a reflection in someone else's mirror, for all the concern that this man showed for him.

'Where am I?' asked Herbert weakly. The question was only the echo of a whisper in his hollow, porous throat.

'In my house,' replied Diaz. 'I would like to ask you some questions.'

'Drink,' said Herbert hoarsely, his mouth as dry as a hay thresher. 'Give me a drink.'

Diaz nodded to the commissionaire, who grudgingly poured some lime juice from the jug on the trolley into a glass, added some soda water and brought it back.

Herbert gulped down the drink, and although almost immediately his throat and mouth were as dry as they had been before, he felt slightly refreshed. He opened his eyes again and this time he could focus them more easily, and he could stand without support.

'Who are you, and why am I here?' he asked.

'Those are questions we might answer later,' said Diaz. 'In the meantime, you will answer some of mine.'

'Will?' repeated Herbert.

This was how older people always spoke to him. Do this. Do that. Get this. Go there. Come here. Never, Please, or Do you mind? The tone of voice as much as the words made all kinds of sullen, rebellious memories riffle through his drugged brain.

'Will,' repeated the man gently. 'What were you doing in that building?'

'I wanted to see someone.'

'Who?'

'A sort of relation.'

'His name?'

'His name?' repeated Herbert dully. He could not think of his name. He should have written it down. When the airline hostess had given him the number, he'd known the name, of course, for he was a relation, he was sure of that. But now the name had flown, like the hostess, to another country, maybe to another world.

'I don't know,' he said. 'I've forgotten it.'

The commissionaire hit him then in the stomach. He was not expecting the blow, and he sagged and retched and sank down on his knees, the lime juice in his mouth again, bitter as bile. The man pulled him up and kicked him sharply behind the left knee. He fell, and this time he stayed down on his hands and knees sobbing with pain and misery and bewilderment.

'Get him up,' ordered Diaz.

The commissionaire and some other man pulled him up and locked their left and right arms through his to hold him vertical. His head lolled on his chest, and a rope of saliva dribbled down his chin and over the front of his vomit-stained shirt.

'What were you taking to him? Why did you want to see him?' asked Diaz patiently.

'I told you,' said Herbert weakly, hardly recognizing his own voice through the flickering red mist of pain and nausea. 'He's a relation. Sort of, anyhow.'

'Have you searched him?' asked Diaz.

The commissionaire nodded.

'He'd nothing on him, sir,' he said. 'Only this, stuck in his belt loop.'

He handed over the damp folded piece of paper to Diaz, who unrolled it and read it.

'X-ray it,' he said, giving it back. 'And do the oxide tests, in case anything is written on it invisibly.'

He turned to the young man.

'Who gave you this paper?' he asked him.

'I don't know her name - a hostess on an airline. I met her in Morocco. We were exchanging drugs. I'd got some morphia she wanted, and she gave me a ticket. I flogged it for some methedrine. I need a fix every three days. At least.'

'So. What you are telling us,' said Diaz, ignoring this admission, 'is that some woman you don't know gives you a piece of paper on which, by coincidence, is written the address of a relation, whose name you have forgotten, in a country many miles away? You therefore go to see this relation. Did you know his address before?'

'No.'.

'When did you see him last?'

'I've never seen him in my life,' said Herbert.

Little fragments of memory, splinters from the past, were floating through his mind now, settling here and there, like snowflakes. He could see part of the picture, but only a small part. The insistence of the hostess in the open-air cafe; the smell of Arab food, chicken slices in saffron rice; the sharp unreal brightness of the stars through the rafters. Then the fix and the sudden, almost overwhelming sensation of peace and happiness as the drug poured round his body with every beat of his heart. The hours of dreams; then waking on the plane with a piece of paper stuck to the palm of his right hand under an Elastoplast strip in case he forgot his part of the bargain. And did he really need a haircut?

'You're being difficult and unintelligent,' said Diaz, drawing on his cigar until it glowed with a hard, red heat, the colour of pain. 'I trust you will regain your memory in due time.'

He nodded to the commissionaire, who hit Herbert once more, this time in the stomach. As he heeled over into the roaring, red whirlpool of agony, the man's fists pounded his kidneys like hammers. Herbert fell, and unseen hands pulled him up, only to knock him down again.

He could feel the blows, each one jarring his body, rock-ing his brain, making him cry out for mercy, but his mind was fuddled. He no longer knew where he was or why they were hitting him or what they wanted to know. If only he knew, he would have told them - anything.

He felt himself falling slowly, and gradually the pain from the blows grew less, and the sound of Diaz's voice with its persistent questions: 'Who are you? What is your name? Can you remem-ber any more now?' - seemed to be coming from farther and far-ther away, like words whispered against a rising evening wind over some endless, shining, moonlit sea.

Herbert wanted to help them, but first they had to stop hitting him, for each blow shattered his thoughts into jagged particles of pain, and he could not speak, even to beg them to stop.

Finally, almost gently, both the pain and the voice re-ceded altogether, and he felt nothing but a soft, ever-deepening dark-ness, and the strange, not unwelcome sensation of a timeless fall, sheathed in silence.

Diaz spoke to the commissionaire, leaning sideways in his chair.

'What's wrong?' he asked sharply. 'Is he going to talk?'

The commissionaire kneeled by Herbert's side. His knuckles were still raw where they had hit his teeth. He was breathing heavily; sessions like this always took a lot out of him; he was no longer young.

He put an ear to Herbert's mouth, listening to him breathe. Then he looked up, puzzled, there was no sound, no breathing.

He ripped open Herbert's shirt and pressed his flattened hand on the damp flesh where he imagined the heart should be, under the necklace and the lucky metal charms, but again there was no beat, no movement of the chest.

'No,' he said slowly. 'He's not talking. He's dead.'

CHAPTER TWO

It was that special hour of evening, when time trembles on its slender pivot between past and present, when summer mists linger longest over the tops of the tallest trees, as though reluctant to drift away, and a man likes best to be alone with his thoughts.

Jason Love, driving home after his last visit of the day, and facing an evening without a surgery, slipped the tiny gear lever of his Cord into neutral as he came over the crest of the old road that runs down from the Quantocks to the village of Crowcombe.

Nostalgia thickened the evening like the songs of unseen birds. The magic alchemy of sight and sound, the smell of summer on the trees, brought back memories of other evenings, girlfriends of long ago, and he allowed himself — as he did once or twice a year - to think, if only, if only ...

He slid the lever into third, and the two hundred tame horses under the long coffin-ended bonnet, blunt as a blue-nose whale, growled as they accelerated the two-ton car through the empty village.

He turned right along the main Minehead road, willingly letting the early summer rash of tourists race past him in their Minis and Minxes, burdened by luggage on the roof, shrouded in cellophane sheets that flapped like the flags of a retreating army.

It was Friday evening, and they had boarding houses and hotels to reach, fractious children to put early to bed, tele-phone calls to make to in-laws, all the ordered milestones of middle-class married lives to observe, while he had nothing but the prospect of a supper on his own; cold salmon, cucumber salad, an iced half-bottle of Dupre's Niersteiner, with strawberries from the garden and coffee black as a blackamoor's backside.

His housekeeper, Mrs Hunter, had already prepared all this for him, for every Friday evening she and her husband took themselves off to Taunton to the pictures.

He turned the car off the main road rather regretfully, feeling that the action was in some way symbolic, an opting out from the rushing river of time to a backwater of his own choosing.

The lane wound between high banks, over intersections where white wooden signposts with fingers carved on the end, pointed to quaintly named places, such as Egypt and Alamein and Over Stowey.

He ran the big white car in gently through the gates of his garden, past the surgery on the right, on to the courtyard paved in the peculiar Somerset fashion of cobbles on end, like rows of grey, hard-boiled stone eggs. He stopped, switched off the engine, and after the beat of the three-inch dual exhaust, silence sang in his ears like the music of the spheres.

He paused for a moment, lit a Gitane. The lawn had been newly cut, and, the scent of grass lay soft on the evening air. All senses, sounds and memories, seemed to focus at this one moment in time, as though the whole world was indeed standing still before swinging on again into darkness and another day.

Maybe he was over-tired to feel this way? Certainly, he was looking forward to a fortnight's holiday which began on the Monday. A locum was arriving on Sunday afternoon, and then for fourteen days he could forget the pressing needs of Mrs Cartwright at Old Manor Farm for her red pills, or Colonel Blenkinsop with his wish for even stronger sleeping capsules, and the medicinal whims of all the other regulars, whom he knew so well and who assured him earnestly that life without his medical ministrations would be impossible; and who, within hours, would be assuring his locum exactly the same thing, with exactly the same sincerity.

Love went into the house, switched on the answering machine in case any messages had come in during his rounds. He heard his own voice say: 'Dr Love is out. If you have a message for him, please speak now.'

The machine hissed, and a disembodied metallic voice began to talk. It belonged to Eddy Miller, who owned the local garage, and who now informed him that two new Goodrich 6.50 x 16 tyres for the Cord had arrived at last, and he could fit them whenever the doctor could spare the car.

Then Mrs Cartwright, as he expected, had suddenly discovered that she had no red pills, not one anywhere, Doctor, and would he please put a prescription on the bus next morning, so that she could collect it from the conductor? Then there was a third voice - one he had not heard before - a woman's voice, which he played back twice to try and place.

'This is Mrs Wilmot from Esdaile House. I have not telephoned you before, Doctor, although we are on your list. We only arrived here about six months ago. I wonder if you could come and visit my daughter? I think she may be sickening for something.'

He played one or two more messages of no importance or interest and then stopped the machine, crossed to the filing cabinet and took out the card for Mrs Wilmot.

Caroline Wilmot, 27. One daughter, Sandra, aged 7. Husband, John Wilmot, 47.

Love could not remember ever meeting any of them, but he knew who they were. Esdaile House stood eighty yards back from the road, screened by trees and a high hedge of rhododendrons, which blazed like a wall of purple flame through the early summer, so there had not been much chance of seeing them casually if they were in their garden.

He had heard in the village that they had come down from London, but no one knew much about them; they were rarely seen in the village shop.

'Sickening for something' was an old-fashioned phrase that he did not greatly like. It could mean the onset of a cold - or cancer. He preferred parents to tell him at least some of the symptoms - a headache, temperature, spots, or whatever.

He glanced down his list of calls for the morning. None of them lay in the direction of Esdaile House. He might as well drive up there this evening. After all, he had nothing better or worse to do, and it could be interesting to meet some new people.

At half past eight, Mrs Hunter rang. They had not enjoyed the picture and so had come out early. She was worried in case she hadn't left the answering machine switched on.

Love assured her that she had, and then, on an impulse, mentioned Mrs Wilmot. His housekeeper's local intelligence service was as good as anything he had ever encountered in MI6, and, in some aspects, a great deal better.

Mrs Hunter sniffed into the receiver.

'Well, she's pretty enough - if you like them like that'

'Some do. Probably Mr Wilmot, for one.'

'And the rest, Doctor. He's at least twice her age. She's got a fancy man of her own who's around when her husband isn't. In a red Italian car. Alfa something or other.'

'Romeo,' supplied Love.

'That's a right name for him,' chuckled Mrs Hunter. "Romeo! Don't say I care for her much myself - or for him.'

'Tell that to your husband,' Love advised her cheerfully, and hung up.

He ate his supper quickly and went out to his Cord. He drove through the village, past the pub with the handful of little cars parked outside it and the flowers gay in the blue window boxes, past the smithy - now disused and about to be converted into a home for a retired bank manager from the Midlands.

Soon, he thought rather sourly, whole villages in the West Country would be populated by retired professional people with careful ways and tiny neat gardens, taking over cottages when the labourers moved out and their families went off to towns or into council houses.

A neat, black, metal fence bordered the curving drive that led from the entrance gates of Esdaile House. A pony — possibly Sandra's - stuck a friendly, woolly and inquisitive head over the fence at him as he went by. A line of washing was strung out behind the lodge, beyond a nest of grey aerials. Whoever lived there, thought Love, should be sure of a good TV picture with that forest of antennae.

He stopped the Cord outside the main house. It was very much smarter than he remembered it when he used to visit the late owner, a widow in her eighties. But then its condition had been so run-down, with gutters blocked and windows cracked and drive overgrown, that almost any change would have been an improvement.

White shutters now framed each window, a polished brass door knocker, shaped like a dolphin, hung by its tail on the door and on either side of the porch, stone urns were reddened by geraniums.

The front door opened. A woman in a dark-green nylon overall stood to one side as he went in. She had a dark, sallow face; possibly Spanish or Southern Italian.

Another woman was coming down the stairs. Her skin was also brown, but with a rather more expensive tan. Nassau or Bermuda or maybe a few weeks in Porto Santa Stefano had supplied that smooth patina. She wore a blue Pucci dress; her hands were slender and smooth as its silk. Beneath the dress, her young breasts bobbed invitingly.

'Dr Love?' she asked.

'None other,' replied Love, moving his eyes up to her face. 'Mrs Wilmot?'

She nodded.

'It was good of you to come out so quickly,' she said.

But it wasn't really good at all, it was his job. The response was mechanical.

'Where's the patient?' he asked her.

'Up here.'

He followed her up the stairs, their feet making no sound on thick Wilton carpet, the colour of Beaujolais. The wall-paper, the eggshell paint, the gilded fittings, were all new, all untouched by time, unscuffed by children's shoes. This was more like a showroom than a house, the sort of place a rich man had, more to show he was rich than because he liked to live like this.

'What's the matter with your daughter?' he asked. 'Has she any particular symptoms?'

'You'd better see for yourself.'

She held open a door for him on the landing. He passed her in a mist of Chanel. He was inside a child's bedroom, painted pale blue, with cut-out pictures from magazines pasted on the walls. A cupboard door was half open, showing a glimpse of expensive toys crammed in on top of each other with casual disregard.

Mrs Wilmot stood behind him. Was she smiling at the child - or frowning at her, trying to will her into some unusually good behaviour? He turned around to see her face, but by then she appeared as beatific as a Botticelli angel.

A little girl was sitting up in bed in the corner. She had been reading, and wore her long blonde hair in two coils on either side of her head. She looked adult and surprisingly old-fashioned - a refugee from Little Dorrit or some other Victorian morality tale where children always appeared to be serious and quiet and well-behaved; not at all as Love knew children in the village, noisy and rough and shouting.

He sat down beside the bed, put out his hand to take her pulse. Seventy-seven; nothing wrong there. He examined her tongue.

Clean and red; full marks in that department, too. Sandra's eyes watched him with a grave, almost clinical detachment. He opened his case, shook the mercury in his thermometer down to 95°, put the end under Sandra's tongue. All this in silence, with the mother watching, as though it were some kind of charade.

He sat for a minute by his watch, then removed the thermometer. As he expected, her temperature was normal.

'I hear you don't feel very well,' he said, closing his case.

Sandra looked surprised, almost guilty, and gave a quick glance at her mother before she replied.

'Don't I?' she asked meekly.

'Well, you should know better than anyone else. Do you feel sick? Any tummy-ache? Headache?'

The girl considered each of these possible alternatives and then rejected them all.

'No,' she said. 'I feel well. My teddy had a tummy-ache last Tuesday, though.'

'Had he now?' said Love. 'Perhaps I should be treating your teddy and not you?'

The girl's eyes flashed briefly towards her mother again, before she replied.

'Perhaps you should,' she agreed, and smiled at the thought, and then seemed to relapse into her own world, re-mote, inviolate.

Love stood up, turned to Mrs Wilmot.

'Perhaps we could have a word downstairs, Doctor?' she suggested, and led the way out of the room.

Years in general practice had convinced Love of the truth of the old Lancashire saying, 'There's nowt so strange as folk.' There was something strange here - but what? The girl was perfectly healthy. Had he somehow misread the message on the answering machine? Could the answering machine itself have gone wrong and missed a line of Mrs Wilmot's message? Both were possible, but unlikely.

He followed Mrs Wilmot into a study, unexpectedly gay with white and gold striped paper. Two sturdy cherubs on a mantelpiece held up an ornate ormolu clock and made a good job of it between them.

Mrs Wilmot walked to a bookcase, heavy with the leather-bound backs of books, each lined with gold. She pressed a concealed button and the whole facade swung away to reveal a rather distasteful bar.

'A drink?' she asked him.

'As I'm not on duty now, yes,' he said. 'Dalmore Highland Malt, if you have it.'

'We have it. Twelve different brands of blended whisky, six of malt. Including yours.'

She said this so casually, with nothing whatever boastful about it, that the words lacked all taint of the nouveau riche. It was simply a statement of fact.

She poured two drinks, clawed up cubes of ice from a gold bucket with gold tongs. They sat down.

'There is nothing whatever wrong with your daughter, Mrs Wilmot,' Love said. 'But I think you knew that when you rang me?'

Mrs Wilmot raised the glass to him in silence. They drank. Her other hand began plucking nervously at the brocaded arm on her chair.

'She wasn't entirely herself when I rang,' she said defensively.

'When are any of us entirely ourselves?' asked Love rhetorically.

Mrs Wilmot said nothing.

'I asked you before about her symptoms,' he went on. 'You told me to see for myself. Well, I've seen. I don't think she ever had any symptoms.

'Was there maybe something else you wanted to see me about, but you didn't like to mention on the telephone - or to my answering machine?'

Sometimes people, especially shy or complicated people, preferred the long way round to the short way home. They were incapable of stating the real worry, the hidden reason for asking the doctor to call. It had to be prised out of them like a reluctant winkle on the end of a pin, and sometimes in more than one visit. He sat, watching her.

"Yes. There was a reason,' she admitted at last. 'You're quite right, Doctor. I didn't want to explain it to a machine. You never know who's going to hear these things. It might be someone who would pass it on.'

Her face wrinkled in distaste at the thought. It was clearly anathema to her that anyone might know something about her or her business.

So what was her business? Love wondered as he waited for Mrs Wilmot to go on. Could it be anything to do with the man Mrs Hunter had called her fancy boy? And what was Mr Wilmot's business, which must be so prosperous that

it could provide a home as exquisite as this, and yet with apparently no sign of him? Was he dead, or divorced?

'No one can overhear us now,' he prompted her gently.

'I know,' she said, 'that's why I asked you here. You're quite right, there's nothing wrong with Sandra, thank God. She's a healthy child, and strong as a lioness. I wanted to see you, not about her, but about her father.'

'Her father?' repeated Love. So there must be a Mr Wilmot. 'What's wrong with him?'

'I don't know,' she said.

'Well, where is he? In bed here?'

She smiled. Maybe she was thinking about the man with the Italian car.

'If he were, I'd have no problem. No. He's in the Middle East.'

'A businessman?'

'Yes and no. He is a businessman, but he has rather retired from active work.'

'Well, how can I help you? What is the problem?'

'I want to know where he is,' she replied simply. 'And how he is.'

'But how can I help you here, in this remote village, if he's in the Middle East? I've never even met him.'

'We're living apart,' she admitted. 'But that's not because we want to.'

'Look,' said Love, 'We're just fencing with words, you and I. If I can help your husband in any way I'd obviously like to do so, for he's technically my patient. But unless you can tell me more, I can't help either you or him. You must see that, Mrs Wilmot?'

'I do. I think he may be in bad trouble. First, Doctor, his name isn't really John Wilmot - it's Jan Wodousky. He's Polish. Mother was Jewish, father a Catholic. Both died in the Warsaw uprising. He came over here after the war when he was about twenty, hardly able to speak any English. There's a strong Polish community in East London and they helped him to find a job with a Polish estate agent.

'He specialized in buying old houses and splitting them up into flatlets. John - I call him that now - stayed for a couple of years until he had made enough contacts to branch out on his own.

'He found someone who would lend him the money to do one conversion. And when he sold that at a profit, splitting the profit with his backer, the word went round that he was trustworthy, and other people wanted to back him. Soon he was buying streets of houses, not just one or two.'

'He must be very rich?' said Love, because he could think of nothing else to say.

'Yes. Anyway, after some years of this sort of development, we met and married. We spent our honeymoon in Spain, which wasn't opened up then. It was a perfect holiday place - cheap food and wine, plenty of sunshine, warm sea. All it needed was people. He was one of the half-dozen or so who foresaw the boom in cheap holidays and he started to build hotels, then apartments and nightclubs. The lot.'

She paused.

'What happened then?' asked Love, because something must have happened, something unpleasant. Otherwise he would not be there now, but presumably Mr Wilmot would.

'I'll tell you what happened,' she went on. 'John began to get anonymous letters. Then phone calls. Then some MP stood up in the House and asked questions about foreign property developers, exploiters, and so on. Money became harder to borrow. What had been very easy for him, within just a few months grew very difficult.

'He'd be promised backing and go ahead, and then the backers would suddenly drop out. He lost deals because he simply couldn't afford to take up the options.

'He began to get depressed. He thought he'd lost his touch. All these worries, plus the strain of borrowing money at changing exchange rates, being promised goods, materials, bricks, whatever, by a certain date, and then having to wait weeks beyond that date until they actually arrived, nearly broke his spirit. At least, that's what the psychiatrist said.'

'Which one?'

'Dr Jackson.'

'Ah, yes. I know him. He was just starting as a consultant when I was a medical student.'

'Really? Well, he advised John to give up work for six months. To do nothing. So we came down here. What made it worse for John was that he was right on the edge of negotiating his biggest deal - opening up a hundred miles of coast in North Africa, virtually from Alexandria to El Alamein.

'The beaches there are absolutely fantastic. The Mediterranean's warm, and you've got a good coast road and water, and the locals are very keen to have the place developed so they can get more foreign currency from tourists.'

'I see all that,' said Love impatiently. 'But why is he in trouble now?'

'You asked for the background, Doctor. I thought it easier to give it to you in detail now rather than have to keep coming back to it.

'Quite suddenly, the anonymous letters increased. So did the phone calls with threats of being deported. All that. We went to the police, but the calls were coming from telephone boxes and couldn't be traced. John grew very morose and depressed.

'He'd never become a British subject. He'd always meant to do so, but he is proud of his own country, and this was quite a step. He kept putting it off. Now he began to worry in case whoever was persecuting him like this could really get him deported.

'I told him he couldn't be put out of England just like that, after being here for about twenty-five years. His lawyer told him the same thing. So did his accountant, and even Dr Jackson, but somehow no one could reassure him.

'One day, John told me he couldn't stand things any longer. I said, if he felt like that he should go away for a few months, and maybe when he came back this pestering wouldn't start again. Dr Jackson seemed to think this a good idea, so he went. To Beirut. He's been out there ever since.'

'As John Wilmot?'

'No. Under the name of this house - Esdaile. In a flat. We telephone each other twice a week, but I never call him by his real name on the phone in case anyone is listening in. I write to him care of the main post office in Beirut.'

'Where do you think he is now?' asked Love.

'He should be in his flat in the El Kantara Building. In the Avenue de Paris, near the sea.'

'But you don't know?'

'No. I've had a fixed time call in every hour for the last five days and nights, but there's no reply. I've sent ten pre-paid cables to the post office, but there's no answer.'

'What do you think has happened?' asked Love.

She shrugged.

'He may have lost his memory, or he may have been hurt in a street accident. If he were taken to hospital, no one would know his real name or who he is, and so they couldn't contact me or anyone else about him.'

This seemed reasonable enough. Too many hospitals all over the world would have one patient with no next of kin, no visitors; someone who obstinately remains an impersonal number on a card, a figure in a column of statistics, because no one cares whether they are cured or killed.

'But how can I help you here in Bishop's Combe?'

"You can't help me here at all, Doctor. But you could -possibly - if you were in Beirut.'

'In Beirut?' repeated Love. 'But that's a couple of thousand miles away, and I'm off on holiday on Monday. To France. St Raphael. I go there every year at this time.'

'Then why not make a change, Doctor. And, after all, Lebanon has very strong French connexions. It was a French possession until the war.'

'I know,' said Love. 'But why don't you contact the local police? Or the British Embassy? Even the missing persons bureau. Can't any of them help you?'

She shook her head.

'The Embassy wouldn't know him, for he's there under another name. I've already made some inquiries, anyway, through a friend in the Foreign Office, and we've drawn a blank. My only hope is to send someone out to look for him.'

'It seems a very expensive way of finding out.'

'Have you anything better to suggest?'

'If I were in your position, Mrs Wilmot, I'd wait for a little longer. He may be away from Beirut for a few days on business.'

'He has no business to do there,' she said dully. 'I do know that.'

'Then maybe he's off on holiday, or moved his flat. Perhaps he's written telling you, and the letter's been lost in the post. There are all sorts of reasonable explanations. And I find that the simplest explanation of a problem is often the right one.'

'Our outlooks must be different, then, Doctor. It's been my own experience that the most unlikely explanation for something is invariably the true one.'

The conversation was turning like a painted fairground swing, getting nowhere. Love finished his drink. She poured him a second. He didn't refuse it.

'Have you been in touch with Dr Jackson about this? After all, he's treating your husband. He must know whether he's likely to have blackouts, maybe, or loss of memory?'

'He takes the same view as you, Doctor. That there's some simple explanation. Maybe it's even another woman.'

It could be that, thought Love. Mr Wilmot would not be the first or the last husband to keep out of contact with a wife for such a reason, especially if he knew that his wife had other outside interests herself. He finished his second drink and stood up; this was territory he did not want to explore. He had enough problems with other patients over their matrimonial complications without seeking any more.

'I'm sorry, Mrs Wilmot,' he said firmly, 'but I don't think that I can help you.'

She stood up and faced him, and he could see that the skin around her eyes was stretched tight as parchment on a drum; she was more worried than she appeared to be. Maybe he should be treating her instead of examining her child or discussing her absent husband?

'I don't think I've made myself clear,' she said. 'What I'm offering, Doctor, is an expenses-paid trip for you to Beirut. Plus a fee of, say, five hundred pounds.'

'That is very generous of you, Mrs Wilmot, and I appreciate it. But, as I've already told you, I'm booked for France.'

'This is a matter of life and death.'

Love repressed a smile. In the last analysis, all human experience must be a voyage between these two extreme and ultimate poles. But was this the last analysis?

'Even if I were to go, how could I possibly find your husband if he isn't in his flat? I don't even know what he looks like.'

'I'll give you photographs of him.'

'But what if he's grown a beard, or dyed his hair? Old photos wouldn't be much good then, would they?'

'No. But I don't think he's done either of those things. I think he may be ill or he's had an accident. All I ask is that you call at his flat, and ask the porter if he's there. Maybe, as a doctor, you could also visit the local hospitals in case anyone of his description has been admitted with loss of memory or run down by a car.'

'If it's so simple,' asked Love, 'why don't you go yourself?'

'I've no one to leave Sandra with.'

'That problem shouldn't be impossible to solve. Mrs Hunter, my housekeeper, might be willing to look after her if you've no relations who could take her for a few days. Because, if what you tell me is true, the whole inquiry will only take two or three days at the most.'

'But it's not quite as simple as that,' she said reluctantly.

'Ah,' said Love. 'Then there's something else?'

She looked up at him defensively somehow, like a young deer at bay caught in the headlamps of an unexpected car on a country road, frightened, yet determined not to show fear against something it did not understand.

In every problem he had ever heard, in every case when someone had sought his help over an apparently simple matter, there always was something else. How rarely did anyone tell all the truth, or even a major part of it? It was bent, shaped, moulded, shaded, sometimes concealed entirely under a patina of self-deception and shame and lies, so as to present what the teller imagined would be a better picture of themselves.

Even what Mrs. Wilmot would tell him now would still be only a part of this something else, perhaps not even the most important part, but as little as she could admit without compromise or too much loss of pride.

'There's a personal reason why I can't leave,' she said. 'I have to stay here for the next two weeks. It's a promise I've made - to Sandra. She's been very unsettled by her father going off for so long.'

Her explanation sounded unconvincing. Love was unconvinced. More likely, the boy friend had suggested a week or two away somewhere together. He could think of half a dozen places where he'd like to spend a week with Mrs Wilmot - if he wasn't her doctor, if she wasn't married.

'I know I could go to a private detective,' she went on, 'but where can I find one I could trust? With a doctor, it's different. Will you go? I'm sorry to be so insistent, but I'm fey about some things.

And I feel my husband's ill or in danger.'

'Let me have a word with Dr Jackson and see if he's any other suggestions,' said Love.

'Say you will go?' she asked hopefully.

'No,' he said. 'But thanks for the drinks. And I'll ring you when I've spoken to Dr Jackson.'

Love walked out to his car. She watched him leave, heard the beat of the two heavy exhausts die away through the lanes, listened for the faint reassuring rumble of the evening train to Exeter run through the cutting miles away. Then she came back inside the hall and closed the door.

She stood for a moment behind it, as though unsure what to do next. She poured herself another drink, and stood looking out over the drive and the lawn beyond, yet not seeing them.

She caught sight of her face mirrored in a window pane, tense and pale, and her hand went up in that reflex feminine reaction to pat her hair. Then she went to the back door, locked it, shot both the bolts, checked all the downstairs windows, and stood uneasily, as though at the centre of a fortress, under siege, listening for footsteps that might never come.

The telephone rang once, but it was a wrong number, and she put back the receiver on its ivory rest, her heart beating like the wings of a frightened bird. It was a warm evening, but she felt cold, as chill as the white mist that rolled up silently from the river, until it covered the lawn like a soft quilt.

She desperately wanted David to ring, wanted to hear the crackle of his Alfa's exhaust, to feel him hard and male against her body, the roughness of his face against her cheek. He was twenty years younger than John and had none of the older man's diffidence and waning self-confidence as a lover. He was urgent and direct and brutal, all the qualities she admired and missed and wanted so desperately.

But David wasn't arriving until later, when he would cut his headlights and drive the last half-mile without them, believing, with a townsman's naivety, that this would mean that no one saw him or recognized his car — quite forgetting the forest of poachers' eyes never missing a stranger in their midst.

At half past nine, as she sat in the big room with the brocaded curtains tightly drawn, and all the bronze safety bolts screwed down in the repainted windows, the telephone rang for a second time.

This time it wasn't David, either; it was the call she had been dreading all day.

CHAPTER THREE

Dr Jackson leaned back in his two hundred guinea chair of black leather and anodized Swedish steel, and rocked himself gently to and fro.

His eighteenth-century partners' desk was covered with polished leather the colour of dried blood, edged with gold - colours, which he liked to tell less successful colleagues, not entirely facetiously, were symbolic of his own individualistic approach towards the practice of psychiatry: you paid with your own blood by being bored by patients' revelations of hatreds and inadequacy; they paid you with gold.

Across this impressive desk, sat another man. The fingers of his right hand drummed an uneasy tattoo on the arm of his chair (a replica of Dr Jackson's but, as a subtle distinction between doctor and patient, as between subject and object, or master and man, rather smaller, with slightly less leather and steel, and a lot less comfort).

They were roughly the same age; in their late fifties. Jackson, in his Squires' suit with the touch of red silk handkerchief in his breast pocket exactly matching his Harvie and Hudson silk tie, thin gold expanding bracelet to his watch no thicker than half a sovereign, appeared, as he always appeared, urbane, detached, his face a mask concealing any emotion and none.

The other man might look equally successful and impressive to his employees, but here he had no need to pretend; here, he wanted reassurance. He came to see Dr Jackson three times a week, at a cost of thirty guineas a visit, to charge up the batteries of his self-confidence. Looked at like this, and at the prodigies of industry he could perform when this confidence returned, the fee was ludicrously little, merely petty cash.

'The fact is,' he said, in the heavy, booming voice that had bullied so many board meetings, 'as I have explained before, I still feel no interest in things. I've got the Rolls, of course, which is fun to drive. And there's the house in Antibes, which we're having completely redone. And, of course, there's Jennifer and the children.'

'And the girl in Chelsea you were telling me about,' pointed out Dr Jackson, just in case the patient had forgotten. 'The one with that - ah - unusual mammary development. Forty, wasn't it?'

'Quite,' said the patient quickly. 'There's her, of course. I still see her about once a week. No, I'm a liar, Doctor. Twice a week. She's expensive, but after all, expense is relative.'

Everything is relative, thought Jackson to himself, but relative to what? And relating his fee to this man's money, he could easily bump up the price another ten guineas a session after today. He'd had enough of his neuroses and his worries, when really he had no proper worries at all.

Ten guineas more, three sessions a week, thirty guineas a week extra, and maybe if I say that the receptionist is away, and could he pay cash as I don't understand all the book-keeping, he'll get the message and go on paying cash. Which is worth probably a hundred a week to me.

Jackson picked up a gold-headed pencil, the (tax-free) gift of another grateful patient, and doodled on the black blotting pad; black, he always told his more sensitive patients, so that no ink would ever show, which meant the utmost discretion in the letters that were so personal, so private, so infinitely discreet that they were delivered to him by hand.

'I think, Mr Paton,' he said gravely, 'that we are only re-tracing our steps. We have gone over every one of your fears and worries and anxieties at our previous sessions together. We have taken each one and analysed it thoroughly, and so have eliminated all traces of reality from these fears that still seem to weigh so heavily on you.

'You have been coming here three times a week for the past year and I have given your case the most serious study, even when you have not been with me. I have discussed it, quite impersonally, of course, with several colleagues, and I must say with regret that they agree with me when I say that there is really nothing more I can do to help you.

'I would, therefore, advise you to break our series of meetings for a time - perhaps for a month or six weeks. And then perhaps you would come and see me and let me know how you feel - whether these fears have stayed with you - or whether, as I hope, they will all disappear.'

'Four weeks is a long time,' said Mr Paton.

From his mean, cold face, impersonal as a bladder of blubber, his eyes, dull as ancient olives, peered out in alarm.

Through the white silk curtains that screened this quiet room from the gaze of the healthy in Harley Street, he could see his Silver Cloud with the chauffeur at the wheel smoking again, although he knew that he hated the smell of cigarette smoke, the bastard.

Why should the man do this to him? And why should this quack, this head-shrinker Jackson, treat him in this way? Wasn't he paying him enough money? Everyone wanted things from him. Everyone either took him for granted or they took advantage of him.

He wanted to weep at the unfairness of the world, but all he did was to grip the sides of the chair more tightly. His face was white now, and damp with a thin film of sweat. Wasn't he entitled to some companionship, some loyalty? Self-pity engulfed him like a tidal wave of tears, and then receded. He'd show them who was boss. He'd give this sod Jackson a couple of weeks, and then he'd phone him.

He'd offer him more money — say, a tenner more a visit — maybe even in cash. Two weeks — or maybe even one; he'd not let it go too long. Maybe Jackson would ring him first? The thought cheered him.

'That's probably the best suggestion,' he said, with what conviction he could manage. 'I'll be in touch with you, Doctor. And thank you for all you've done so far.'

He put his hand inside his pocket, and pulled out a cheque book.

'Shall I settle up now - to save you the business of sending a bill?'

Jackson shrugged, as though money was the last thing that interested him.

'As you wish,' he said. 'By chance, I have your account in my drawer.'

He pushed it across the desk.

By lucky chance, thought Paton bitterly.

Both men stood up, Jackson carefully not looking at the cheque. They shook hands.

Paton went out to the door, where the flat-footed old ex-nurse, who also operated the telephone board for all the doctors in the house, slid back the bolt for him and told him it was warm outside but they'd pay for it later.

We pay for everything later, thought Paton, as he tapped angrily on the window of his Rolls. That bloody chauffeur and his cheap cigarettes. If he had to smoke, why couldn't he choose Sobranie?

Jackson glanced at the cheque, then tore up the bill, for he saw that Paton had deliberately made it out to 'bearer', and there was no point in paying these things into the bank if you did not need to. He put it thoughtfully into his back pocket, lit a cheroot. His secretary came to the door.

'Dr Love is here,' she said.

'Ah, yes. Show him in.'

Love sat down in the still-warm seat that Mr Paton had just left.

'Professional or social, Jason?' asked Jackson, offering him a cheroot.

'A bit of both,' said Love, taking it, for Jackson's parsimony was as well known as his address. 'I'm in town for the day, as I explained on the phone, and I thought I'd seek your advice. About an interesting proposition.'

'How interesting?'

'A trip to Beirut. All expenses paid.'

'Alone?'

'Absolutely on my tod. Only snag is, I've to look for one of your patients - and mine, too. At least, he's on my list, although I've not met him yet. A Mr John Wilmot — real name, Jan Wodouski. His wife lives in my village. She called me out on Friday night, saying her daughter was ill.

'But the child was quite well. Her mother seemed to have some problems about her husband, who's in Beirut and can't be contacted. Said he was under you for treatment, and wondered if I'd go out and see what had happened to him - if anything.

'I told her I wasn't interested, but, let's face it, I don't pick up a trip like this every day of the week, or even every other day. It's five hundred quid's worth.'

'Wish she'd offered it to me,' said Jackson enviously. 'But as she didn't, let me fill you in with a few facts. On a professional basis, if you like. You pay for information, eh?'

He laughed as though this was a joke, but Love knew he never joked about the most serious influence in his life: money.

'Let's have the information first,' he said. 'Then we can see.'

'Well. Wodouski. I knew he was in Beirut, but I didn't know he'd disappeared.'

'Mrs Wilmot said she'd told you she couldn't get in touch with him.'

'That's so, but not being able to get in touch with a husband for a few days is rather different to claiming he's disappeared. I mean, the number of times my wife tries to get in touch with me when I want to avoid her for one reason or another, doesn't mean to say that I've pushed off. At least, not permanently.'

He stood up, crossed to a filing cabinet, opened it, thumbed through the files, and pulled out a buff folder.

'Here we are. Jan Wodouski. Born Warsaw, 1923. Parents were both killed in the uprising, but he survived somehow. In and out of camps. Eventually came to Britain, 1945. Learned English. And, like so many others like him, he made a fortune. Sharp customer, though, I'd say.

'He'd got on to the Rachman idea of buying up old houses with sitting tenants, putting in some rough West Indian to make a lot of noise and commotion until the original tenants got frightened and moved out, and then he'd fill the whole house with tarts, or coloured immigrants who didn't know they were being swindled - all paying cash. Mrs Wilmot tell you that?'

'No. She made it sound much more pleasant.'

'Funny thing is, when you meet him he is quite a pleasant fellow.'

'Sounds charming.'

'Well, he's generous in some ways,' retorted Jackson defensively. 'Always paid my bills, anyhow. And sent me a case of a dozen Scotch last Christmas. And another on my birthday. But he's terribly insecure. Imagines he's being persecuted or swindled or something.

'Had a chauffeur who was really his bodyguard at one time. Then a private detective who would follow his car. He even had his own phone tapped in case people called up when he was away. Done by some firm of private eyes. Wanted to know what everyone said and who was calling when he wasn't there.'

'Does he trust his wife?' asked Love.

Jackson stubbed out his cheroot.

'He's older than she is, but then he's very rich. If she's playing around, she has to consider who else will pay her bills if he found out. He never admitted any worries on that score. But, off the record, I think that maybe she had the odd good friend from time to time.'

'She told me he received a number of anonymous letters and telephone calls, threatening he'd be deported.'

'I know,' said Jackson. 'I put them down to some nut who was jealous of him and envied his prosperity. I didn't think they were serious.'

'He did, though, or he wouldn't have ducked out to Beirut,' Love pointed out.

Jackson nodded.

'You know how it is with some of these people who make a quick fortune. They get a sudden rush of blood to the conscience, and then they either give a hundred thousand to a hospital or charity, or else they shoot themselves. It's all a compensatory thing. In Wodouski's case, he had a persecution mania, and I just couldn't shift it.

'His wife and I discussed the whole question. She suggested that he took off if he was so anxious to go. I agreed. Told him to stay out of the country for a few months. He's been there for nearly six-months. There's no reason whatever why he shouldn't come back, so far as I know.'

'Maybe there really is a reason,' said Love. 'Maybe some-thing in his background that you don't know about? What few people I've met who've made millions from nothing are all perfectly willing to be quizzed on every step up the ladder — except one. That's the most interesting part of their whole career - the time when someone got skinned, or they married for money, or someone they'd swindled killed themselves. Maybe there's a little dark patch in friend Wodouski's otherwise sunny life.'

'Maybe,' agreed Jackson. 'I've no doubt he's swindled numbers of people, but so have most men who have made his sort of money. He's also slept around a lot. Pays a couple of retainers to women, and I think he had an illegitimate child. But again, these things aren't uncommon. Especially when you're as rich as him.'

'Would you go to Beirut?' asked Love. 'I don't know this woman, although she's technically a patient of mine. I've never met her husband, and even though they're both rich as Croesus, I still don't want to take five hundred pounds off her for nothing.'

'My dear Jason, you do me too much wrong,' said Jackson. 'I wouldn't dream of taking five hundred off her. If I were you, I wouldn't get off my bed for less than a thousand. And if you've still got a Presbyterian conscience, and don't want to pay my fees, look at it this way.

'Everything, all through our lives, is relative. If some poor devil comes to your door, and you give him an old suit or 25p for a meal, it probably means very little to you. But it could mean a hell of a lot to him.

'So far as Mrs Wilmot is concerned, you're the poor man at the back door. Five hundred quid to people like her is small change - what she'll spend on cigarettes.'

'She must smoke a lot. But I take the point.'

'Then take her offer too. Forget the money side altogether. You're doing her a good turn if you accept. She's probably genuinely worried about her husband, either because she likes him, which is always possible, although unlikely, but more likely because he's a good provider, and she owes Harrods for the past six months.

'Consider the profits old Wodouski makes - he told me that on one deal alone before capital gains tax came in he made three-quarters of a million - without even moving out of his office. Simply buying and selling something on option which he never had to take up.

'Put your five hundred quid against that sort of money, and

you'll see it in its proper perspective.'

'I'm seeing it,' said Love. 'Mind if I use your phone?'

'For a local call, I hope?' said Jackson anxiously.

'But of course. To my travel agent. To cancel my trip to France, and book instead to a former French possession — Lebanon.'

CHAPTER FOUR

St George's Bay, Beirut, rimmed with tall white buildings, sharp-edged and white as a giant's filed teeth, turned slowly on its side as the plane came in to land.

Love had brought with him the 1890 edition of John Murray's Handbook to the Mediterranean. As the safety belt sign flashed on, he read: 'The situation of Beyrout is beautiful. The promontory on which it stands is triangular - the apex projecting 3 miles into the Mediterranean, and the base running along the foot of Lebanon.

'The south-western' side is composed of loose sand, and has the aspect of a desert. The north-western side is different. The shore-line is formed of a range of deeply-indented cliffs, behind which the ground rises for a mile or more, when it attains the height of about 200 ft.

'In the middle of the shore-line stands the city - first, a dense nucleus of substantial buildings; then a broad margin of picturesque villas, embowered in foliage, running up to the summit of the heights, and extending to the right and left.'

You couldn't have it much better than that, he thought, wondering how eighty-odd years had changed the place, and whether locals would still agree with the Victorian writer of the guide-book that 'its prosperity is entirely due to foreign enterprise. The European mercantile firms have infused new life into the natives...'

The only natives one can write about safely now are Whitstable oysters, he thought, as the red desert around the airport rushed up to meet him. A strip of road, grey as a solder ribbon, stretched to an infinity of buildings. Somewhere, down among those anonymous houses and blocks of flats, or maybe in one of the cars that crawled like toys, was his patient's husband. Doubtless, he would have a very simple explanation for his wife's inability to contact him - probably, as Dr Jackson had suggested, that he simply did not want to be contacted. He was very likely shacked-up with some girl, and the last person he wanted to speak to was his wife.

But years of dealing with the frailties of human nature had made Love realize long ago that, while the simplest explanation is often the right one, what may appear to be a complete explanation, is, in fact, only an answer to part of the problem.

A patient might complain of stomach pains, but the real cause could lie in worries which he could not control, or in an unsatisfactory relationship between a wife and her husband.

This, in turn, might stem from the husband being unhappy in a job - and he was unhappy because a superior also felt insecure or inadequate, and took out his resentment on him. The causes wound back, one behind the other, like carriages on a railway train. The case of Mrs Wilmot's disappearing husband could well be another example of this.

The plane's wheels bumped once, twice, as the Caravelle landed, and the roar of the engines grew as the pilot reversed his jets. They taxied to a halt outside the long sandstone airport building, with the big neon sign, 'Welcome to Lebanon'.

Love waited patiently in his seat while the other passengers stood up with that nervous compulsion of all air travellers to be out of the plane, although the doors were not even open. He was thus one of the last across the sun-dried concrete and into the customs hall.

Some visiting dignitary was inspecting a guard of honour to the left of the main entrance. A band in khaki fustian, with shabby boots and unpolished instruments, played a sonorous march as this dark-skinned gentleman, incongruously dressed in swallowtail coat, and carrying a top hat, his black hair glistening like a seal's backside in the hot sun, walked ponderously along the ranks, looking each soldier up and down as though he wanted to recognize him again.

Who he was or where he came from was no concern of Love's. Half the airports of the world must be receiving or saying farewell to similar foreign visitors, all guests of local taxpayers, with retinues of secretaries and servants, and to no good purpose whatever.

A customs officer chalked a hieroglyph on Love's bag without asking him what it contained, and Love was out in a hollow square, where taxi drivers touted for trade by braying on their horns and waving at him through the windows of their cars. He chose the nearest, a green and black Mercedes.

'Where to, sir?' asked the man.

'The Bristol,' said Love, and sank back on the old plastic seat, carefully covered by transparent cellophane.

The man handed a grubby card over his shoulder.

'Best night club in the city. They give you special price if you mention my name - Ali Akbar.'

'Thank you very much,' said Love insincerely, handing it back. Next to an early death; the last thing he wanted was a night club where a lot of middle-aged men would sit in half-darkness, only half alive, like etiolated creatures of the night, watching the jiggling breasts of the belly-dancers; drink and watch, but do not touch, and back to reality in the morning.

The driver kept up a one-way barrage of facts and misinformation about the city, its past, its future, the riots, the Arab refugees, El Fatah.

Did the Englishman know that a deputy of the President of Egypt, an influential gentleman, Ahmed Hussein - one of the most important men in the Middle East and therefore the world — was coming to Beirut on the day after tomorrow? The Minister of Culture and Development, he was called, but he was really chief of the Egyptian Secret Police. That was his deputy reviewing the guard of honour at the airport. Did the Englishman know that? The Englishman didn't.

Ah, then did he not wish for a special place on the route overlooking the Deputy President's deputy's drive through the city? That could be arranged by Ali Akbar - and at a very cheap rate - if the Englishman understood?

'I understand,' said Love resignedly. 'But I didn't come here to see visiting firemen. I came for a holiday.'

'Visiting firemen?' the driver repeated in amazed dis-belief. 'This is no fireman, this is a most famous and powerful Arab. If his deputy has a guard of honour, what will not the great man receive himself?'

The question was theoretical, Love thought, and as such did not need answering.

They pulled in under the canopy of the Bristol Hotel. Waving away the porter, Love carried in his single suitcase. His room was on the tenth floor. Two single beds, pale green hessian walls, a bathroom with a slight smell of chlorinated water, but modern German taps, a small verandah that overlooked a square with gardens and fountains (not working) in the centre.

He ordered a fresh lime juice from room service, and when the drink arrived, stood leaning over the balcony, feeling the sun on his face, the concrete rim of the balcony warm through his sleeve.

He would find this character Wilmot, telephone his wife that all was well, and then spend the rest of his time on the beach, or by the hotel pool.

He had promised Mrs Wilmot to stay for five days at her expense in Beirut, and then, whether he could find her husband or not, he would move on for the second part of his holiday to St Raphael.

If he could not trace her husband within that time, then surely he must have left the country - or gone to that other country from which no traveller returns.

LOVE-ALL

Love decided that his first visit should be to Wilmot's flat. If he hadn't been there for a week or so, then he would call at the Middle East Airlines office and see whether he had bought an air ticket. They could also check through the central booking register with the other airlines that served Beirut.

If this produced nothing, then he would try Wilmot's bank - his wife had given him a letter of authority to show to the manager. Finally, he would try the British Embassy, although he agreed it unlikely that they would know the whereabouts of someone who was not a British subject, living in Beirut under a different name.

Love finished his drink, went downstairs, bought a guidebook to the city from a stall in the foyer. From the map in the back, he found he could walk to Wilmot's flat as easily as take a taxi.

The El Kantara Building was like half a dozen others on either side of it - maybe a dozen others for all he knew - an upended slab of precast concrete twenty storeys high, with rows of blank windows facing the ocean, some shielded by striped plastic blinds against the reflection of the sun from the sea. Most of the windows had no curtains, which prob-ably meant that the flats were empty.

Half a dozen people waited outside one of the three lifts. They looked at him incuriously as he crossed to the commissionaire's office. A man inside was reading an Egyptian newspaper, his lips moving with each word as though he was speaking to himself.

Love tapped on the glass. The man frowned at the interruption, put down the paper, opened the door, raised his eyebrows.

'Do you speak English?' asked Love.

'Yes.'

'I'm looking for a friend. Mr Esdaile. In flat one seven nine two.'

'Mr Esdaile has been away for some days. But I am not really the commissionaire. He's off duty this morning because he worked on Friday, which is our holy day. Perhaps you could come back in the afternoon - after five? He should be here then. Maybe he can help you more?'

Love shook his head. He had suffered in this way before in the Middle East. He would come back after five, and find that no one else was there, either. They had all gone home, or hadn't arrived, or were on holiday, or out of town, or seeing their mother-in-law's aunt's cousin.

He would then be advised to return at ten on the following morning, to be greeted with smiles, enormous politeness, and the information that the person he sought was now not here, didn't work here any more, or was not known; and sometimes all three explanations for his absence.

'I can't come back,' Love told him. 'I also have other business to do. Perhaps I could leave a message?'

The man turned up his hands, palms towards heaven, to show that Allah had not been over-generous in backsheesh, although, through his infinite mercy, that situation might conceivably be remedied. Love remedied it with a Lebanese fifty-pound note.

The man put aside his newspaper, opened a drawer, pulled out a sheet of writing paper with the name of the building printed at the top in English and Arabic script.

'Thank you very much,' said Love. 'I'll take it up myself and put it in Mr Esdaile's letter-box.'

This seemed an admirable solution. They shook hands with each other and bowed.

Love crossed the floor to the lift, went up to the seventeenth floor.

Five doors opened off the landing. He pushed open the vertical letterbox in the door of 1792, trying to squint inside, but all he could see was a small length of painted-cream corridor, and an etching of some seventeenth-century French provincial scene.

He took out a dental mirror, the size of a shilling, on the end of a small nickle-plated handle, and held this at an angle through the letter-box to see whether any other letters lay on the floor. There was nothing but a small square of Turkish carpet.

All this did not add much to the sum of human knowledge, so he scribbled a note on the piece of paper: 'John Esdaile. Was just passing through. Brought some good news from your wife. Can you please telephone me at the Bristol. Room 1021. Sincerely, Jason Love.' He read this through and added the word Dr.

Then he folded up the paper, dropped it through the letterbox, waited on the landing for a few more minutes in the hope that, perhaps, Wilmot might return. But although the lift went up and down several times, it did not stop.

Love pressed the button for it, and went down. The entrance hall was empty. He crossed to the commissionaire's office. This was empty, too. He pushed open the door with his elbow, having a basic wish to leave no fingerprints on the handle.

Inside, above the desk at which the man had been reading his newspaper, hung twenty rows of keys, a set for each floor. They had plastic tags, and he turned over the seventeenth row until he came to 1792.

He glanced over his shoulder. The hall was still empty, and beyond the glass doors, cars fled to and fro, glittering like huge bright beads between the building and the beach.

He took down the key, pulled a visiting card out of his pocket, traced the outline of the key on the back of the card. He wiped the key and the tag with his handkerchief, hung them back on their nail, slipped the card into his pocket. Then he went out and crossed the hall into the street.

It was hotter now, as though the sun before had only been running at half power. The sea lay sluggish under the heaviness of its heat, the waves too lazy to break. A jet, coming in from the West, pulled a trail of white vapour behind it down the sky.

On the way back to his hotel, Love passed a travel agency,

bright with pictures of the Caribbean, Niagara Falls and long, empty beaches near Bombay. An alert young man with a sallow face and an out-dated moustache, a throwback to the film star dream of the handsome young man in the 1930s, looked up brightly at him from behind his desk.

'I'd like a map of Lebanon,' said Love, 'and any details of tours you might have.'

The man pushed a wadge of folders across the desk.

'Is there anything else we can help you with?' he asked.

'Yes, there is,' said Love, as though in an afterthought. 'Where can I get a key cut? I always like to keep a spare.'

'There's a shop in the Rue Hamra. Only a hundred metres from here,' said the man. 'You can't miss it.'

Love didn't miss it. He had a key cut while he waited, then walked back to his hotel.

What he proposed to do might not be entirely legal, but then, if everyone lived their lives by the absolute letter of the law, while the world might arguably be a better place, it would also take so much longer to get things done.

If he could search Wilmot's flat, maybe he would find an address for him, or some clue why he was unobtainable. He might even find Wilmot himself.

He ate a lunch of red mullet and salad with a bottle of iced Sauterne, and spent the afternoon sun-bathing beside the pool, until the sun suddenly burned itself out, as though overstrained after supplying so much heat for so long.

The brief twilight grew loud with the braying of car horns as traffic built up at intersections. He had a Dalmore Malt on the rocks, then a cold lobster, half a bottle of Chablis, and afterwards sat on a wicker chair on the terrace overlooking the water, watching the sea turn dark and lights begin to twinkle, like fallen stars, in the little fishing boats.

A surprisingly chill wind blew out from the desert, carrying the scents of a dying day; olive oil, a sharp nostalgic bitterness of crushed herbs, a faint smell of woodsmoke. The neons were lit now on all the buildings, flickering Catherine wheels of colour. Hands lit six-foot cigarettes, and the basic international exhortations, Bebe Fanta, Fly BOAC, reflected in the oily waters of the bay.

The Lebanese, like most Mediterranean people, eat late -Love had been one of a handful dining early in the restaurant — and so he calculated that nine o'clock would be a safe hour to visit Wilmot's flat. The commissionaire would probably be off duty having supper, and other residents, who might notice and remember a stranger, would also be in their own flats.

At quarter to nine he went up to his room, emptied his money out of his pockets, with his passport, his driving licence, three hundred pounds in travellers' cheques, pushed them between the pillow and the pillow-slip in his bed, and then moved his pillow under the bolster.

He took a pair of rubber surgical gloves from his case, dusted some talcum powder into the fingers, rolled them up into a ball in his back trouser pocket, put his pencil torch in his inside jacket pocket.

The idea of finding someone who might not want to be found in an international city on the edge of war or rebellion intrigued him. It was probably absurd to feel like this, but then, if examined too closely, some of the most exciting and entertaining episodes in life were the epitome of absurdity.

He wondered how his locum was making out, and glanced at his watch. Allowing for the time lag, he should be finishing his evening surgery at any minute. He examined the key he had had made in the locksmith's, rubbed a few drops of hair oil along the rough edge, for a rough key could jam too easily in the lock. Then he turned out the light, took the lift down to the entrance hall.

A coachload of Americans on a package-deal holiday was just arriving. Dozens of people with plastic covers over their hats, carrying string bags and cameras, some even wearing goloshes, milled around the reception desk, very conscious of being in a foreign, faraway land, all eager to book in and reach the air-conditioned, iced-water safety of their rooms.

The promenade was jammed with cars. There had been an accident half a mile up the road, and drivers sat hooting impatiently, as though by sheer volume of noise they could resolve the situation, like those Old Testament trumpeters who ended the siege of Jericho by bringing down the walls in one climactic burst of sound.

Love took fifteen minutes to reach the El Kantara Building. The commissionaire's office was closed, the light was out; he had been right in thinking the man would be off duty.

He took the lift to the seventeenth floor, pulled on his rubber gloves, pushed the key in the door lock. For a moment, he thought it would jam. Suddenly, almost unexpectedly, it turned and the door opened. He pulled out the key, closed the door gently behind him and stood against it, listening.

The flat smelt fusty, as though all the windows had been closed for too long. A machine began to hum and tick and whirr somewhere and, for a moment, Love's heart jumped, and then he realized it was only the refrigerator. He must be getting old if such homely noises sounded sinister; old, or more careful.

He took a couple of deep breaths to steady himself, walked through the first door he saw. It led to a living-room. He switched on the main light.

The room was furnished impersonally and without taste; a cheap, varnished, wood bookcase, a four-legged coffee table with some magazines jumbled on it, three chairs upholstered in imitation leather, brass ashtrays on the arms.

He didn't know quite what he was looking for, so he had no idea where he would find it, but surely Wilmot must have had an appointments book or a diary?

After all, even though he was in virtual, if self-imposed, exile, he would probably still be in touch with his property company, if only on the basis of letters and telegrams? May-be one of these would give him a lead to his whereabouts. He opened a handful of books on the built-in bookcase and shook out the pages, but there was nothing - not even an envelope as a bookmark. The room could have been occupied by anyone or no one.'

He turned out the light and went to the kitchen. This was walled with blue ceramic tiles. He opened the refrigerator. It was empty. The food cupboards contained two tins of baked beans, half a pound of tea, a tube of condensed milk, and a small packet of salt; hardly the basis for a gourmet's meal -or even the larder for a man on his own.

Love lifted the lid of the waste-bin; it was empty. So Wilmot was obviously not in residence. He had moved, and presumably he was not coming back quickly, otherwise he would not have cleared out the kitchen so thoroughly.

Something niggled at Love, like a thorn in his thumb. Then he remembered what was missing: the note he had written and pushed through the letter-box had not been in the hall. Someone had been into this flat since afternoon.

Perhaps the caller had been Wilmot? This seemed the most reasonable assumption. Maybe Wilmot was at that moment trying to contact him at his hotel? With the new arrivals, the telephone might not be answered. He'd have a quick glance around the rest of the flat and then go back, just in case.

He went into the next room, flicked on the light. Nothing happened. He moved the switch up and down half a dozen times, in case the contact was loose, but the light still did not work. The bulb must have fused.

He flashed his torch. The room had fitted carpets and the curtains were drawn, as much against the heat of the day as for privacy, because who could overlook a flat seventeen storeys high, and facing the sea? He shone the torch around the room. The beam picked out two suitcases on the floor, both half-empty of clothes, a bunch of keys, some small change, a bottle of hair oil on the built-in dressing table.

The little white finger of light moved round to the bed, and there it stopped.

A man was lying on the bed, his face turned away from Love, a coverlet pulled up over his right shoulder.

'Mr Wilmot!' called Love softly.

The man did not reply. Faintly, from seventeen floors below, Love heard the wailing rise and fall of a police siren as an ambulance bored its way through the clogged traffic to the accident. Music began to play in a flat next door, and then died, and he heard an announcer say, 'Ici Paris,' and go into a long spiel in French - about what he didn't know and didn't care.

Love cleared his throat, and called again: 'Mr Wilmot!'

He moved towards the bed, put out his hand and pulled back the coverlet.

The man was wearing a shirt, open at the neck, with a string of cheap metal charms. Love shook him.

'Wake up,' he said. He pulled against the shoulder and, for a moment, the weight resisted him, and then the man rolled over on his back. He had a thick beard, with long black hair that came down almost to his shoulders. His ears were pierced with rings, his face was young and unlined.

This certainly wasn't Wilmot, as Love knew he would look from his photographs.

Which was just as well, from Wilmot's point of view, for this man was quite dead.

Love lifted up one eyelid, and a blue eye with its pupil diminished, even in death, looked out at him, and saw nothing but the endless mists of eternity. He pulled up the sleeve. The skin was blotched with bruises and tiny pin-point scabs of dried blood where he had injected himself. So he'd been a junky. Had drugs killed him?

Love ran his hand under the man's beard and his hair, and felt small scars beneath his fingers. He shone his torch again on his face. The skin was puffy with bruises; traces of blood had dried in his nostrils and around his lips. He had been hit, and probably fallen, maybe in an accident, more likely in a fight.

Was this the reason Wilmot was keeping under cover?

Had he been killed in Wilmot's flat in mistake for Wilmot? Love pulled up the coverlet, glad he was wearing gloves, and switched off his torch.

As he turned, the room exploded into light.

A man was standing in the doorway, looking at him and smiling, as though he found him amusing. He was a big man, and he almost filled the doorway.

But it was not this that Love noted particularly, or his hippie clothes, the dirty jeans, the sandals, the shirt without buttons, or the inevitable necklace round his neck - it was the .32 FN automatic he held in his right hand, aimed at his navel.

Love cleared his throat. He had nothing else to clear; his mind felt clogged and blocked and dull.

'Who the hell are you?' he asked in a voice that sounded like a stranger's.

'I was going to ask you that,' the man replied, pleasantly and in English.

'I'm a doctor,' said Love, as though this helped matters; if it didn't, it could scarcely make them worse.

'So? And you're visiting your patient in the dark, Doctor, carrying a torch, and wearing rubber gloves, letting yourself into someone else's flat with your own key? It seems to me that you've also arrived a bit too late to help this particular patient.'

'So you were already here?' asked Love.

'I was.'

'So whose is this body - and where's the owner of the flat?'

'This is the body of a man I met two days ago. Seemed a harmless enough bum. Name of Herbert Ellis. Like you, he wanted to find the tenant. So did I. And when I arrived at the front door I found Ellis already there.'

'And then?'

'And then I rang the bell. But no one was at home. We went out, and the commissionaire conveniently turned up in a car and asked if we'd found the tenant. We hadn't. So he kindly gave us a lift up the road, and there I left them.'

'Why are you telling me all this?' asked Love.

'Because I know you, you old pox-doctor. Even if you don't recognize me under all this hair.'

'You know me?' Love asked in surprise and disbelief.

'Surely. Remember Teheran and Damascus?'

The man in the doorway grinned, slipped the FN into his back trouser pocket, and held out his hand.

Something in the movement, linked with the names, unlocked Love's memory.

'Richard Mass Parkington!' he said, in relieved amazement. 'Of course I know you, you old bastard.'

'Flattery,' remarked Parkington smugly, 'will get you nowhere.'

They had first met in Teheran some years before, when Love was there as a delegate to a medical conference. A wartime acquaintance, Colonel Douglas MacGillivray, who had since risen to become the second-in-command of the British Secret Intelligence Service, had asked Love to try and find a British agent who had fallen some days behind with his routine recognition signals.

Parkington, a professional secret agent, had also known this man, and, on his way home from an assignment in Singapore, he had stopped off in Teheran, hoping to see him.

Love and Parkington had met more recently in Damascus, *(for their experiences, see Passport to Oblivion and Passport for a Pilgrim where Love)*, visiting the grave of a daughter of one of his patients, had discovered, to his amazement, that the coffin held an entirely different corpse.

'So what really brings you here now?' said Love. 'Don't tell me this fellow Esdaile is involved in your world of spies?'

'I'm not telling you anything. My orders are simple - to find Esdaile and get him out of Beirut. As quickly as possible. Quicker if I can.'

'Is he that important?'

Parkington shrugged; offered Love a cheroot; lit one himself.

'Not to me, he isn't,' he said. 'I've never set eyes on the bugger. But I've been virtually camping out on his door-step here for three days. I've even taken a flat in the next block to this, with a camera with Takumar telephoto lens locked on to these windows.

'It's got a neat Japanese attachment, worked through a photoelectric cell, that makes it take a picture every time there's any movement. But it hasn't registered a thing. So whoever else has been here must have kept the curtains drawn.

'I decided I'd have a closer look and got a key. And look who I find. Two people I know. One dead, the other still alive.'

'That's the way I mean to stay,' Love told him. 'With that in mind, what do we do now?'

'First thing, get the hell out of here. The place is obviously being watched. I reckon we've got no more than minutes before whoever killed this character is on to the police, saying there's a body in this flat, and we're right here with it. Which means quite a bit of explaining for us to do - especially as we haven't been invited in.'

'Let's go,' said Love.

Then he remembered the note he'd written.

'Did you pick up a piece of paper I pushed through the letter-box, asking Wilmot to ring me?'

'No,' said Parkington. 'There was nothing on the floor when I came in, only minutes before you. When I heard the front door opening, I hid in a kitchen cupboard. I thought it might be the police already, and, once they were in the bedroom, I could nip out. Then I realized it was just someone looking around, like me, and I thought I'd discover who. What are you doing in Beirut, anyway?'

'I'll answer that back in the hotel,' said Love.

As he spoke, the telephone rang. They both waited, looking at each other, half expecting that it would somehow be answered without their aid.

Parkington shrugged. Love walked through the corridor, picked up the receiver.

A voice asked in French, 'Monsieur Esdaile?'

'His residence,' said Love, also in French.

'Lebanese Post and Telegraphs Department,' said the voice. 'We have a telegram for you. From Morocco. Shall I read it?'

'Yes,' said Love.

'Knowing your interest in ancient history suggest you follow Grecian example and advise haircut where necessary to anyone who asks.'

'Is it signed?' asked Love.

'No, Monsieur. No signature. We have telephoned you before, but we had no reply. Do you wish confirmation?'

'Not necessary,' said Love, and replaced the receiver.

He scribbled down the message on a visiting card, stood irresolute, hearing a clock tick somewhere, and the distant sound of traffic far beneath.

'Who was that?' asked Parkington uneasily. They were staying too long; every second diminished their chances of escape.

Love told him.

'That can wait,' said Parkington, "but we can't.'

They went out of the flat, climbed down the service staircase for two flights, rang for the lift.

As it arrived, Parkington handed Love a pair of horn-rimmed glasses with blue-tinted lenses.

'Put them on,' he said. 'Hunch your shoulders up a bit. Walk with a limp. It's much easier than wearing a false beard.'

'After you with that false beard,' said Love.

The foyer was still empty, but as they went across the marble floor, Love limping dutifully, a white police car swept up the crescent-shaped drive-in and squealed to a stop.

Two uniformed policemen, revolvers at their belts, jumped out, followed by a plain-clothes man. They ran through the outer swing door.

'What's the betting they ring for the seventeenth floor?' asked Parkington.

'I never bet, unless on certainties,' said Love.

'You'll never have a better,' said Parkington, hailing a taxi.

In Love's room in the hotel, with a couple of bottles of whisky on the table, sitting close to the radio with the volume turned up, just in case anyone had had the idea of concealing a microphone in the room, Love told Parkington why he was there.

'Now,' he said. 'Your turn. Why is Wilmot so important to your lot - as well as to his wife?'

'I don't know. I only know I've got orders to get Wilmot out of here as fast as possible.'

'Who says so?'

'MacGillivray, who else?'

'Old Mac! How is he these days?'

'Pretty fair. Just back from leave.'

'I bet I know how he spent it,' said Love.

'You're right,' said Parkington. 'Looking for a house. If I had all the money he's spent on letters to house agents, and advertisers in Country Life and The Field over the last thirty years, looking for the perfect, goddam' house, I'd retire immediately.'

MacGillivray's dream was to find the ultimate in country houses; a stream within the grounds, stables, garage block, clock tower with weather vane and louvred wooden panels; a house that looked small outside and yet had large rooms. Every time he found something that nearly approximated to his dream, he discovered, with almost equal feelings of disappointment and relief, that some convenient and unbearable fault - wood rot, wet rot, foot rot, maybe just its price - mercifully put it beyond his reach. For MacGillivray wisely realized that if he ever achieved his ambition, if his dream should finally become reality, then he would have nothing left to wish for; and as Bernard Shaw had pointed out, the only thing worse than not having what you want is having it.

'Are you in touch with MacGillivray?' asked Love.

'I have a call from Control every evening,' Parkington explained. 'It's tape-recorded and run through at a different speed every time. Sometimes they play it backwards.'

'How do you translate it?'

'Each week I receive a bulb catalogue from a firm in East Anglia.

On the last page is an index of the prices for daffodils, tulips and gladioli and all that rubbish. These prices tell me what speed the tapes will be played at for the next seven days.'

'Do you think Wilmot knows you're after him?'

'Maybe that's why he's scarpered. Could be he's working for the other side. Or he may have stumbled on to something that makes him dangerous to them - or us.'

Love smiled inwardly at Parkington's description of all who were not in sympathy with the aims of Her Britannic Majesty's Government as The Other Side. He had heard MacGillivray use the words, as though they were spiritualists, or a rival team. In one sense, they were the latter; Kipling used to refer to spying as 'the great game'. Maybe it had been in his time, but not now. From Love's point of view, it was a game for pros, and one in which he had no wish to become further involved.

He had set out from Somerset, hoping for a few days in the sun at the whim of a wealthy patient. Instead, he appeared to have run into a web of intrigue completely unimagined in Bishop's Combe. Or did Mrs Wilmot know or suspect that her husband might be more than a self-made tycoon with the beginnings of a persecution complex?

Maybe, if he was working for the other side, this could explain his anxiety to leave Britain? Maybe the calls he had received were not threats at all, but simply warnings that a net was closing around him?

The permutations multiplied like amoeba; the best advice Love could give himself was to stick to his original intention of making a few calls, and if these produced no results, admit he could do no more, and move on.

But was this advice still possible to act on? If Wilmot's flat was being watched, as Parkington believed, then he would have been seen and followed. In that case, instead of being the hunter, Love could soon be the hunted.

But if Wilmot was in deadly danger, either because of what he had done, or what he had discovered - whether deliberately or by chance - to whom could he appeal as a stranger, living under a false name two thousand miles from home? Who could he trust with either his secret or himself?

The answer was, quite simply, no one. So — if Wilmot knew about the body in his flat, or worse, was responsible for killing the hippie - he might be driven to risk contacting his wife, simply because he knew no one else he could trust.

He might not ask for help, because what help could she provide from such a distance? But he might at least give her some indication of his danger, or, more useful to Love, his whereabouts.

Love stubbed out his cigarette, his mind made up.

'If you're in touch with MacGillivray,' he said, 'could you get on to him now?'

Parkington looked at his watch.

'In about half an hour,' he said. 'What do you want to say to him? That our case comes up next Tuesday week - number two court?'

'With a bit of luck, we won't be in any court. I'm guessing that Wilmot is on the run because he knows he's in danger - either from your people, or from who you call the other side. The only person he can trust in this situation may be his wife. So, when you speak to MacGillivray, ask him to check whether Mrs Wilmot has made or accepted any overseas telephone calls in the last two days, not necessarily from here, but from anywhere.

'I'm assuming that her husband has tried to get in touch with her. Or maybe he's left a number where she can ring him. If we could find that number, maybe we could also find him.'

'It's an idea,' Parkington allowed.

'And when you're speaking to MacGillivray,' Love continued, 'see how soon he can reply. I've a strong feeling in my bones and water that the police here will be asking us some questions about that body in Wilmot's flat. We haven't much time to fanny about. Get your fellows off their beds and let's have a reply within an hour.'

'We'll make it half an hour,' said Parkington. 'After all, that's what they're bloody well paid for.' He poured out two more whiskies.

CHAPTER FIVE

The automatic gates outside the lift at Covent Garden underground station hissed open with a rattle of loose trellis-work joints.

The crowd of young people who had been crammed inside it, walled in by advertisements for swimsuits and girdles, all incongruously dressed in permutations of maxi coats and mini skirts, boots, bell-bottomed trousers, cast-offs from jumble sales, and the remnants of what had once been fashionable on North American Indian reserves, swept out and over Floral Street, down past The Nag's Head. In a chattering tide they poured unseeing between the lines of cars, jam-packed, half on the pavement and half off, towards the Royal Opera House.

From an upstairs window, through the double panes of , glass which effectively insulated all noise from market porters by day, and such opera-goers by night, Colonel Douglas MacGillivray stood and watched them, and wished he were young again.

It was a wonderful world now, he thought, when you could fly anywhere within hours, change jobs at will, be sought after, admired, and held up as a mirror to past and future generations. But youth only lasted, like the bubbles in champagne, for a very short time, and soon even these bright, chattering young people out beyond the double panes of glass, would feel, as he felt now, on the outside, looking in.

He did not really envy them - he would only change places if he knew what the years had taught him - but they irritated him when they threw away the chances and opportunities that had not even been imagined when he was then-age. And despite their much publicized permissiveness, he found that, when he met the sons and daughters of his friends they seemed curiously innocent about other aspects of the world.

Here, hundreds were rushing to see some work of musical fiction, which was infinitely less astonishing than the mysteries with which he dealt every day, and for much of each night. But such is the curious ambivalence of human nature, they would never have believed this if they had been told.

Usually, MacGillivray was back by this hour in his flat off the Brompton Road, where his wife would have had a meal ready for him from seven o'clock on the Salton trolley, not knowing whether he would be delayed or not. And there he would sit, his mind back-tracking over the events of the day and the troubles of the morrow, while she prattled on brightly with the inconsequential, one-dimensional chatter of childless couples in middle age.

Mrs Parker in the flat underneath had been burgled again; the porter had said he thought the whole block was coming down soon in a redevelopment scheme; she had been absolutely the ideal house for them, advertised in that morning's Daily Telegraph, and would he ring the agent as soon as he could?

But by each evening, MacGillivray, whose days were spent sending telegrams to the only agents with whom he ever did business, secret agents, had no wish to speak to anyone else.

On that morning, an agent in Morelia, in Mexico, had been killed in a car crash. Apparently, a drunken driver had swerved his van into the agent's Jaguar almost outside the church of San Augustin. He had been killed instantly. But was this a genuine accident, or was it one of the many staged murders that take place all round the world, all round the clock?

For the real diplomacy is not acted out in the elaborate charade of embassy receptions and banquets and visits, but by unknown men who move like shadows across a dusky landscape, acting now for one side, for one country, now for another, sometimes only for themselves. MacGillivray had to find a relief urgently, and the only possible man was a courier in a travel agency in Durango, nearer the United States border. He had telegraphed to him from one of his own cover addresses, a travel agency in the Edgware Road, but had received no reply. He was obviously out with a band of tourists, women with blue-rinsed hair, middle-aged men in baggy suits and clattering false teeth, padding their way in plastic raincoats around the wide, empty hills, their ears popping with the altitude.

MacGillivray wondered whether the scene of the incident - he would not dignify it by the description of accident until he was convinced it had been accidental - had any significance. The church of San Augustin contains an effigy of a black Christ. Had this some political symbolism?

At first, he had thought it might have, but then he remembered seeing other coloured Christs in different Mexican churches - green and yellow in Puebla, red in San Diego, blue in Atotonilco. He was becoming jittery, imagining complications where probably none existed, even though he had just returned from a week's holiday in the Kyle of Lochalsh and Skye. Maybe he was growing old, and not just feeling old, which was quite a different thing.

MacGillivray's office was, to outward appearances, the office of an importer and exporter of soft and dried fruits. The name above the shop front, where indeed this legitimate business was carried on at a nominal profit, was Sensoby & Ransom, but this firm was simply a cover, as an apparently empty sea-shell can conceal its secret tenant, a hermit crab.

The Secret Service needed such legitimate enterprises where people could come and go at all hours, where tele-phones could ring through day and night without any interest or suspicion being aroused. They therefore used, as convenient shells, a timber firm in the City, a travel agency, a garage that exported vintage cars, and so on.

Sometimes, these firms died, simply to rise again, Phoenix-like, from their own ashes, with a new image, a new name, a new address - but the same hidden reason for being in business.

MacGillivray poured himself another whisky and stood drinking it, wondering what the weather would be like now in Scotland, with dusk turning the purple heather to the colour of a Roman emperor's robe and the burns clear and bright as liquid glass.

He wondered whether he'd like the country so much if he spent fifty-two weeks in it every year, and not just three or four. On this disturbing thought, he finished his drink, locked the bottle away in his desk cupboard.

He'd give this Durango man ten more minutes and then switch on the answering machine and go home.

Janet had told him she was preparing one of his favourite meals - salmon steak, with cucumbers cut thin as round razor blades, new potatoes and peas, and a bottle of Riesling between them.

There was some reason, he knew, for this special celebration and, with an enormous spasm of guilt, he suddenly remembered that it was the eve of their wedding anniversary, and he had bought nothing for his wife, and now it was too late. That seemed to be the story of his life, he thought sourly: too late.

The telephone rang. He picked it up, pushed over the lever that switched on the recording machine.

The international operator said, 'Sensoby and Ransom, London?'

'Yes.'

'We have a call for you from Beirut.'

'Who's speaking?' he asked, disappointed it was not from Durango.

'Personal call to Douglas MacGillivray from Mr Carter. Are you Douglas MacGillivray?'

'Yes,' he said resignedly. Who else could he be after all these years? In fact, who else would he want to be?

He watched the green light flicker on the recording machine.

Whatever they said now would be taken down and typed out by his faithful Miss Jenkins tomorrow, and so would last for ever - or, rather, for as long as the records of the British Secret Service lasted, which might not be quite the same thing.

Parkington's voice came on the line.

'This is Carter speaking,' he said. 'Sorry to ring you so late about the consignment of dates, but I've had difficulty settling up things at this end. Before we go any further, I just want to confirm that your buying price is four shillings and thruppence a pound, landed.'

'I confirm, four and three,' said MacGillivray, and moved the speed control on the tape recorder. There was a pause, and then Parkington's voice, shrill and incomprehensible, speaking at four and a quarter times the speed of ordinary speech, jabbered like a maniacal parrot in his ear.

Then another pause, in which he wound the speed control back, and Parkington's ordinary voice said, 'Sorry about that. This is a bad line. I'll ring you again tomorrow at the same time. Before I go — have you received the last consignment?'

'Yes,' said MacGillivray. 'They are in good condition. I'll await your call tomorrow. Goodnight.'

He replaced the receiver, rewound the tape, set the control at the speed of speech and listened.

Parkington's voice said:. 'One. Our subject here has proved impossible to find. A mutual friend, Dr Jason Love, was asked by subject's wife, Mrs Caroline Wilmot, of Esdaile House, near Bishop's Combe, Somerset, to find her husband because she could not reach him through letters or telephone calls. Dr Love has also been unable to make contact.

'Two. Love suggests we discover whether Mrs Wilmot has received any, repeat any, foreign calls in last seventy-two hours. If so, please advise country, city, exchange and number of origin.

'Three. Commissionaire at subject's block of flats has use of

1966 Mercedes 220 SE saloon. Investigation shows this registered in name of Akbar Casinos Inc, local subsidiary of Pan-World Developments registered in Panama through discretionary trust, Carlos Investment Trust, operating from Netherlands Antilles. Trustee and principal owner named here as Carlos Diaz. Appreciate action soonest. Otherwise, NTR.'

Nothing to report. How many agents sent this consistently as their only contribution. Parkington was not usually one of them. MacGillivray wondered where Wilmot was, whether he had already been caught and killed. Beirut could be an unhealthy place for wanted men; Kim Philby had fled from it to Moscow. Had Wilmot done the same thing - or been taken against his will?

MacGillivray switched off the machine and stood up and looked out into the street. The crowds had gone; the opera would now be well into its first act. Rain had begun to fall, soundless and soft. Looking through it at the rows of parked cars, glistening like coloured glass under the street lights, he wondered whether the drama that must be playing around the elusive Mr Wilmot was also in its first act — or its last.

He had never heard of Wilmot, until his name had unexpectedly appeared in a signal from an agent in Cairo and a check with the Foreign Office had made him divert Parkington from an otherwise routine trip to Morocco. And was this man Diaz any more than an international tax-dodger who, after the manner of his kind, had built up a legal wall around his activities, whatever they might be? Was it important that the commissionaire of the flat where Wilmot had been living used a car belonging to one of his companies, or wasn't it?

The only thing to do was to find out. What a bore that events always seemed to grow more complicated at night. Who had said, history was made at night? It was, of course; it had to be; it was always night somewhere in the world.

MacGillivray gave a sigh of irritation, picked up another telephone, dialled a number. An old colleague, Inspector Mason of the Special Branch, answered.

'Yes?'

He was at home and in the middle of supper. A congealing and unappetizing mass of frozen fish fingers, frozen peas, and frozen chips, not altogether satisfactorily thawed out, huddled together, as though for companionship, on his cold plate. His wife was not a cordon bleu cook. In fact, she wasn't really anyone or anything special, except a woman to whom he had foolishly proposed twenty-five years earlier, never really imagining that the proposal would be accepted with such alacrity. Now, in his semi-detached house off the Barnet by-pass, but not far enough off, because the heavy lorries going north made all the loose panes tremble in the windows, Mason was secretly glad of any interruption, even if it meant work.

'MacGillivray here. Can you get someone in the Post Office to put a hook on a line belonging to a Mrs Wilmot in Somerset? Actual address is Esdaile House, near Bishop's Combe.'

'Of course,' said Mason, scribbling it down on the back of an envelope. 'But this is getting a bit dodgy now. All these civil rights people and so on. One really needs a magistrate's permission.'

He said this automatically, because he liked to give every difficulty a good chance of arguing for itself. That way, he appeared to be better at overcoming them than he was.

'I know that,' MacGillivray replied. 'But why not put in some bloke as an engineer? Say he's testing a line, doing market research, some rubbish of that sort? I also want to know - if you can find out - whether this good lady has had any overseas calls in the last seventy-two hours. If so, where from and what was the number. And who she speaks to in the next seventy-two.'

'Have you her phone number?'

'Sorry,' said MacGillivray, smiling to himself, because he was not in the least repentant; life was being hard on him; why should he make it easy for anyone else? 'You'll have to ask Directory Inquiries. You can get me at home within half an hour.'

'Thank you very much,' said Mason sourly, and banged down the receiver.

The fish fingers looked even less appetizing than before. He pushed away the plate, and his wife, in her dull, heavy, middle-aged voice asked him: 'Is anything wrong, dear?'

What was there in his life, at work, at home, anywhere, to encourage in either of them the illusion that anything was right? Did every marriage taste like his after so many years? Where had all his dreams gone?

'Nothing,' he said stoutly, driving such dangerous, saddening thoughts from his mind. 'It was lovely. But I've got work to do.'

'Work, work. That's all you think of, work,' said Mrs Mason.

She was a fat woman, sitting with a cat on her knees, stroking its tortoise-shell fur mechanically, watching their tiny TV set.

Shadowy figures chased each other in and out of card-board alleys. A gun fired unconvincingly and a car accelerated wildly down a long, wet, studio street. Never did she imagine that this one-dimensional drama in black and white, scaled down to their minute screen, could conceivably bear any relation to the way in which her husband earned his living.

Mason shut the door of the hot, dowdy little room quietly behind him as he went out. He was glad to feel the fresh cold rain on his face.

Love turned to Parkington, half a packet of Gitanes and nearly a whole bottle of Dalmore Malt later.

'That hippie,' he said. 'Who was he again?'

Parkington poured himself the last of the bottle.

'I told you. A nut named Herbert Ellis. You've seen his passport, in any case.'

'That doesn't mean to say he was who the passport said he was.'

'Obviously not. But, so far, I've no reason for doubting it. Have you?'

'Why did you dress up as a hippie?'

'I didn't particularly mean to be a hippie. I just wore what is virtually international dress nowadays, if you don't want to be remarked on. If I'd appeared with striped trousers, black jacket, and short back and sides haircut, I'd have stood out like a live man at an undertakers' reunion.'

'But why would Ellis call on Wilmot - out of all the thousands of other people in Beirut?'

'Why wouldn't he? We're not calling on any of those other thousands ourselves, are we? Maybe he was a friend of Wilmot, or even a relation. Although, I must say, he didn't seem to know much about the man.'

'I've got several relations I've never even seen,' Love pointed out.

'And lucky you. Maybe he was some casual acquaintance, just passing through, who thought he'd touch Wilmot for the price of a ticket or a fix.'

'It's possible. But my feeling is that Ellis was probably trying to see Wilmot for some special reason of his own.'

'Like what? I said, he didn't give me the impression of being on very close terms with the man. Had more of the attitude of a door-step caller.'

'What if he didn't know Wilmot, but he knew Mrs Wilmot - maybe through some mutual friend? And what if she asked him to look up her husband, just like she asked me?'

'It's an idea,' agreed Parkington. 'But it's not much more.'

'And that message about the Greeks and a haircut that was phoned from the post office? What do you make of that?'

Parkington reached down for the telephone.

'Nothing. Not a damn thing. But I'll have another word with MacGillivray, and put him in the picture. This time, we'll be selling figs. Nothing like a good dish of figs to get a man moving.'

The dark blue Ford Cortina turned into the drive of Esdaile House as the church clock struck half past nine on the following morning.

It was driven by a young man with black hair and side-boards, a well-pressed grey suit and a white drip-dry nylon shirt. He looked like any of those other ageless young-old men who overtake each other on main roads, their jackets usually hanging in the back of just such a Cortina or Vauxhall Viva, as they drive in shirtsleeves from one appointment to another, selling paints, chocolates, or a new line in soft plastic coverings for kitchen tables. Sometimes they stroke their ear lobes as they pass, or smooth back their hair, as though to emphasize that passing a slower traveller does not warrant their full concentration.

They are the new Mercurys of the age - the so-called 'young executives' for whom featureless mock-Georgian houses and maisonettes, red brick outside, breeze-block walls inside, are spawned by the thousand in north and south-west London. They are anonymous, aseptic, plastic, made from moulds, conditioned by the Sunday colour supplements, as lacking in personality and character as the goods they sell.

This particular young man climbed out of his car, reached in again, and pulled out a slim leather briefcase, with a zip around the edge. Then he glanced into a pocket diary, and looked up at the house to make doubly certain he was in the right place, checked the time with his watch, just as he must have been taught on the business management course (The Importance of Punctuality and First Impressions). Only then did he stride purposefully towards the front door. His sharp sloe-gin eyes took in the polished door knocker, the newly painted shutters, the festoon of aerials on the lodge roof.

He rang the bell and stood back from the door, so that he would not appear to be crowding the client (The Psychology of your First Successful Sell).

Mrs Wilmot opened the door.

'Well?' she asked. 'What do you want?'

He carried with him an air of being a visitor of a type she would prefer to avoid, someone who would attempt to sell her the unsaleable, who would urge her to try a new washing powder, or ask what breakfast food she preferred.

'I represent the Midland Widows Insurance Company,' the young man said gravely, as though this was a serious admission to make, and produced a card to prove the point.

She took it, without looking at the name engraved in the corner. Surely this goon was not about to sell her a life policy?

'I believe you have a relation,' he went on. 'Mr Herbert Ellis?'

He said this more as a statement of fact than a question.

The reels in the wire recorder, the size of a slim cigarette case, which he had switched on when he took out the card, were already turning in his right hand pocket. A wire, thin as a thread, led down from the Rotary Club badge in his lapel, which concealed the microphone.

Mrs Wilmot nodded.

'Yes, he's my brother.'

'Then I wonder if I could see you, madam?' the young man asked again, making the question seem like a statement.

'You are seeing me,' Mrs Wilmot pointed out. 'I'm sorry, but I'm in a hurry. I have to go to Taunton. Couldn't you put whatever all this is about in a letter?'

'Your brother took out a considerable insurance on his own life in your favour,' the young man went on, as though she had not spoken.

'I didn't know,' she said, face puckered with surprise, and some interest. She'd never known Herbert to have any money. Usually, she was the one who would send him a surreptitious tenner folded inside a sheet of carbon paper in case the Customs in whatever remote country he might be were X-raying overseas letters; or a gift token he could sell at a discount for cash, simply to keep him away. The hope was always that one day Herbert would find a steady job, or even marry a rich wife; anything rather than just to keep on drifting, living on other people's pity or spasmodic generosity.

'Perhaps we could go inside, instead of discussing this outside?' the young man suggested, and took a step towards the door.

'Well, of course, if it's important,' Mrs Wilmot said hesitantly. 'But I've an appointment, and I'm late already. Will this take long?'

'I don't think so,' he said. 'It's purely an exploratory meeting.'

They were in the hall now, surrounded by the Canalettos and the Gauguins, which the young man noted with interest were bolted to the walls. The rich are generally careful; the careful are not always rich.

Mrs Wilmot opened a door into a small study lined with books bound in shiny brown and maroon and deep green leather, the titles all in gold. They stood by a desk, the size of a billiard table, but rather more expensive.

'You knew nothing about your brother's insurance?' said the young man.

'Nothing,' Mrs Wilmot agreed, mystified. 'But what's all this about?'

'Have you seen your brother recently, Mrs Wilmot?'

'No.'

'Do you know where he is at this moment?'

'He was in India. He's travelling. As a student, you know. He has an allowance from a trust fund.'

'I see. And you haven't heard from him recently, either?'

'Not for some time.'

'Well, I'm sorry to tell you, Mrs Wilmot, that I must, therefore, be the bearer of very bad news to you.'

'Bad news? What do you mean? Has something happened to him?'

He nodded, watching her face. Her surprise certainly appeared genuine.

'I regret to say it has, Mrs Wilmot. He's been involved in an accident.'

'An accident? What sort of accident? Where?'

'He was walking along a street - in Beirut. Apparently he stepped off the pavement and was knocked down by a hit-and-run driver. Out there, people rarely stop after accidents if they don't have to. There have been some ugly instances of drivers being lynched by the crowds.'

'In Beirut? Lebanon? Are you sure you're talking about my brother?'

Her concern now was obviously genuine. The young man nodded. 'Quite sure.'

'Has the man who knocked him down been traced?'

'I understand from contacts out there that he is a man of considerable local influence. There were no witnesses. It would only be your brother's word against his.'

'Well?'

'Unfortunately, Mrs Wilmot, your brother cannot give his account. He was killed.'

'He's dead? Are you serious?'

'I am most definitely serious, the young man assured her gravely. 'My company naturally wish to extend to you their very deep condolences on your bereavement. I just had to check that you were, in fact, the Mrs Wilmot named in the policy.'

'Of course I am, but I'm not interested in the money. What about Herbert? Who was this influential man who ran him down?'

'You will understand, Mrs Wilmot, that our information is necessarily very brief. We have only received a night letter telegram from our office in Beirut. We have, of course, asked for further details, but they may take a little time to arrive. The name of the man means nothing to us - and probably not to you.'

'Well, who was he, anyhow?'

'His name was Carlos Diaz.'

'And what did she say then? How did she take that?' asked MacGillivray, with interest.

He sat back in his green leather armchair, offered the young man a cheroot, which the young man, knowing the Colonel's idiosyncrasies, refused, to MacGillivray's pleasure. He allowed himself a packet of five a day. If he gave one away, this would only leave him with four, and the day was still young.

'She seemed amazed, sir,' said the young man. 'She wanted to know more details -- anything I could tell her. But, of course, I stuck to my story that we'd only had a telegram with the bare facts. She kept saying, "No, I just can't believe it."'

'But did she believe it? You convinced her?' MacGillivray asked quickly.

'I did my best, sir. And, of course, I've got it all down.'

He tapped his pocket.

'I felt a bit mean, sir, actually.'

'A feeling that does you great credit, but which you must not indulge too much - especially in our profession. After all, we now know that the man Ellis was her brother - something we didn't know before. And she knows that her brother is dead, which she didn't know before.

'So it's been a kind of mutual exchange of information. The only point of error is the way in which this unfortunate young man died. And, of course, the little matter of the insurance.'

The Midland Widows did not exist as an insurance company, although their office address appeared in heavy black type with several numbers in the London telephone directory. All rang one telephone in a small flat in Notting Hill where a middle-aged spinster, lately retired from the WRNS, answered callers most efficiently. There were not many - for how many people look up an insurance company in the telephone book to put some business their way? The company was simply another of MacGillivray's shells, useful on occasions like this, for it provided a reason for visiting a suspect.

'I suppose that's one way of looking at it, sir,' agreed the young man; he had been brought up to tell the truth, and lies bothered him, even if told in the cause of duty.

'It's the only way,' MacGillivray assured him. 'Have you been with the Special Branch long?'

'Three years.'

'Do you find it interesting?' MacGillivray asked the mechanical question almost without meaning to do so.

'Very varied,' the young man replied diplomatically.

'Ah, yes.'

It would certainly be varied, although some things never varied, such as the greed and weakness and immeasurable vanity of the human animal. 'Well, I'll certainly put in a good word to Inspector Mason about you. Thank you for corning along so quickly.'

MacGillivray stood up to end the interview, shook hands. The young man went out. As he closed the door, the light above it turned green to show that MacGillivray was once more on his own.

He walked across the worn carpet, stood looking out over Covent Garden at the lorries piled with grapefruit and cabbages in orange nylon nets. He wondered what was happening to Parkington and Love in Beirut.

Why was Mrs Wilmot so surprised that a man named Diaz had killed her brother in a car accident? The green telephone trilled like a metal nightingale on his desk. He picked it up.

Mason's voice said, 'Don't say we never give you nothing.'

'I never do,' replied MacGillivray, 'but then I ask for so little, it's almost impossible for you to refuse me.'

'Balls to that,' retorted Mason. 'You asked for a hell of a lot and I'm giving it in full measure - pressed down and running over, as the Good Book says.

'Now, Mrs Wilmot's calls. She's taken two overseas telephone calls in the last three days. I don't know what she said in them or who they were from, because we hadn't got a hook on the wire then.'

'Do you know where they came from?'

'Of course. That's easy. From Beirut in Lebanon. Both from the same number - 735738. You got that?'

'All of it,' said MacGillivray, scribbling the number down on a memo pad. 'Were they long?'

'The first was eight minutes. The second, twelve. She took the first at eight our time on Friday evening, and the second at six our time on Saturday. She called an overseas number this morning. At five past ten.'

'Ah,' said MacGillivray, 'I think you're going to tell me she called a Mr Diaz in Beirut?'

'Check,' agreed Mason in a puzzled voice, 'But how did you know?'

'Extra-sensory perception. We never know the powers we possess - until we need to use them. Then, too often, we find we haven't got any. I'd still like Mr Diaz's number from you.'

'It's Beirut 578221. Anything else?'

'Nothing for now,' said MacGillivray, 'but if there is, I'll be back. I'll do the same for you some day.'

He replaced the receiver, pressed the button for Miss Jenkins. She came in, with the pages of her shorthand book held down, by the wide rubber band she always used, an impersonal, sexless, supremely efficient creature, brown hair smoothed back, face innocent of make-up, eyes blue and faded, like a carpet that has seen too much sun.

Not for the first time, MacGillivray wondered how she had spent the weekend. Was it in her one-room flat in Dolphin Square, overlooking the Thames? Or was it walking in the Chilterns - or maybe taking brass rubbings in some West Country parish church, where the plate was so valuable that the churchwardens, retired majors and naval commanders to a man, kept the doors locked most of the week?

He would never know, and he did not really want to know, because truth is so much sadder than imagination. The reality was probably that Miss Jenkins was resigned to looking after a widowed mother, and wondering where her youth had gone.

He stubbed out his cheroot, cleared his throat, and brought his mind back to the present problems.

'Ah, Miss Jenkins,' he said, as though he had not seen her sixteen times already that day. 'Can you do a Most Immediate for Parkington? He's in Beirut. Under the name of Carter. Send it from the travel agency...'

Parkington gave the little page-boy, his eyes black with kohl, a Lebanese pound note as a tip, took the telegram into his room, locked the door, opened the envelope. He read aloud to Love:

MISTER JOHN CARTER ADELPHI HOTEL RUE SALADIN BEIRUT STOP REGARDING YOUR QUERY FOR PACKAGE HOLIDAYS CYPRUS STOP TOTAL NUMBER OF PASSENGERS SO FAR CARRIED

BY CYPRIOT AIRLINES IS 264262 STOP REGARDING ONWARD BOOKING FACILITIES YOU SHOULD KINDLY CONTACT OUR MISTER KYRENOS CARE OF LEDRA PALACE HOTEL NICOSU PRIVATE TELEPHONE 421779 AFTER TEN FIVE DAILY STOP ASSURING YOU OUR BEST ATTENTION AT ALL TIMES ALPHA TRAVEL AGENCY LONDON ENGLAND.

'So what's all that about?' asked Love, who did not greatly care.

Parkington took out a pen, wrote down both numbers, then subtracted them from a million.

The first is the telephone number from which the good Mrs Wilmot has received a call. The second is the telephone number she called at five past ten today.'

'So now we've got to find the addresses for these numbers?'

'Exactly. Which should take all of five minutes.'

'In England, yes,' agreed Love. 'Because you simply ring up and say you're Harrods or John Lewis, and you've got a hamper or a set of candlesticks to deliver, and can they help you with the address as the clerk dealing with this is in hospital. What do you do out here?'

'Much the same,' said Parkington, picking up the tele-phone. 'I'm on this beat because I speak French and Arabic. I'll simply ring both numbers, say it's the local office, and a telegram has come in which is marked with the phone number but it must be delivered, and we can't find the address in the street directory.'

'Will they accept that?'

'Why shouldn't they? Everything is so damned inefficient here, they'll believe it.'

He dialled the first number. Love heard a man's hoarse voice acknowledging the call in Arabic. Parkington spoke quickly, clearing his throat now and then, as though he were about to hawk, presumably in his intention to impersonate how he imagined a Lebanese postal clerk might speak.

He scribbled down an address, rang off, dialled the second number.

This time, a woman answered, speaking French.

Parkington changed linguistic gear. He might have been a French dancing master or a hairdresser, thought Love sourly, watching him write down another address. He replaced the receiver.

'There we are,' said Parkington. 'Ararat Hotel, Rue de Montparnasse. That's the first one. A bum area, and so I'd say a pretty bum hotel. The next is in a different place altogether. A suburb just outside the city - Ramlet el-Baidd. The rich man's end. Which shall we take first?'

'The hotel,' said Love.

They had another whisky on that, checked both streets in Love's guide to Beirut, then went downstairs, hired a taxi, told the driver to drop them off at the end of the Rue de Montparnasse, where it crossed the Avenue du President Charles Helore, near the old part of the city.

Traffic flared and blared at them in a blaze of colour and noise. The palm fronds trembled slightly in a haze of heat down the centre strip of grass and flowers that divided the two tracks of the Avenue de Paris.

They sat in the back of the cab, shielded from the sun by the pleated silk blinds, watching the white squares of the new buildings shrink away as they approached the docks, until they were among old-fashioned three-storey buildings with washing hanging out from the upper windows on wooden poles, over streets lined with parked lorries. The driver pulled into the side.

'Here, monsieur,' he said.

Parkington paid him, watched him drive away. They crossed the road into the Rue de Montparnasse, a narrow street, with the edge of the pavement painted in black and white segments.

'I'll go to the hotel,' said Love. 'You follow me and have a look at the place from the outside, then over to the rich man's end.'

He walked on his own down the street, hands in his pockets like a tourist, looking into shop windows, resisting the men in shirt-sleeves who came out of the carpet stores and the little open-fronted shops with windows full of beaten gold ear-rings.

'Just to look, sir, not to buy. I promise you good price. You're English, yes? American? I have many friends in New York. I give you good discount...'

The Ararat entrance was simply a wide doorway between one shop selling American magazines about souped-up cars, and another filled with tennis racquets and shotguns and grey rubber decoy pigeons.

The 't' in the hotel sign was missing, and no one had swept the tiled step outside the door that week. Love walked past the entrance, fifty yards up the street, in case he was being followed by anyone except Parkington. Then he walked back and went inside.

The hall smelled of cheap hair oil and curry, one overlaid on the other. To the left was a reception desk with a frosted-glass screen, and rows of keys hanging from pigeon-holes, under an ancient brass light encrusted with grease and dead flies.

Across the hall, a staircase led up to the next floor, its dirty red carpet held in place by tarnished brass rods.

An old man rose to his full five feet two behind the screen. He had thinning grey hair on his head, and a lot of thick grey hair sprouting out of his nostrils and ears.

'Monsieur?' he asked, as though surprised anyone should come into his hotel.

"You speak English?' Love asked him.

He inclined his head gravely, as if this was a serious thing to admit.

'I hear you have a good restaurant here,' said Love. 'I'm a tourist passing through. I wondered if you could serve an early lunch?'

'But, of course. This way.'

He padded ahead of Love in his pointed plastic shoes, pierced with ventilating holes. He breathed heavily as though the hair in his nose was suffocating him. His suit rustled like dead leaves as he walked.

They went up the stairs along a corridor, as gloomy and oppressive as the rest of the hotel. It suddenly ended in two glass doors, and beyond these soared a gigantic ballroom, the size of a tennis court, its glass roof spattered on top by bird droppings.

Six or seven tables were set up in one corner of the tessellated floor. A waiter, half as old as time and twice as slow, was pouring cloudy water into glasses on each of the tables.

'Here is the restaurant, monsieur,' said the old man, rather as Moses might have indicated the glories of the Promised Land. 'Gaston will look after you.'

At the mention of his name, the waiter fluttered rheumatically towards them, empty jug in his hand.

'You have a table?' Love asked him, as though anyone else was likely to have booked here.

The waiter indicated the nearest. Love sat down, his back against the wall. The waiter brought him a menu card, heavily thumb-printed. Love glanced through it, choosing the dishes that seemed to have the greatest chance of being reasonably fresh. He settled for a mezze, the local variety of hors-d'oeuvres, and a bottle of Almaza beer.

'You're English?' asked the waiter.

'Yes,' said Love.

'There's another Englishman staying here. You are a friend of his?'

The waiter's mind obviously worked on the principle by which he naturally assumed that two foreigners from the same foreign country would know each other.

Love inclined his head, neither confirming nor denying.

'He'll be down for lunch in a minute. He lunches very early. Perhaps you lunch early in England, yes?'

'Sometimes,' Love admitted. It usually depended how busy he was.

The waiter went off to shout the order through a swing-door into the kitchen. Then he came back to continue pouring out the milky water into the thick glasses.

The main doors opened and a man came through. He wore glasses, was dark-skinned, of medium height, middle-aged, in a light-weight tropical suit. He walked quickly, lightly, almost on his toes, as though at any moment he might suddenly break into a run. He glanced across at Love, eyes narrowing, obviously wondering about his nationality.

Then he sat down at the table farthest from Love, and began to read the Lebanese Daily Post avidly, as though he had been waiting impatiently for weeks for just this chance.

The waiter padded in, wheeling the mezze trolley, put down a cold plate in front of Love, nodded across towards the other man.

'There he is - the other Englishman,' he announced in a conspiratorial whisper tinged with pride, as though he had somehow arranged for him to materialize.

Love drank some beer, selected lobster cooked with saffron rice, olives and sour cheese, and then walked across to the other man's table. He went on reading, as though he expected Love to pass by.

Love stayed. The man looked up, half surprised, half wary. His face was lined, and his eyes lacked brightness. He had all the symptoms of a worried, unhappy man.

'Excuse me,' said Love, feeling a bit like Dr Livingstone. 'You must be Mr Esdaile - or Mr Wilmot?'

'And if I am?'

The question seemed an accusation, rather than an admission.

Love pulled out a chair, sat down at the table beside him.

'I'm Dr Jason Love, your wife's doctor - and yours. She asked me to look you up. Which I've done. It's time we met.'

'Dr Love!'

Esdaile pushed back his chair and half stood up, a smile creasing his face, as though this was the one happy moment in a day of deep depression.

'Tell me, Doctor,' he said, sitting back in his chair. 'How is she?'

'Your wife?'

'No, my daughter. Sandra. She's ill.'

'What were you told was wrong with her?' asked Love.

'Leukaemia. She's asking for me. Do you think she'll pull through, Doctor?'

Love looked sharply at his worried face, at the dull, unhappy eyes, the stubble on the chin. He had seen the child again just before he left, and although leukaemia, like syphilis, can wear many false faces, he was convinced that Sandra Wilmot was completely healthy. Yet this man, two thousand miles away from home, sincerely believed she was already under the ever-deepening shadow of death. Why?

'Who told you this?' he asked.

'I'd rather not say here,' said Wilmot, glancing uneasily about the enormous ballroom.

'Upstairs,' he said. 'I'll tell you there.'

'Let's go,' said Love.

The waiter rushed in; he must have been watching them

through a peep-hole.

'Charge the meals to my account - room four-oh-two,' Wilmot told him.

'But you have eaten nothing,' said the old man, bewildered.

Truly, as they always said, the English were mad. Yet he might profit from their waste and folly. He now had two complete meals, paid for but not eaten, which he could serve to the next two guests — and pocket their payment himself. In truth, Allah was generous to his followers. At least, he thought more realistically, he would be if he sent along another two customers to the restaurant.

Love and Wilmot went out of the ballroom, down the corridor, up two flights of stairs and into a large wood-panelled bedroom with an uneven floor that sloped away towards one corner. The air smelt sour with wood rot and stale cigarette smoke. The shutters were closed, and a huge antique fan batted the air rhythmically above them with long, square-edged blades.

'I'll call you Wilmot,' said Love, when he had shut the door.

'Call me any bloody thing.'

Wilmot crossed to the dressing-table, opened the door, took out a bottle of whisky and two glasses. He rinsed them carefully under the cold tap of the wash basin, dried them on a towel, poured four fingers of whisky into each.

Wilmot sat down on the bed, gripped his glass with both hands.

'Now,' he said. 'Sandra. What's your opinion?'

'That she's perfectly fit. There's nothing wrong with her at all.'

Wilmot's face creased with incredulity.

'Are you serious?' he asked.

'Of course.'

'There could be no doubt, Doctor?'

'I'm telling you. She's fine.'

Wilmot's face softened in relief. He finished his drink, poured out another one.

'You wouldn't lie to me, Doctor?'

'No,' said Love. 'But someone else was lying to you. Whoever told you she was ill.'

'I can't understand it,' said Wilmot evasively. 'I was desperate when I heard. I rang my wife from this number. She confirmed Sandra wasn't well, but she wouldn't say what was wrong with her.'

'Why did you leave your flat? Your wife was very worried about you. She asked me to come out and find you.'

Wilmot paused for a moment, as though in doubt whether to go on; then he made up his mind.

He said: 'You must hear lots of secrets, Doctor, and keep them?'

'Sometimes,' agreed Love.

'Well, I'll tell you some more,' he said. 'Caroline's probably told you how I felt I was being hounded out of Britain. I came here because it's a neutral place. You can move money in and out. No questions asked. And I wanted time to think.

'I've made a lot of money, Doctor, and a good deal of it, in the early days, in pretty unsavoury ways. A lot of us in the property field are like that. It's all very respectable now, but it wasn't when I started, just after the war.

'There's no doubt I probably could be deported, if the immigration people knew exactly how some of my early money was made, running whore-houses and so on.

'Anyway, last year I met a fellow in the same line of business I'd not seen for years. He'd got a concession with the Egyptian government virtually sewn up for about a hundred miles of coast in North Africa.

'He'd been in the camp with me. I think he'd been a British agent once, that's how he got British nationality. He lived in Cairo. He was very friendly with our Egyptian Minister - who wanted his cut, of course.

'If we got this, we'd have the biggest holiday development in the world — and, geographically, nearly in the centre of the world. Only hours away from London, New York, even Australia.

'I was in touch with him out here, and expected he'd call on me in my flat. But instead I had a visit from two British policemen.'

'In Beirut?' asked Love, surprised.

'In Beirut. Plain-clothes men. They'd been looking into various financial deals, they said, and since I was technically an alien, without this permit or that authority, I could be deported.

'I told them I'd always had the best advice from British accountants and lawyers, and if I was guilty of these things, it was unintentional. They did not appear impressed.'

'How do you know they were policemen?' asked Love.

'They showed me identity cards. They advised me not to contact my wife, not to reply to her letters for the time being - unless I wanted to involve her in unpleasant publicity. I moved out - again on their advice - and came here.

'Yesterday, one of them came to see me again. He told me that Sandra was seriously ill with leukaemia and was asking for me. Yet I couldn't go to see her, because if I landed in England I'd be arrested immediately - and put on the next plane out - presumably back here.

'But then he came up with a suggestion. If I'd do a job for the British Secret Service, then the Home Office or the Foreign Office, or whoever was involved, would drop all these charges. I could even become naturalized.'

'What was the job?' asked Love.

'To shoot someone.'

'Dead?'

'Dead.'

'Do you know who?'

'Only that he arrives tomorrow. I'll be told all I need to know before then.'

'Why can't they shoot him themselves?'

'Because although both the British and the Americans wanted the man out of the way, they simply couldn't afford to become involved if anything went wrong. They've too many commercial firms here that would suffer. If someone else shot him, though - and got caught - they could deny all knowledge convincingly.'

'Do you believe that?' asked Love.

'Do I believe anything?' replied Wilmot. 'The fellow showed me a letter on Home Office paper addressed to me and signed by some Under-Secretary, which said, in round terms, without specifying in detail, that if I collaborated with them over a project about which I'd be told, then my nationalization request would receive favourable and speedy consideration. That was as far as they could go officially in writing, the policeman said. He had a pass, a warrant, every kind of thing. He was genuine, all right.'

'So. Are you going to shoot him?'

Wilmot nodded.

'Someone is coming to see me here in about an hour to brief me — when I saw you in the restaurant, I thought you might be him. A man named MacGregor.'

'Good old Scots name,' said Love. 'Met him before?'

'Never. I've shaved off my moustache since I saw the policemen, and I'm wearing these glasses, too, just in case someone recognized me. Well, that's my story, Doctor. What do you think?'

'I don't know,' said Love. 'But it smells to me.'

Yet, even as he spoke, he recognized the smell of authenticity.

The SIS and the CIA frequently used ordinary people - newspaper reporters, travellers, businessmen who might have some legitimate reason for being in a strange part of the world - to pass on a coded message, or to pick up information, maybe to bring back a tiny package hidden in a book or a bar of chocolate. To seek such help in a political assassination was only taking a further step.

'Are you a good shot?' he asked.

'I should be. I've a thousand acres in Perthshire. I spend a month there every year. I've also a place in Dorset for the pheasants. And they're giving me a Belgian FN rifle with a telescopic sight, which is about the best there is.'

'What else are they giving you?'

'I'll learn that from MacGregor,' said Wilmot. 'But they've a foolproof scheme laid on for my getaway - special car, private plane out to Cyprus! The lot.'

'It's murder,' Love pointed out.

Wilmot shrugged his shoulders.

'Millions of people are killed in wars, Doctor,' he said. 'That's murder, too. Only under another name. This could go under the same name - if names mean such a lot. Patriotism.'

Love lit a Gitane and sat, head down, thinking. He knew that MacGillivray was sometimes forced to use amateurs, either through lack of agents in the right place, or money, or simply through bad planning, for he sometimes worked for him in this capacity.

But for an act of political murder, an amateur, even a skilled shot, offered many hostages to failure. He might have a sudden rush of blood to the conscience, and at the last moment, decide not to shoot, or, worse still, he might shoot and miss.

'What name are you registered under here?' Love asked Wilmot.

'Ford. Douglas Ford. It was their suggestion, too.'

They seem to think of everything.'

'That's what they told me.'

'Ever killed anyone before?' asked Love.

'No.'

'When were you last in your flat?'

'About a week ago. Why?'

'I was there this morning.'

'How did you get in?' asked Wilmot, surprised.

'Had a key copied. Looks, like someone else also has a copy.'

'What do you mean?'

'There was a body on your bed.'

'A body?' repeated Wilmot. 'What do you mean - some-one drunk?'

'Someone dead.'

'Are you joking?'

Love shook his head.

'Never been more serious. A young man. Long hair, hippie clothes. He'd been badly roughed-up. Bleeding from his mouth and his nose. I left pretty quickly after that - just quickly enough, in fact. The police were coming in the building as I went out.'

Wilmot sagged, like a balloon with a leak.

'I don't know what you're talking about,' he said weakly. 'I don't know any hippie. I hardly know anybody in Beirut, in any case.'

'You'll have a hard job explaining that when the police come around.'

'My God, do you think they will?'

'I found you. So can they. And they will.'

'But only if I'm here,' retorted Wilmot. 'And I'll be out by tomorrow. They should have enough to keep them busy then.'

'So should you - if you get involved. Remember, they'll be after you then for two murders. One private, one political.'

Wilmot put his head in his hands and shook it, as though trying to drive out the fearful thoughts that flooded his brain.

'You must believe me, Doctor,' he said at last. 'I know nothing about this man in my flat. Do you think MacGregor does?'

'I wouldn't ask him,' said Love. 'In fact, if I were you, I wouldn't even see him.'

'But I've got to,' said Wilmot desperately.

'You're sure you've not seen him already?'

'Absolutely.'

'Well then,' said Love. 'Keep your head down and I'll see him - as you. He doesn't know you. If he's seen a photograph of you, it's as you used to be, with a moustache and sideburns, not as you are now.'

'What good can that do? He'll be back, and we haven't a lot of time. The man I'm to kill arrives tomorrow.'

'Here's my proposition, Wilmot. I'll see MacGregor - as you. If I think it's a sound proposition from your point of view, I'll come with you tomorrow. You may need a friend.

'If, on the other hand, I think there's no chance for you, and the whole thing's just an invitation to write your own death certificate, I'll tell you. And you can think again.'

Wilmot looked at him in surprised gratitude.

'Why are you doing this, Doctor?'

'My job is to save life, not take it. I may bury my mistakes - but at least I don't kill them deliberately. And your wife's paid me a lot of money to find you. I feel I owe her this.

'You go out now and book in at a cinema. Sit for half an hour in one seat, then cross over and sit in another on the other side of the house for ten minutes or so, and then go out through a different entrance before die interval.

'Take a bus ride round town, and find another cinema and stay there until it's dark. Then come back here. It might be better if you used the service entrance. Just in case both the front and the back doors are being watched.'

'By whom?' asked Wilmot.

'If we knew that,' said Love, 'we might know the answers to a lot more questions.'

He glanced at his watch.

'Now get out while you've the chance. I always prefer my patients to walk out rather than be carried.'

Wilmot crossed to the chest of drawers, took out a wallet of travellers' cheques, a silver hip flask of brandy, put them in the inside of his jacket, buttoned down the flap on top of them. Then he picked up a light-weight straw hat, pushed it on the back of his head, shook hands with Love, crossed to the door.

'I'll await your call, Doctor,' he said. 'And thank you.'

'You won't thank me when I put in my bill,' said Love. 'I charge a pound a mile travelling to private patients, and I'm two thousand miles away from home.'

'Be my guest,' said Wilmot. 'I'll pay that for your journey home, too.'

'It's a deal,' said Love, hoping it was.

Wilmot went out, closing the door quietly behind him.

CHAPTER SIX

Love made a quick examination of the suite. Beyond the bedroom was an old-fashioned bathroom roughly the same size, with a big blotchy mirror and louvred white shutters, pegged back against the wall. A leaky tap had stained the inside of the ancient bath, which was supported on four metal claws grasping white balls. The wall tiles, and the mosaic floor, were chipped and cracked.

As a doctor, Love had heard many strange stories in unlikely surroundings. But this was the first time he had waited to be briefed on an act of deliberate murder by a man he had never met, whose real name he would probably never know. However, there must be a first time for everything.

He sat down again in the chair, lit another cigarette, and waited, mind switched off, for whoever might arrive.

After about twenty minutes, when he had begun to wonder whether the whole thing was a hoax, he heard a tentative knock at the door, and called, 'Yes?' thinking it might be a chambermaid coming to turn down the bed.

The door knob turned, the door opened. A man came in, closed it, and locked it behind him.

He was of medium height, of any age between thirty and. forty, the sort of man you ride next to in a bus, or see across a street, and. never recognize again because he has the chameleon-quality of fitting into any background as though he belonged there. He wore a deep blue Dacron suit, a button-down shirt, a dark red tie that matched the dark red handkerchief in his breast pocket. His face could have been anyone's; it just happened to be his.

'Mr Wilmot?' he asked.

'Yes,' said Love, not getting up.

JAMES LEASOR

The man crossed the room, sat down on a dressing-table stool, spun it round towards Love. He had not offered to shake hands.

'My name is MacGregor,' he said. Love thought this unlikely, but let it go. It went.

'You know why I'm here?' MacGregor went on.

'To tell me the set-up for tomorrow.'

'Yes.'

'Are you also a British agent?' asked Love.

MacGregor nodded.

'I'd deny it in a court of law,' he said, 'because, as you know, the Secret Service doesn't exist officially. So if any of us are caught or killed, we don't exist, either.'

'Do you have any pass or identity card?' asked Love.

'Nothing,' said MacGregor. 'You wouldn't expect me to, would you? But I can tell you a few things about yourself which may show I've done my homework.'

'Go on.'

'You were born in the Sisters of Mercy Nursing Home, Warsaw, on December 20th, 1923. Your mother had high blood pressure, but it didn't kill her. She died with your father in the uprising in 1944.'

'You could have found that out easily,' said Love. 'It doesn't prove you know much about me.'

'Well, does this? You did your first property deal when you were twenty-four. You bought a greengrocery shop off the Fulham Road, with a flat above it. You rented it out as a restaurant.

'The flat came empty and you put in three whores, each paying you ten pounds a week clear, tax free. This you paid into a branch of a bank in Leicester. You opened the account there in the name of Walnut Securities. You liked walnuts, so it was an easy name for you to remember, even if you didn't speak much

English then.

'After this venture, you opened several more whore-houses. At the last count, you had probably twenty or thirty. I believe that the last bank statement for Walnut Securities showed you had nearly one hundred thousand pounds in cash there. Do you want to hear any more?'

'That will do,' said Love.

So maybe Wilmot did have something to fear. Living on immoral earnings, on such an organized scale, was a deportable offence.

'Right,' said MacGregor, 'so we understand each other. Now I'll tell you what's going to happen tomorrow.

'As you probably know, the visitor to this country is politically unacceptable both to the British and the American governments. More than any one man, he is responsible for keeping up the tension in Egypt against all kinds of rapprochement with Israel. He's also the main link with the Arab guerrilla organizations, their chief front man - and he has a retainer from China paid into a Geneva bank account every month.

'If he were removed, a lot of steam would go out of that whole situation. With results that could be of immeasurable value to the West. You will remove him.'

'Why couldn't he simply be discredited in some way? Or maybe bribed to retire through convenient ill health?'

'These have both been tried, without success. There's only one solution. He has to die.'

'That's murder,' said Love.

'I wouldn't argue,' agreed MacGregor, and didn't.

'Right,' he went on. 'At eight-ten tomorrow our target arrives at the airport, is met by the diplomatic corps, an emissary of the President, and all that swallow-tailed-coat crowd. He then drives in an open Cadillac convertible, with police outriders, through the main streets, along the coast road to the Great Seraglio. It's a former Turkish barracks where the Prime Minister has his office.

'At one point on this road, he passes directly underneath a new and empty skyscraper, which still has a lot of builder's rubbish on the roof.

'You'll be on top of that skyscraper, Wilmot, with a rifle I will supply. It will have three bullets, a silencer, and a telescopic sight that can magnify the target fifty times. You'll also have a special alarm watch synchronized to mine.

'You can't be overlooked by anyone, for you'll be on top of the tallest building for nearly half a mile in any direction.

'When your alarm watch rings, the car with your target will be about to turn a corner right beneath the building. As it turns, you will fire one shot.

'If you miss, you can fire the other two. But you'll only be the height of the skyscraper away from him, and with that telescopic sight, and your natural eye, you'll be able to pick out the hairs in his nostrils. There'll be no risk whatever of you missing.'

'Seems like a hell of a risk getting away from there afterwards, though?'

'We've thought of that.'

'Tell me.'

'At quarter Jo eight tomorrow morning, you will walk into the building, wearing ordinary outdoor clothes, but with some simple facial disguise - a moustache, dark glasses, something of that kind. You'll also carry a leather briefcase, which I'll provide. It will contain the black robes of a Coptic priest - black stovepipe hat, black beard - and the rifle which is designed to fold up.

'At the precise second you fire, we will start two diversions in the street. First, six thunder-flashes thrown out of an office window will explode just behind the leading outriders, and in front of the Cadillac. And a smoke-bomb detonator, which we'll hide with a timing device in one of the litter bins at the bottom of a lamp-post, will go off two seconds later.

'Everyone will assume the man's death is somehow tied up with these very loud explosions.

'In addition, to add to the confusion, we've a third diversion. All the lamp-posts on the route have loudspeakers on them to play martial music. We have another amplifier which we'll plug into this circuit, out in the suburbs, and boost the music from the loudspeakers tenfold. The noise will be fantastic.

'Right? After you've fired, you get into the lift, put on the robes and disguise, come down, and walk slowly out of the building with your hands folded, as in prayer.

'With all this blare of music, the explosions, the smoke from the bomb, there'll be chaos down there in the streets. Who is going to question a quiet priest, walking in a parallel street, not even in sight of the main action?'

'Don't ask me,' said Love. 'I hope no one does.'

'No one will. At the back entrance to the building we'll have a police car ready. You simply climb into the back and are driven out to the airport. Finish.'

'Do we have a rehearsal?'

'Yes.'

'Like when?'

'Like now.'

He stood up, opened the door. Love followed him down the stairs, through the seedy entrance hall, out into the bustling street.

A beige Hillman Minx pulled out from a side alley. Mac-Gregor opened the back door. They climbed in and the car shot forward. A dark-skinned man sat at the wheel, the pocks of old boils pitting his neck.

MacGregor said, 'Everything's been timed, but just to set your mind at ease, we'll run through it from the time you arrive.'

'Who's the driver?' asked Love.

'One of ours,' said MacGregor enigmatically.

The driver pulled into a vacant space between two parked Plymouths. MacGregor jumped out, held open the door for Love. The car moved on instantly and was gone before he could memorize its number. And even if he had done, he knew it would almost certainly be changed, so what was the point?

They walked up the pavement for fifty yards, and then turned into the entrance of a new office block. Floors of empty anodized window-frames gazed blindly across the teeming street.

The entrance hall had a gigantic sculpture in bronze on one wall, still covered with polythene sheeting to protect it against the decorators' spray guns.

The floor was littered with planks and saw-horses; power cables lined the main marble staircase like giant black serpents.

They took the lift up to the sixteenth floor. MacGregor wedged open the door with a piece of wood, and they walked the last flight of steps to the roof. A wall about four feet high, made from grey plastic slabs held by aluminium uprights, was fixed around the edge.

Two sections were missing, and here the contractors had been mixing. concrete; paper bags split open, half-full of cement and sand, formed an escarpment. Rough wooden scaffold poles, tree trunks sticking out of the concrete, like the stumps of long thin teeth, gave the bags extra strength. Love could see that the protection, both from other eyes -or other bullets - was sound as a row of sandbags.

It was very hot up there, without any shade, and no wind at all. The sun bored down on them dizzily, and Love felt his shoulders grow damp with sweat under his thin shirt.

He glanced cautiously over the wall, because he hated heights. Far beneath them, midgets moved along the pavements, bent on miniscule missions of their own, and cars darted about like brightly coloured mechanical mice.

A haze of heat shimmered over the distant rooftops. Be-yond the white new buildings and the red terracotta roofs of the old part of Beirut, the sea merged with the sky's only slightly lighter blue.

'Here's where you'll be,' said MacGregor. 'In this gap. The only way anyone could see you here - unless you stand up - would be from a helicopter, and there'll be none tomorrow. The police have forbidden any overflying. They're very jittery with all the trouble on the borders and El Fatah guerrillas and so on.

'Lebanon has always been a gateway country between East and West. Now the Arab-Israeli trouble nearly has the gate off its hinges.

'What you have to do is to keep down behind these bags and poke the rifle through this hole here.'

He indicated a small space about three inches square, which had been wedged up by pieces of wood under the cement bags.

Love lay down and squinted through it at the street inter-section hundreds of feet beneath. All that would be visible from street level would be the snout of his rifle, and even that only at the moment of firing.

'Now,' MacGregor went on, 'when your watch alarm rings, the car will be turning that corner. It's a right angle. They're only clocking fifteen miles an hour in the motorcade, so they'll be doing even less as they turn.

'As I said, you'll have three bites at the cherry. You can't miss. See for yourself.'

He took out from an inner pocket a matt-black Jasco telescopic sight, handed it to Love.

Love put the sight to his right eye, focused it. Against the crosshairs on the lens he could see the faces of people at the street corner as clearly as if they were standing next to him. One man spat in the gutter; another was lighting a cigarette; a third picked his teeth with a match.

He handed back the sight.

'Right,' said MacGregor again. "Now, assume you've just fired, and the smoke and the detonators and thunder-flashes have all gone off down below. Everyone's shouting and screaming. Police sirens. The lot. You slide out backwards, and go down the flight of stairs we've just come up. Let's see you do it.'

Love pulled himself back over the hot, rough concrete, feeling it warm to the palms of his hands and against his knees. He followed MacGregor down the stairs. The lift was waiting for them. MacGregor pulled out the wedge. The lift swept them down into the basement.

'Now, out this way,' said MacGregor. 'You'll have put on the priest's robe by now. Throw the case away in this junk.'

He nodded towards the packing cases, the drums of paint and creosote and stacks of newly sawn planks; all the impedimenta of a building nearly finished.

The back door led into a side street. As they came out into the sunshine, a black car with white doors moved up from a parking meter. The driver, in khaki uniform with a red top to his cap, leaned over the seat and opened a rear door.

They climbed in. The car sped away through the traffic. A policeman on point duty, standing on a wooden pedestal under a flashing amber lamp and a sunshade, waved to them as they went by.

'See that?' said MacGregor proudly. 'The cover's pretty good if it even takes in the real thing.'

They followed the airport road. The older buildings wore their shutters pinned back against their walls. The influence of provincial French architecture was strong in shutters and wrought-iron fences, their paint powdered by years of sun-, shine. Soon they were out amid the flat lands and the red earth and the international signs : Coca Cola; Pan Am Makes The Going Great; BOAC Takes Good Care Of You.

Ahead of them, airport buildings sprouted in the distance; blue glass in the control tower, the long sand-coloured stretch of the restaurant and booking hall, the giant clock facing the entrance road lined with cedars.

The car turned into the main car park about fifty yards from the terminal, under the concrete lamp-posts and the strips of well-watered grass.

'We get out here,' said MacGregor. 'From this point, we're only fifty yards from the private section of the airport. That's about as near as we need go now, just to show you where it is.'

They walked between the lines of parked cars. A few small private airplanes - a Cessna, two Rapides, two Pipers - were drawn up in line, wheels chocked, wings weighted by ropes to concrete blocks. One of the Rapides, silver fuselage reflecting the sun like a mirror, bore British markings.

'That will be ready for you tomorrow,' said 'MacGregor.

Love put his hand in his pocket for the stub of pencil he always carried there, along with one of his visiting cards and, as he walked, hand still in his pocket, he scribbled the number on the card.

'Pilot up front, engine running, permission to take off secure,' MacGregor continued.

'It's taken us exactly ninety-five seconds to walk from the car to here. If you run, you can do it in a minute. The plane will be airborne in another fifty seconds.

'The pilot will have had his route passed and checked by Control. His story is, he's flying up to Baalbek with a geologist - that's you. Five miles north, he turns west, and out over the coast to Cyprus. When Control asks him what he's doing he simply delays replying for as long as he can. Then he reports oil-feed trouble, and says he's going up to gain more height. When they ask him a second time, he doesn't answer.'

'Couldn't they catch him with a fighter?'

'Of course. But who the hell's going to send up a fighter plane after a geologist on his way to Baalbek in a plane with engine trouble? Use your loaf. Any other questions?'

'Only one. What if I don't do it?'

MacGregor stopped and looked at him. They stood very close together, two men surrounded by hundreds of empty cars, the sunshine sending wild heliograph- signals from their windscreens.

'My colleague told you yesterday,' MacGregor reminded him gently.

'I'd like to hear it from you.'

'If you don't do it,' said MacGregor quietly, 'that's the end of the matter. We can't make you. We're simply offering you the choice of two things you appear to want rather badly.

'One, British nationality. Two, a chance to return home without any trouble, bother, or inquiries of any kind. I would say it's a reasonable exchange. We know you're a first-class shot, or we wouldn't have bothered with you in the first place.'

'OK.' said Love. 'I'll do it.'

'Right,' said MacGregor, without any show of emotion whatever. He appeared neither pleased, relieved, or surprised.

'This afternoon, when you get back - and you'd better make your own way back, in case we're seen together - you'll receive a parcel from the Speedy 12-hour Dry-Cleaning Service.

'It'll contain the rifle, three rounds of ammunition, the gear you've got to wear tomorrow, and a pair of flesh-coloured rubber gloves. Wear them all the time. We don't want any fingerprints.'

'Does it matter, if I'll be in Cyprus?'

'In a deal like this,' said MacGregor, 'everything matters. You either do it professionally or you don't do it at all. I'll ring you tomorrow, just to check all's well. Goodbye.'

He did not shake hands. Love watched him walk towards a grey Fiat 500. He climbed in behind the wheel, started the engine, and drove off, without a backward glance.

Smooth operator, thought Love admiringly, and began the hot trudge over the baking brick pavement to the airport building to hire a taxi.

Parkington was waiting for him back in his hotel room, feet up on the dressing-table, a dozen stubs of cigarettes in an ashtray by the side of his chair, two bottles of Dalmore Malt on the table, with a tooth glass. One bottle was half-empty, the other half-full.

He poured himself another drink, gave one to Love.

'So what happened?' he asked.

Love told him, then took out the card on which he had written the airplane number, picked up the telephone, asked the operator to get him the British Embassy.

When the cool, remote voice replied, a long way from Kensington, and probably loving it, Love said, 'I wonder if you could help me with a query? I'm an English doctor on holiday. A friend of mine is flying out in his own plane. I've seen one at the airport and I wonder whether you could check whether this plane is, in fact, owned by a Mr Jackson?'

It was the first name he could think of. But he was sure the psychiatrist would not mind being promoted, however, temporarily, to the status of someone who flew his own airplane.

'One moment,' said the girl, as though she dealt with questions like this every day, as possibly she did. 'I'll put you through to the air attaché's office.'

Love repeated his question, this time to a man, giving him the aircraft's number.

'I think you've made rather a mistake, Doctor,' said the man, almost confidentially, as though he was not often in a position to point out the mistakes of others. 'The plane with this number belongs to the air attache himself.'

'Are you sure? It's a Rapide. Silver, with a red flash down each side and red spats on the wheels.'

'That's it,' said the man. 'It's his private property.'

'Is it now? Does he fly it very far?'

'Oh, yes,' said the man. 'A lot. Matter of fact, he's just come in from Cyprus today.'

'When does he go back?' asked Love.

'I think some time tomorrow.'

'Well, I've obviously made a mistake,' said Love. 'Thank you so much.'

He put down the phone before anyone could ask him for his name or number, turned to Parkington.

'That plane belongs to the air attaché. He's flying it to Cyprus tomorrow. This thing begins to look genuine.'

Parkington lit another cigarette from the stub of the one he was already smoking.

'It may bloody well be,' he said. 'But I know nothing about it.'

Perhaps this enterprise had been organized by one of the other clandestine secret arms, civil or service, that sometimes worked without knowledge of each other's actions, and not always with successful or even predictable results.

Sometimes, Parkington thought, they spent so much time and

effort and ingenuity in scoring points off each other — always with the ultimate aim of a 'K' or, at least, a GBE for the Director concerned - that they had little enough strength left to fight the Queen's enemies, the purpose for which they were originally recruited.

'Could you ask MacGillivray whether he knows anything about it?' asked Love.

'Too risky,' said Parkington. 'But why this interest? You aren't going to shoot this Egyptian bugger, are you?'

'I'm afraid my patient may. He's desperate to get home, and this seems to him to be the only way. I'll try to talk him out of it, though, but he seems adamant. And while we're on the subject, what's your interest in getting Wilmot out of Beirut?'

'Nothing personal. Only that I'm supposed to have done it by eight tomorrow morning. Presumably before he can shoot.'

'Then you're not making much progress,' said Love.

'I could say the same for you,' said Parkington. 'But at least I've got two seats booked for us out to Cyprus by the early morning plane.'

'In your own names?'

'No. I'm travelling as Captain Brooks and he's Major Hall. There's a lot of military traffic between here and Cyprus. This is a leave centre for the United Nations Force there. I've even arranged military passes for both of us. Now all I've got to do is to get him, which shouldn't be hard now I know where he is.'

'When do you propose picking him up?'

Parkington looked at his watch.

'Very early tomorrow morning - about three or four. If I pick him up any earlier, I'll only be lumbered with him for the night. And he could be followed. If it's so important for our people to nab him, it must be equally important for someone else to keep him here. So, I'm leaving him where he is until the last possible moment.'

'If he's not physically in Beirut, he can't shoot this character tomorrow,' said Love.

'Exactly,' said Parkington. 'You're coming on. So I can't see what all the worry is about. My only difficulty was finding him, and even that wasn't very hard.'

'You didn't find him,' said Love. 'I did. And maybe it was lucky you didn't. Look what happened to that hippie!'

Parkington swung his legs down, stubbed out his cigarette.

'My God,' he said. 'I'd completely forgotten about him. Who the hell was he really, I wonder?'

'We've been through all that before. I can't help you. We were never introduced. Either he knew Wilmot, or he came to see him about something that concerned them both.'

'Maybe Wilmot surprised him and they had a fight, and Wilmot won?'

'Wilmot denied it.'

'Of course,' said Parkington. 'What was in it for him if he admitted killing him?'

'I believe him,' said Love. 'Maybe Ellis was simply dumped in his fiat as a lever to make Wilmot do what he was told.'

'Or maybe,' said Parkington slowly, 'you were right earlier on. Maybe Ellis came to tell Wilmot something. Perhaps to warn him of the danger he must be in, though from whom or why I've no idea - yet.

'Someone's obviously keeping a watch on the place, and perhaps they picked up Ellis just because they wanted to know why he was there, what he wanted to see Wilmot ' about. Maybe they killed him. What could be valuable for them may also be useful for us, I suggest we go back to Wilmot' s flat and see what happens.'

'I'll tell you exactly what'll happen,' said Love. 'If it's being watched, we'll be picked up, probably by the local police. And what sort of excuse have we got for being in someone else's fiat with a copy key?'

'Let's decide that when we're asked the question,' said Parkington, standing up. 'Right now we're wasting time.'

He picked up the telephone.

'The British Embassy,' he said when the hotel operator answered. 'Yes, I know. Again.'

Love watched him, for he knew the cardinal rule of the Secret Service that at no time should an agent contact any member of the overt staff of the local British Embassy in connection with an assignment, although, under one guise or other, most Embassies maintained one official who, in dire emergency, might be approached by certain round-about means.

When the Embassy operator answered, Parkington said, 'My name is Carter. I'm an insurance agent out here with the British company, the Midland Widows. Unfortunately, one of our clients' has been killed in a street accident and I have to identify his body. Can you tell me if there's any central mortuary where the victims of accidents are taken?'

The girl said, 'This is a little out of my province, Mr Carter. Hold the line, I'll put you through to someone who can help you.'

Some clicks in his ear, and a man's voice said, 'Yes?'

Parkington explained the situation to him.

'Hell,' said the man. 'That's a bit of an odd one.'

Parkington said nothing; he could imagine him sitting, shirt-sleeved, under the slow-turning fan in one of the minor offices in the Embassy. His accent somehow made him think he would not have one of the bigger air-conditioned offices, complete with the Annigoni portrait of the Queen, and a signed Christmas card from Buckingham Palace, which overlooked the Avenue de

Paris and the sea.

'I'll try to help you, old fellow,' the man went on.

Parkington waited. He heard voices, the rustling of pages being turned.

The man said, 'I think we may be on to something now. There's a central mortuary in the Rue de Massey. I am told that bodies are kept there for two days for identification purposes, or autopsy if there's been an accident. If your client's body isn't there, perhaps you could ring again, and we'll see if we can help you?'

Parkington thanked him, replaced the receiver.

'Did you hear all that?' he asked Love.

'Enough to guess that if we can't find the body there, it'll be in the bay with a chunk of concrete tied to it. I'm on my way.'

Love went out of the room, took the lift down to the entrance hall. The city blazed with lights, like a meteor on the edge of the sea. Touts for night clubs clustered round him, falling in step as he walked, thrusting cards and chits at him, promising him ten, fifteen, even twenty per cent discount on all drinks for cash.

He brushed them aside, caught a cruising taxi, and when he was fifty yards up the road, told the driver where he wanted to go: the public mortuary.

'You have suffered a sad bereavement, yes?' the driver asked, watching his face closely in the mirror for any sign of grief.

'Not me, personally,' Love told him. 'A friend.'

'Ah, yes. A friend.'

This was not quite the same thing as suffering yourself, but maybe he could weep by proxy. And why did people always assume that bereavement must be sad? Sometimes the tombstone inscription - 'A happy release' - was true both for the living as well as the dead.

The taxi ploughed its way through the thrombosis of traffic, stopped outside a high building designed in the old French colonial style with tall, fluted columns, proud arches, and giant lanterns filled incongruously with electric bulbs.

Love paid off the driver, walked up the main stairs. The vast entrance doors were shut, but a small wicket-gate let into one of them was pegged open, and a light burned in the reception office at one side. A clerk of some kind, wearing a cast-off khaki uniform, open at the collar, sat writing on the porous paper favoured by lower grade Lebanese government officials, with a pen that scratched and blotted with every line. He breathed heavily while he wrote, as though the act of writing demanded a greater physical than mental effort.

Love tapped on the desk. When the clerk looked up irritably at this interruption, Love took a Lebanese five-pound note out of his pocket and laid it on the desk. The clerk's eyes bulged, as though he had never seen one before. Perhaps he hadn't; at least, not there.

Love said gravely in French, 'I must apologize for disturbing you when you are so busy, monsieur. But I wonder if you could help me?'

He pushed the note slightly nearer to the other man, pressing it down firmly on the desk with the tips of his fingers, just in case the clerk had too many ideas too soon.

'If I can,' said the clerk, watching the note as though it might suddenly take off in some other direction.

'I am a doctor, and a friend of my wife, possibly - you know how these things are - more than a friend, met with a sad accident only yesterday.'

It was the most unlikely tale he could think of, for he had no wife, but he hoped it might appeal to some streak of male vanity in his listener; a cuckold collects even a clerk's contempt.

'I am very grieved, monsieur,' said the clerk. After all, sympathy cost nothing, and this could happen to the nicest possible people, and, all too frequently, did.

'I wonder if you could possibly tell me whether you admitted his - ah — body? He was a young man with long hair.'

'They all have long hair these days, monsieur,' said the clerk. 'It would take hours. You must come back in the morning. It is impossible to help you now. I am here on my own, as you see.'

Love put his hand in his pocket, took out another five-pound note, crackled it between his fingers, and laid it down next to the first, smoothing it.

'I understand how late you are working, monsieur,' he said. 'I do not seek to give you more work without, perhaps, the cost of a meal and a bottle of wine.'

'It would take a long time,' the other man pointed out, but he was standing up now; he was beginning to see there might be a profit in it for him.

'Here are ten pounds,' said Love. 'I'll give you another ten on top if I can identify the body of my wife's friend.'

'What was his name?' asked the clerk, pocketing the two notes, and buttoning down a frayed flap on top of the pocket.

'Ellis. Herbert Ellis. He was English, I believe.'

'English, eh? There are very few English here. That should help us.'

He went back to his desk, pulled out a book, and began moving his stubby finger, thick as a chippolata, down the pages.

'Ah,' he said at last. 'Here we are. The body came in this morning. Cause of death - accident. Struck his head on the pavement.'

He looked up at Love, who wondered how many more Lebanese pounds had been paid to which doctor for such a verdict. And who had paid them.

'Can I see the body?' Love asked. 'As a doctor, I am used to such things.'

'That I appreciate, monsieur. But I am on my own.'

'I need not take you from your desk,' Love assured him, holding up two more notes to the light as though to reassure himself of their value.

'I could spare a moment, monsieur,' the clerk said quickly. 'It would only be a moment, and you must not tell anybody. I have my pension to consider.'

'The thought is ever in my mind,' said Love.

The man came out through a side door, led him across a wide empty courtyard, where two small Citroens were parked close together in one corner, as though for company in such ghoulish surroundings.

All the windows were shuttered inside. It reminded Love of walking through the Palace of Versailles, but this was a palace of the dead.

How ironic is the homage everyone pays to the dead, when the living lack so much, he thought, as they crunched across the marble chips that covered the courtyard. Death touched even the poorest with the illusion of importance; how many men who had walked to work every day of their life rode by Rolls to the cemetery?

The clerk opened a small door with a key he carried on a chain, ushered Love through, and locked it behind him. They were in a corridor now, lit from the roof by bulbs in white china reflectors, shielded by metal grilles. A strong smell of formaldehyde hung heavily in the unexpectedly cold air. The chill did not come entirely from the stone flags of the floor, or the walls scored with parallel scratches exactly the height of the sides of a trolley used for carrying a corpse.

One more door to be unlocked and locked behind them, and they were in a white-tiled room, with herringbone sluices out in the floor, leading down to metal gratings.

An air-conditioner droned, and fluorescent strip lights bathed the corpses that lay side by side on the marble-topped tables in a faintly green and ghostly light.

Their faces were exposed, their bodies were covered. Some, brought in naked, had their trunks wrapped in bed sheets or waterproof rubber squares. Others still wore street clothes. On their way to some appointment, death had unexpectedly established a prior claim to their presence.

Some dragged out drowned and sodden from a river or the sea, were still wet, and bloated, with water leaking from body orifices. Dye from their clothes had run with the water, so they seemed to be bleeding with blue or green or purple blood.

'Monsieur Ellis. Number two four eight.'

They walked down the rutted marble floor and stopped by the hippie's body. His long hair half obscured his face, as though he had died in a high wind.

'Here he is, monsieur. You recognize him?'

'Yes,' said Love. 'Had he anything in his pockets?'

'Nothing, monsieur. He was found in a different part of the city. The police brought him here. They only gave me his name, and his nationality.'

We bring nothing into this world, thought Love, and we take nothing out, but sometimes we can leave a little behind us. If only he'd left a watch, there might be a message inside, or a card in a wallet, an address or telephone number in a diary. He looked down at Ellis, wondering where he had lived, and how and why he had died.

'We had better get back, monsieur,' said the clerk nervously. 'Someone may have come. I am alone on duty. Please. It is very irregular.'

'Life is irregular,' said Love.

There was no need to hurry, now he'd persuaded the man to do what he wanted.

'That is so, monsieur. But I am only three years away from my pension. And if I were found ...'

'You won't be,' Love assured him.

He moved the hair back from Ellis's face. The eyes had been closed, and the face looked pale as the marble on the floor. Odd, how the young set such store by long hair, he thought. It was part of the battle between youth and age, an outward physical sign of disagreement, the rejection of one generation's ideas of smartness. Hair. The word had even been given to a musical. Hair.

He suddenly remembered the cable that had been telephoned to Wilmot's flat about the Greek and a haircut.

Of course; it was an attempt to advise Wilmot what to do when a long-haired caller arrived. King Xerxes, in the Persian-Greek war, had sent a long-haired bedraggled slave through enemy lines, guessing that he would not be molested. But when the man reached his destination, his orders were to demand a haircut, for written on his scalp was the message that swung the outcome of the war.

'Please,' repeated the clerk nervously. 'It is enough. You have seen the body. We must go.'

Love nodded, ran his hand through Ellis's hair. At the parting he could see a tiny bead of dried blood. He moved the hair across to the other side of his head and read the faint outline of figures, apparently written in indelible ink : 134262426.

He had used his last visiting card. He wrote the number with his small stub of pencil on the lining inside his jacket pocket.

'I quite agree, monsieur,' he said reassuringly. 'You have been very kind and understanding.'

'It is my pleasure,' said the clerk, thankful that the risk was over.

He led Love back to the wicket-gate. They shook hands and bowed to each other carefully.

So. Love had discovered something - a number on a dead man's scalp. But what did it mean? Was it a telephone number? A code? Or a combination that could open a safe -perhaps in Diaz's house?

The possibilities cheered him, for they were possibilities. He was moving forward or, at least, he was moving, and not just running on the spot. Now for Wilmot. Maybe the number would hold some significance for him?

He hailed a cruising cab and told the driver, 'Ararat Hotel.'

The street was busier than it had been during the day. A lorry had overturned at an intersection and two police cars and a fire engine, with sirens wailing, and blue lights flashing from their roofs, were parked up on the pavement beside it. Lines of cars, headlamps ablaze, horns braying, were jammed bumper to bumper in both directions.

The shops on either side of the hotel entrance were still open, and stalls had been set up outside some of the others, where the shutters were down. A brisk business was being done in doughnuts shaped like quoits, and square slabs of syrupy pastry, piled up, glistening and golden. Under the hissing, flaring naphtha lights, moths and night insects buzzed with tiny trembling wings.

Love pushed his way through the swing-doors. The reception desk was empty; a dim night-light burned above the counter. Obviously, the Ararat Hotel did not run to a night porter.

Love walked slowly up the stairs. Under the feeble yellow glow of the ancient electric bulbs set high in the ceiling, the mirrors on each landing, dull and stained and faded, looked like windows into a fog. Dust lay everywhere, thicker on the rubbery green leaves of the potted plants.

The air felt heavy, used and re-used, as tired as the decorations; hope had died here too often and for too many people.

Love tapped on Wilmot's door, and then stood back, waiting. In the next room, a radio was playing high-pitched French marching music, which suddenly stopped to a burst of applause. In a room across the landing, a little dog began to bark, and was cuffed into silence.

Love knocked again, more loudly this time, and then turned the handle. The door opened easily enough, and the light was on inside. A radio was playing dance music of the Thirties; from the bathroom, he heard the cascading rush of water. Steam billowed out from the bathroom door, which stood half open. Love tapped on it.

'Mr Wilmot,' he called. 'Dr Love here.'

Again, no answer. He pushed open the door. The bathroom was empty, filled with steam.

So, where the hell was Wilmot? Maybe he'd gone out for a packet of cigarettes, leaving the door open and the bath running. The water was up to the overflow, bubbling and gurgling through the circular brass escape grille. Maybe Wilmot had been held up somewhere, perhaps he couldn't cross the road because of the jam of cars?

Love leaned over the bath to turn off the tap. In that instant, as he gripped the tap, the antennae of survival in his mind sensed an almost imperceptible movement behind him. He ducked and turned, seizing the wire soap-rack from the side of the bath as a weapon.

The rubber cosh missed him by an inch, and boomed on the side of the bath, echoing like a giant gong.

Behind him, through the billowing haze of steam, he saw a Nubian, face black as polished coal, hair cropped like dark dust sprayed on his huge skull. The man raised the cosh for a second attack, lips drawn back over his too-white teeth. As he moved, Love whipped up his right fist into the Nubian's groin and, as his face came down, smashed the soap rack against the bared teeth, and the snout-like nose with its sunken syphilitic bridge.

The Nubian growled in pain and rage and surprise, and struck again with the cosh. This time he hit Love on the shoulder, but Love twisted, and gripping the Nubian's wrist with his right hand, he brought up the edge of his left in the Karate movement under his elbow. The tremendous force

of the Nubian's downward blow, doubled by Love jerking his wrist and hitting the elbow from underneath, snapped the bone like a stick of glass.

The Nubian's face contorted like a black gargoyle in his giant agony. Veins on his forehead stood out like knotted cords. He sagged forward, moaning, the cosh rolled down into the bath under the steaming water. He reeled, turned away, his left hand instinctively going up to ease the shattered, splintered bone which had punctured the flesh and stood out, jagged and pink, like a bone on a butcher's slab. As he turned, Love gave him a direct left upper-cut. He fell heavily across the bath and rolled back on to the tiles.

Love slipped the Beretta out from the man's back trouser pocket. As he straightened up, someone else spoke from the door, in English, in a quiet, almost bored voice.

'An interesting performance - for an amateur. But now you're among pros, Dr Love. Drop that gun!'

Love straightened up, holding the gun against his right leg, muzzle to the ground.

Two Europeans stood in the bathroom doorway. They wore dark suits, and could have been businessmen, but their business was violence and death.

Their cold, hard eyes belied their neat appearance; so did the muzzles of the guns they held in their right hands. One stood well over six feet; the other was slightly smaller, but broad-shouldered. Muscles bulged beneath the thin cloth of his sleeves.

'Who are you?' asked Love.

'We'll ask the questions,' said the taller man. 'Drop that gun!'

Love's brain stopped working.

The three of them seemed to stand frozen in a timeless tableaux. Only the rush of the hot tap, the steam fuming off the water in the bath, the unconscious Nubian on the tiled floor, were real. The rest belonged to a phantasmagoric dream world, a nightmare come to life.

A trap had been set, and he had walked blindly and stupidly into it. Simple, harmless, homely sounds - radio music, a bath running - had lulled him into a false security. Wilmot was probably still in some cinema on the other side of the city - if these men had not already found him.

The man's voice jarred his thoughts like a blunt electric drill.

'For the last time, drop that gun! I'll give you three. One —'

Love's index finger tightened slightly around the trigger of the Beretta. If he could only swing up the barrel another thirty degrees, he could hit the first gunman. Then, if he dropped immediately, he might shoot the second man's gun out of his hand. It was a chance, thin and remote, maybe, but he had nothing else. Could he risk it? The thought spun uselessly in his brain, disengaged from the gears of action.

'Two.'

In Love's brain, wheels meshed and turned. His gun whipped up, but just too slowly.

'Three,' said the man in the doorway very softly. 'Never say I didn't warn you, Doctor.'

His gun jerked slightly as he fired.

CHAPTER SEVEN

Mr Diaz had been asleep, and he awoke now to find his tongue and his mouth dry, his throat slightly raw.

He must have fallen asleep in the easy chair with his mouth open, which always irritated him. He associated sudden dozing with senility, and breathing through one's mouth with slackness and over-indulgence, and he abhorred these signs of weakness, for weakness marked the start of caution, and caution was the end of everything.

He sat up slowly, shaking sleep from his head. A servant stood framed in the doorway.

'Well?' asked Diaz shortly.

These fellows standing about, you never knew how long they had been there, or how much they saw - or, worst of all - whether you had talked in your sleep. Your brain burned on, even in slumber; you could speak your thoughts and others could hear them and steal them - just as he had so often stolen the ideas of others when he was young, to forge them into gold.

'You asked to be called at nine o'clock, sir,' the servant said gently in his soft, well-brushed voice.

'Ah, yes,' said Diaz. 'And it's nine already?'

The servant nodded.

Diaz thought he had just dozed off, and yet here he must have been asleep for nearly three hours. Perhaps he was growing old, or maybe he was just weary of the sameness of life. He missed the excitements, the sharp, splintering ecstasies of earlier years. Maybe this was also an unwelcome part of the pattern of growing older, more mature, careful.

Nine o'clock. In twelve hours, a politician he had never seen would be murdered. As a result, another man, whom he knew well, would certainly be appointed to his position, and a decision which had been promised in favour of someone else would almost immediately be reversed in favour of himself.

And, as a further refinement, the man who would have benefited by the original decision would be accused of the murder! The delicate and ironic convolutions of the scheme intrigued him. He had always preferred the longest way between two points, it gave him more time to enjoy the journey.

Twelve hours, and he would be potentially one of the half-dozen richest men in the world. Surely such an aim was worth the price of a few human lives? The world, after all, was only an enlargement of the jungle; the weaker fell prey to the stronger, and the stronger, in turn, to the strongest.

All life was an allegory of violence. In ten or twenty years, someone else would be in his place, as rich as he was, possibly richer, savouring his power and possessions. Yet now that unknown was probably envying him his wealth, just as years ago, barefoot in the slums of Bohemia, he had also envied the rich going past in their spidery-wheeled Daimlers and Benzes. That was the order of things; like death itself, it was inevitable.

Diaz stood up, ran his hands through his hair to massage the ache of receding sleep from his skull. He pressed a foot button near his chair and a male secretary came into the room, sleek and impersonal as a two-legged seal; a man without views, ambitions, or even opinions; an intellectual eunuch, not even his master's voice, only his echo.

'Has anyone been to his flat this evening?' Diaz asked him.

The secretary shook his head.

'No, sir. We've taken a, flat opposite, removed the spy-hole in the door and put in a fish-eye lens to cover the entire landing. No one has called.'

'I see. What happened when the police came?'

'Our informant with the force, sir, telephoned me earlier this afternoon.'

'Of course he did,' said Diaz irritably. 'That's what he's paid for. But what did he say? I don't want to know how he rang, or where from, or how much you pay this miserable police sergeant, or whoever he is. Just give the facts that concern me.'

'I'm sorry, sir.' The secretary bowed slightly, like a shop-walker to a rich but tetchy customer.

'When the police received the anonymous call saying a body was in the flat, they sent four officers, two plain-clothes men, two in uniform. The body was removed in an ambulance. It is now in the mortuary.'

'Was the young man identified?'

'Fingerprints were taken, but they didn't match up with anything on the police files. Which isn't surprising, really, for he had only just arrived in Beirut.'

'I'll decide whether it's surprising,' said Diaz irritably. 'Go on.'

'The police are contacting all European and the American and Canadian embassies in case one of their subjects has been reported missing.'

'How long does the body stay there?' said Diaz.

'No more than forty-eight hours, sir.'

Diaz wondered why the hippie had been trying to get into Wilmot's flat, when he had claimed he did not even know the man.

He suddenly wondered where the hippie's spirit was now, whether his spirit was anywhere, whether, indeed, he possessed a spirit. These were unusual thoughts for him, but then he had always prided himself on being unusual.

Even as a boy, when other children had spun their hoops or jumped on the joins of paving slabs, he had deliberately stayed apart, disdaining such pastimes, because they were only passing time, they held no profit for him at the end of the game.

LOVE-ALL

If you won, what did you win? Nothing, except chalked crosses on the wall of the tenement buildings where he lived. If you lost, what did you lose except a little prestige, to be forgotten as soon as the next game began?

Bearing these elemental points in mind, why waste time on make-believe, when you could use that time so profitably for producing something for yourself? He had always been a producer, even when he had nothing but his own. ingenuity to turn, first into money, then into power, so that others could harness their efforts for his enrichment. His father had been a carpenter, a craftsman of skill, secretly surprised, sometimes even worried, by the cupidity of his eldest son, who scorned to learn a trade.

When Diaz was eleven, he was spending his evenings writing out pages of impositions by oil lamp in the bedroom he shared with two younger brothers and a sister : 'I must not eat sweets in class'; 'I must do my homework more carefully'; 'I must not be late for school'. He sold them sometimes for sweets or pocket money, but usually for bundles of out-of-date schoolboy magazines, that his richer contemporaries had read. With these he ran a simple lending library — charging five centimes for the use of a magazine for one week - and to make sure that the reader brought back the magazine on time, he had to pay a deposit, a propelling pencil, two school meal tickets, maybe even a fountain pen or a cheap watch, anything that could be sold.

Sometimes, boys lost their magazine, but never a second time, because they also lost their pencil or pen or watch.

When he left school at fourteen, he ran a paper round, and discovered how easy it was to superimpose the rules he had learned on a more adult world.

On his own, he could only deliver as many papers as he could squeeze into the brown canvas bag fitted on his cycle handlebars. But if he employed other boys and girls, then there was no limit to the number he could distribute.

They were all willing to work for him, because they were even poorer than he was. He also discovered means of persuading people to do what he wanted, apart from paying them, and sometimes instead of paying them. They could be coerced, threatened, punched-up.

By the time he was sixteen, Diaz controlled a gang of boys who were willing to persuade others where their real interests lay, and if they doubted, then two black eyes, a bloodied nose, a few broken teeth or a smashed window in their homes could work marvels to make them change their minds.

At eighteen, he moved out into still more adult dealings; he discovered which girls did, and which girls didn't, knowledge that was instantly exchanged for cash. He learned what prices he could charge for the services of these girls, how much or how little to allow them; and he also learned of the vastly greater sums that husbands and sometimes wives would pay for secrecy and silence in such matters.

By twenty, he had proved the truth of what he had suspected ever since childhood, if he had ever had a childhood; you couldn't earn money, you had to make it. And to make it on any scale, you had to have others making it for you.

He was also learning the truth of the other adage, that you either had no money at all, or you could never have enough, for as his income grew, so his needs increased in proportion.

Now, at sixty, every sense seemed jaded, except that timeless, inner compulsion that burned on, consuming him: the need for more and more money to buy more and more power.

He had enjoyed everyone and everything he had wanted, but with each repeated experience the pleasure diminished. He was fat and old beyond his years, but then what if he had stayed slim and looked younger? How could he have borne those agonies of frustration, driving a third-hand car, wearing last year's suit, tied down by the humdrum chains of a family, with children's clothes and school fees to pay?

He had no friends, but then what use were friends to him? They either wanted to borrow money, or asked him to invest in their schemes; maybe, at base, they really hated him, and sought to bring him down to their level?

In this world, you had to be like a rock or a lion - alone. You trusted no one, because no one was worthy of your trust. You needed no one for themselves, only for their qualifications and skills, and these were for sale, and so you bought them in the market place at the best price, along with everything else that was on offer.

His empire of hotels, his blocks of flats, his shopping precincts and casinos stretched along the North Mediterranean shores from Italy to Portugal. Money made in whore-houses in one place paid for new apartment blocks in another. Rents, from these repaid mortgages on vast sites to be developed into holiday villages and young people's camps, through which drugs could be passed and disseminated. Everything in his enormous web of activities was correlated, cine merging into another like the dovetailed joints in the wooden cabinets his father used to make.

And now Diaz faced the ultimate coup that would make all that had gone before seem nothing more than a rehearsal for the deal. With one signature, he could expand his empire. and, at the same time, make it impregnable to all rivals, all opposition.

He had used politicians often, in the past, of course. Knowing instinctively how much to bribe this minister or that oiled the wheels of progress in so many countries where building permits and planning decisions could delay work indefinitely and expensively.

But this was the first time that Diaz had deliberately used politics as a weapon. He had never meant to do so, but one day in the bar of Shepheard's Hotel in Cairo a stranger had introduced himself. He gave the name of an acquaintance in Rome, with whom Diaz had done some business just after the war.

He seemed a pleasant, cheerful fellow, plump, with gold tips to his teeth, and rough hands, as though he had not always been rich. He said he was a tourist, and in a sense he was; for Diaz made his own checks on his background, and although Mr Iskenderun was originally Turkish - he joked that the town was named after him - he toured now on a Polish passport, and wherever he stayed, the Iron Curtain influence was furthered just a little.

It might be, as in Egypt, that Polish and Russian technicians arrived, apparently to advise on the building of dams and the laying of roads, the setting up of airfields, but in reality to prepare the way for Soviet troops. They would follow, initially in civilian clothes, and always, in the beginning, as military or defence advisers. Sometimes, Mr Iskenderun would arrange loans, which could only be ratified through the country concerned buying Tatra trucks or Skoda cars or Russian guns.

Sometimes, a surprised local politician who was not not-ably sympathetic towards Mr Iskenderun, would be given a new American car, that symbol of ultra prosperity, the mark of success in every under-developed country. And sometimes, too, Mr Iskenderun, with every appearance of outward regret, would show such politicians small snapshots of themselves in embarrassing company, which, sadly, he said it would be his duty to make public unless they could cooperate with him — of course, for the benefit of their people - in this direction or in that, but always in the way he wanted.

Outwardly, Diaz and Iskenderun looked much alike. They had both survived, when others with similar backgrounds and early handicaps had gone under. They both represented opposing poles of enterprise, and they both knew exactly what they wanted, and how much they would have to pay to get it.

What Diaz wanted was money, for money meant power, and power was what his life was all about.

What Iskenderun wanted was a follow-through of the old imperial dictum - divide and rule. If he could splinter a country's unity, fracture its economy and rock its confidence, then the forces he represented so astutely would move in; all criticism would gradually be quelled, all opposition bought or stamped out. So another part of the world would become secure for communism and lost to any kind of individual freedom.

In long discussions that took place between them in such unlikely spots as walking around the Sphinx, or on the beach at Alexandria - sites chosen, Diaz shrewdly guessed, because they gave least chance of being overheard — Iskenderun made clear exactly what he wanted, and what he could guarantee to Diaz in return.

The Russians were already strong in Egypt, and steadily increasing in numbers, with whole areas containing troops and air force personnel sealed off from civilian contact.

Tank and other Army convoys moved at night, without lights, along roads closed to other transport. Syria was already within their enclave, Jordan would follow, and the last to roll would be Lebanon.

Now the Lebanese people, for centuries poised between East and West, playing one against the other, and taking a percentage from both, always with a discount for cash, were reluctant to surrender all that their links with the West had meant to them, materially and economically, for so long. But their Government was weak. It had been unable to drive out the Communist-inspired, financed and equipped Arab guerrillas, for Arab could not publicly be seen to fight Arab, when the common enemy should be Israel.

What Iskenderun needed was a sudden Lebanese uprising, some unexpected insurrection, when all outside radio and press links would be cut, if only for hours. In those few hours, troops from other Iron Curtain countries, all wearing Arab uniforms, could take control. And once in, no other country in the world could drive them out, short of going to war - and who in the West would do that?

Lebanon had for centuries been occupied by some other, stronger nation; Romans, Turks, the French - as he pointed out in his persuasive way to Diaz.

'They are one of the world's subject peoples,' he assured him. 'Like women, they need to be dominated.'

Diaz let the polemic pass him by.

'What's in it for me?' he asked more practically; and so Iskenderun had told him, describing each stage in his plan, one following the other in obvious sequence, as one onion skin rests upon another.

There were no hostages to fortune or error. The plan was based on a sound study of human psychology and past riots. One thing would lead on naturally to another, just as life must inevitably lead on to death.

Diaz lit a cigar, remembering their meeting, squeezed the match out between his thumb and the stump of his right index finger. He had been born without the nail, and one of his secret interests was to seek out examples of others who had overcome some physical disability; blind Milton, deaf Beethoven, Nelson with only one eye, Roosevelt paralysed. They had succeeded, either despite their disabilities, or because of them; he was not quite sure which, and it did not matter greatly. The main thing was that they had succeeded, just as he would succeed now, as he always would.

Now he had to deal with Wilmot - or Esdaile or Wodouski, or whoever he really was. This was his side of the bargain and it would be resolved easily. But for the moment, like a thorn in a thumb, it produced an irritation out of all proportion to its size and importance.

Years of anticipating and avoiding trouble, as a shrewd sailing ship captain steers around rocks or whirlpools, had made him recognize dangers afar off that others, without his inner eye, could never see.

This hippie, for instance. Why had he wanted to see Wilmot? Was he really a relation, as he claimed? If so, why did he not know more about him? The Israelis, and even the Americans or the British, had very good Intelligence systems. Could he not have been one of their men - maybe planted as bait, knowing that he would lead them eventually to Diaz?

Or was the truth what he had been assured, simply that the boy was a junky; that his mind was fuddled with drugs, his blood eroded by the destructive metabolism of methedrine and mescalin?

That fool of a commissionaire had been far too rough with him, but you had to use what people you could find, with all their faults and imperfections. If he had only dealt with the boy himself, he would have found out something, however small, that he might fit into the mosaic of events. He could discover nothing from the dead: their secrets always died with them.

His secretary coughed apologetically. Diaz looked up at him, annoyed at having his thoughts scattered.

'A telephone call for you, sir,' the secretary said. 'From England.'

'Who?'

'Mrs Wilmot.'

'Put her on,' Diaz said. 'And tape the call.'

He picked up the golden telephone by the side of his desk, listened briefly to the squeaks and crackles of a trans-European connexion. Spirit voices spoke in English and French and German, and then he heard Mrs Wilmot, her voice strangely hollow over the distance, as though she was speaking in an echo-chamber.

'Hello? Can you hear me? Hello!'

Diaz turned up the amplifying control that was set into his desk.

'I can hear you perfectly,' he said. 'Can you hear me better now?'

'Ah, yes. I thought that we'd been cut off.'

'Why are you telephoning?' he asked.

He always hated the unessential preamble with which so many women clogged their communications. It added nothing, except expense, to the call.

'It's about Herbert,' she said.

'Herbert?'

The name sounded ludicrously provincial booming over two thousand miles of telephone line, yet he had heard it before, and very recently. Herbert.

'Yes,' she said. 'My brother. I hear there's been an accident. You've killed him.'

Her voice was rising now, almost hysterically. Diaz caught sight of himself in one of the large ormolu mirrors that ringed the room: the heavy forehead, the dark, oily hair, the completely expressionless countenance that might be a mask of wax, were it not for his sharp, black eyes, shaded, as ever, with shadows painted by years of self-indulgence.

Herbert. Of course. The hippie. How could he have been Mrs Wilmot's brother? How couldn't he be? He could be anyone's brother. And how could she possibly know he had anything whatever to do with his death? The implications hammered into his brain like nails.

'What do you mean?' he asked carefully.

'I've just heard about the accident.'

Accident. The word held some comfort for him. Maybe she didn't know the truth; but how could she know any-thing?

'Tell me,' Diaz said, not wishing to admit he did not know what she meant.'

'The car accident, of course, what else? He was insured. And I was mentioned in the policy. So a man from the insurance company came to check just what relation I was before they paid out. Don't you know about the accident?'

Her voice was hardening with suspicion and distrust.

'Go on,' said Diaz.

When in doubt, it was always wise to order others to speak. Never admit any lack of your own knowledge; let them fill the gaps with their own garrulity.

'I can't understand how you don't seem to know about it,' Mrs Wilmot said plaintively. 'The insurance man said he was knocked down by your car. You were the actual driver.'

'But you know, Mrs Wilmot, I never drive myself. I am always driven. So your insurance company has made a mistake'.

'Perhaps it was your driver, then, who killed him?'

'I think we are speaking at cross purposes, Mrs Wilmot. You telephone me to say that I have run down your brother in my car. I know nothing about this. I have never met your brother. I didn't even know you have a brother.'

'Had,' she said bitterly. 'He's dead now.'

'What does he look like? Where did He die?' He changed tense halfway through.

'He was young. Twenty-two. A student. Wore his hair long.'

She could think of nothing else about him. They had not been in close contact for a long time. She remembered him from a photograph he had sent her several weeks previously, when he was still in India.

'Would he wear sandals and an open-necked shirt and a metal necklace?'

'I expect so,' she said. 'I know he had a necklace like that - he mentioned it in one of his letters.'

'When and where did this accident take place?'

'With you in Beirut yesterday. These insurance companies have offices everywhere. The local office in Beirut found he was insured through London - the Midland Widows. They cabled here and someone came down to see me. I've just told you.'

'I will look into it and telephone you back,' he promised. 'Are you at home?'

'Yes.'

'Stay there until you hear from me.'

He put down the telephone before she could say any more. His secretary reappeared at the door.

'You heard that?' said Diaz. 'That hippie was Mrs Wilmot's brother. Now, what the hell was he doing trying to see her husband? He was going to warn him about something. Maybe us.'

The secretary said nothing. He was not paid for views and opinions; he was only a verbal whipping boy, a sounding-board for Diaz's thoughts. He waited for a moment and then cleared his throat deferentially, testing the air, to see whether it was safe for speech.

'Well?' said Diaz.

'Our people have just discovered someone else in Wilmot's room, sir.'

'Really, who?'.

'An Englishman. Dr Love.'

'Who is he?'

'He arrived yesterday, sir. From London. He went to Wilmot's flat yesterday and, according to our man there, when he could not get a reply, he left a message for him.'

He pulled out the note Love had written and read it aloud: 'John Esdaile. Was just passing through. Brought some good news from your wife. Can you please telephone me at the Bristol. Room 1021. Sincerely, Jason Love. (Dr)'

'Where is he now?'

'Outside, sir.'

'Then bring him in. And find out who represents the Midland Widow Insurance Company here.'

The secretary beckoned over his shoulder. Two servants wearing white alpaca jackets with brass buttons and black trousers manhandled Love into the room and stood, one on each side of him, their arms linked through his to hold him upright.

The pistol that had shot him in Wilmot's room had not fired a lethal bullet. The barrel had been carefully bored out to take a paraldehyde dart, the type that big-game hunters use when they wish to stun a wild animal so that they can capture it unharmed.

The dart had struck Love's left cheek; its anaesthetic had knocked him out immediately. Now he stood sagging between his captors. The walls of the room advanced and retreated, writhing as though they had a life of their own. Beneath his rubber leg, the carpet rippled like waves on a Wilton sea.

Through the mist that clouded his unfocused eyes, he could vaguely make out Diaz, behind his desk, but to Love's tired, drugged brain, he seemed as remote as a mandarin figure wreathed in fog, growing larger and then smaller with each receding heart beat.

Diaz surveyed him, his face concealing all feelings.

'Who are you?' he asked.

Love tried to speak, but the message for speech was lost somewhere in the scattered files of his central nervous system.

All he could murmur thickly through lips that felt as large as rubber bananas, were two words: 'A doctor.'

'Were you visiting Esdaile?'

Love shook his head to try and drive out the muzziness in his mind. Diaz motioned to one of the men to give him a drink. A servant poured a lime juice and soda and passed it to him, just as he had done hours earlier to Herbert Ellis.

The acid drink stung his throat and sharpened his senses. Now he could see Diaz more clearly, and recognize the richness of the furnishing of the room.

'Who are you?' Love asked in a voice more like his own.

'Never mind that,' replied Diaz. 'We have an interest in flat one nine seven two in the El Kantara Building. It was until quite recently occupied by a business colleague. How do you account for your presence in it?'

'I came through the door,' said Love.

'So I would assume,' said Diaz.

'We found a key on him, sir,' pointed out the secretary.

'Did you get it from Mr Esdaile?' asked Diaz.

'No.'

'What were you doing in there?'

'Mrs Esdaile is my patient in England. She asked me to visit her husband.'

'And did you find him?' asked Diaz.

'No. He was not in his flat.'

'I see.'

The secretary came in, bent over Diaz's left shoulder and whispered in his ear. Diaz nodded, his face still empty of all expression.

'I hear you are also a friend of Mr Carter, another Englishman?' he went on.

'I know him,' agreed Love.

'Then you probably also know that he is a dangerous man?'

'I didn't know that,' said Love, looking as surprised as possible in his condition and his surroundings.

'Then you should choose your friend's more carefully,' said Diaz. 'Mr Carter, I learn, claims to represent the Midland Widows Insurance Company. I believe he is also a British secret agent. I think that you also are probably involved, in some way, with some such organization.'

'That's ridiculous,' said Love, because at that precise moment, it was; at least, the last part.

'How did you know that Esdaile had moved from his flat to the Ararat Hotel?'

'I had a phone call telling me,' said Love.

This was not true, but if Pilate did not know what truth was, how could he? Anyway, it was the best he could do in the time.

'Did you find anything on him?' Diaz asked the secretary.

'Nothing hostile, sir,' the man replied. 'Money. A key ring. Nothing else.'

Diaz glanced up at the French carriage clock on the marble mantelpiece. Nine-thirty. Within twelve hours, whether Love was simply a country doctor, or an agent, or both, would be completely immaterial and irrelevant. But those twelve hours between could be dangerous, and if he were not who and what he seemed, they could also be disastrous.

The easiest thing would be to kill him now, but this meant further complications; the disposal of a body, the possibility that one of his own men might speak too freely, for murder was rarely simply something between two people, the killer and the killed. Others were nearly always involved, and the risk of discovery multiplied immeasurably with every precaution taken to ensure secrecy.

In his early days, he had made instant decisions to black-mail one man, to kill another, to force a third to agree to his terms by threatening to maim or disfigure his children; but life was not direct or simple any more, even for him.

The safest solution would be to hold Love prisoner for the next twenty-four hours and so allow themselves a safety margin. But in the meantime, they would find out what he knew.

Diaz raised the palm of his right hand half an inch from the arm of his chair. Love could see that the tip of the index finger was missing; as a doctor, he wondered instinctively when and where he had lost it, who had performed the operation, if there had been an operation.

Diaz's secretary approached deferentially.

'Find out why he's here,' said Diaz. Don't kill him. But make him talk.'

'I've told you all there is,' said Love.

"You've told me nothing,' said Diaz. 'Nothing. But you will, Dr Love. You'll tell me everything...'

CHAPTER EIGHT

Parkington sat on in Love's hotel bedroom until the light suddenly dwindled and deepened outside the window into the short, sharply fading twilight that led, within minutes, to the dark.

He did not switch on the bedroom light. A man on his own can think as well, and possibly better, in the dark. And he had plenty to think about.

He sat, sunk down in the chair, the fingers of his right hand gripping his glass of whisky, his mind freewheeling over the events so far.

As a professional, he preferred to let events guide him, until, like a man in a small boat, gauging tricky currents at a harbour bar or river mouth, he could decide which to ride and which to ignore.

Usually, so his years in the strange, shadowy, unmapped half-world of double- and treble-cross had taught him, a sign appeared - and he could go this way or that. It might be a look on someone's face, an inflexion in a stranger's voice, an apparent coincidence involving events that could never naturally coincide. Immediately he recognized this pointer, warning bells would ring in his brain, all the free-wheeling gears would lock and mesh and turn, and, like the man in the boat, he would take control.

Parkington had not reached that point yet in this case, and he wondered why. Perhaps he was growing old? Once or twice in recent years it had struck him that his zest for action was diminishing. Before, he had always welcomed a fight, a chance of clashing physically with the other side. But now he sometimes felt like a gladiator who has fought with the lions too often. The lions were always young and new to the arena; he was the only one growing old. Too few of his friends would live to draw their pensions and retire to grow roses in the gardens of bungalows on the south coast, for with each new assignment they multiplied and ex-tended the element of risk. He had been lucky so far in so many ways. He had survived, and this was possibly his greatest achievement.

This particular assignment could be simple, but if so, its simplicity was being fairly effectively concealed.

Who was this hippie, and why should he be in Wilmot's flat, either alive or dead? And who exactly was Diaz, and the man MacGregor who had briefed Love so carefully for an act of murder? Could they be the same man, under two names?

The red neon sign blazed above the hotel window, flashing on and off, painting the far wall alternately with blood and darkness.

He stood up and drew the curtains. As he did so, he heard a faint movement outside the door. His hand went automatically to his shoulder holster, feeling the rough reassuring serrations of the butt of his Smith and Wesson .38. He heard breathing beyond the door, then a timid tap on the panel.

'Come in,' he said, half withdrawing the revolver, ready to fire the instant he saw the blue flash of reflected light on another gun barrel.

Instead, he saw the grubby page, whom he had already tipped, holding a silver-plated tray with a telegram on it.

Thankfully, Parkington let the revolver slide back under his armpit, came across the room from the window, turned on a reading lamp. As his heart beats slowed, relief poured through his body; the dull pain in his guts, a compound of years of drinking and tension, eased temporarily and melted away.

'Mr Carter?' asked the page.

'Yes,' said Parkington.

'I thought you might be here, sir. I knocked at your room and there was no answer, but I knew you were a friend of Dr Love.'

Did you now, thought Parkington. If this was true, then he was growing slack as well as older. No one should have seen them together. They should have gone through all the safe, cautious routines of travelling separately in the lift two floors beyond the ones they wanted, walking down back stairs, wearing spectacles, meeting in darkened cinemas. Instead, he had done nothing. It was a bad beginning to start underrating your enemy; your enemy almost never made the same mistake about you.

He gave the boy a Lebanese pound, waited till he had gone, opened the telegram. It was from the London office of the Midland Widows Insurance Company, and it came in clear.

He read:

MISTER CARTER ADELPHI HOTEL RUE SALADIN BEIRUT HAVE TO INFORM YOU POLICY CLAIM ON LIFE OF HERBERT ELLIS DECEASED HAS BEEN FILED BY HEAD OFFICE IN FAVOUR OF HIS SISTER MRS CAROLINE WILMOT ESDAILE HOUSE BISHOPS COMBE SOMERSET STOP BENEFICIARY SEVERELY SHOCKED WHEN ADVISED DIAZ OTHER PARTY IN FATAL ACCIDENT STOP REPORT CLAIMS SETTLEMENT PROGRESS SOONEST MANAGER OVERSEAS CLAIMS DIVISION

Parkington read it through for a second time, then lit the corner of the page with his cigarette lighter, carried it across to the bathroom, flushed the black and burnt paper down the lavatory pan.

So the hippie had been Wilmot's brother-in-law. Presumably, Mrs Wilmot had not known he was visiting her husband, for, if she had, there would have been no reason to ask Love to find him.

She must also know Diaz, which would have made the news that he had apparently run down her brother in a car and killed him, even more astonishing.

Had her brother wanted money from Wilmot? Or had he come for an entirely different reason, perhaps bringing a warning, or as a go-between? If so, against whom or from whom?

He poured himself another drink, went up to his own room. He could wait, endlessly, turning out permutations of possibilities like a computer, or he could try to find the truth by going in search of it.

He made up his mind, emptied his pockets of all money except for five Lebanese pounds and a few small coins in his back trouser pocket. Then he examined his revolver, checked that the six shells were oiled in the breach, opened his suitcase, and unscrewed the lid of a Max Factor talcum powder tin.

The whole top came off with the lid, and, from the assorted weapons concealed inside in sponge rubber so they would not rattle, he selected a thin throwing knife in a plastic sheath. He slipped two elastic bands over his left shoe and up his calf and pushed the knife in its sheath through the bands. It felt hard and comforting against his flesh.

From his suitcase he took out another metal box, marked 'Views of Lebanon - Gateway to the East and West', with which he had been provided before he left London, in the (accurate) belief that no Lebanese customs officer would examine such a very commendable package of home projector slides'.

Parkington opened it now, put his wristwatch in the box, and in its place took out another and a metal bracelet engraved with the name J. R. M. Carter, his blood group and date of birth. He slipped one on each wrist. He opened a cigarette tin and scooped out some grey putty-like goo, rolled it into a ball, wrapped a sheet of notepaper around it, and put this in his jacket pocket. Plastic explosive could be useful in blowing open a door or for causing a diversion. He filled his cigarette case, slipped this in his trouser pocket, checked that his pencil torch was working.

Then he looked at himself in the big illuminated shaving mirror above the basin; a hard, cold, well-used face looked back. He could be anything or nothing. He preferred to be nothing. Life was safer that way.

Parkington went out, took a taxi along to Abdullah Has-san Boulevard, paid off the driver, and walked back three streets to the road where Diaz lived,

There was nothing unusual about it, except that he lived there. Palm trees sprouted like green feather-dusters from the pavements, and concrete lamp standards held up sodium lights on curved arms. Cars were parked on both sides of the street.

He walked slowly along the opposite pavement to Diaz's house, hands in pockets, stopping now and then to glance into a shop window, any European or American tourist with time on his hands in a strange and alluring city.

When he drew level with Diaz's house, he glanced into the windows of a restaurant, hung with deep-red curtains, that provided a mirror in which he could examine the outside of the house, while apparently reading a dimly lit menu.

It was built in the French colonial style. Shutters were closed behind the windows, making it impossible to tell whether anyone was in the rooms or not. He was not quite sure how he would get inside, and half hoped that someone might, conveniently come out and leave the door open - taking a dog for a walk, or posting a letter. But no one did.

And who or what was he looking for inside the house? He had no idea, but he felt convinced that somewhere inside this darkened shuttered house lay a key to the secrets he sought. He had no proof, only that extra inner sense that most policemen, lawyers, newspaper reporters and spies possess. They are like water diviners; when they approach that tender, often disputed, dark-edged area between fact and fantasy, nerves bend in their brains towards the heart of the mystery.

Once he was inside the house he was certain he would find some lead to follow. He had to; he had nothing else.

But how to get inside the place?

He could knock on the door and, according to whoever answered, take events from there. He might pose as an insurance man, or an electricity inspector, any of the stock, accepted excuses for crossing someone else's front doorstep without arousing either alarm or inquiry.

But this would mean that whoever answered the door would probably accompany him while he examined the meter, or discussed some ludicrous technical point. He would have no opportunity of being on his own, of seeing whether a locked desk or a safe could be opened.

Alternatively, he could knock on the door, club whoever opened it, and then go straight in. But this meant a body to be rid of, and the added risk that more than one person might hear his knock, and wonder why whoever answered it did not return.

The third possibility seemed the only feasible one: to enter the house unseen, and search it.

Forcing a window would be impossible, because the shutters were closed, and the house stood in a terrace of similar houses, which meant he could not try one of the back windows. As he walked past the line of cars, the driver of a small green Citroen, with only inches to spare, began going forward to butt the car in front, then reversing to push the one behind, until he forced enough room for his own vehicle.

As he accelerated away, muttering under his breath at the stupidity of other drivers who parked so unreasonably close, Parkington saw a round manhole cover, about two feet across and studded with dulled diamonds of green glass.

In the years when expatriate French colonial officials, port executives, and the like had lived in these houses, the central-heating systems needed for the two cold months of each year had been fed with coal through these covers, just as it was in

Paris and Lyons.

This would be his way in.

He crossed over the road, walked back past the house. Two cars were parked outside the door; a shabby grey Cadillac with a tattered vynide hood and an almost new Ford Mustang. Both had fairly good ground clearances.

The manhole cover opposite Diaz's house was just behind the Mustang's gearbox. The road was dry and appeared to be clean. He bent down, as though to pick up something, and then rolled sideways into the gutter and under the car.

He lay there on his stomach for a moment, watching the wheels of other cars swish past within inches of his face. Then he turned on his side, took out his knife, began to prise round the rim of the round cover. He dug the blade in through the accumulated dust and twisted it.

For a moment, he thought the blade would break. It went back like a spring. Sweat poured from him, then the lid began to move, slowly but steadily, like a giant oyster-shell opening.

Parkington slid one hand under it, slid it carefully to one side, and flashed his pencil torch down inside the mouth. The faint beam showed ancient bricks, blackened years ago with coal-dust, and now hung with grey secretions and soft mushroom-like growths. He swung his legs down the hole and gradually levered himself into it.

He hung by his right hand, shining the torch with his left. An empty cellar stretched away beneath him. In the far corner he could see the outline, of some crates of wine.

Parkington pulled the manhole cover over his head, and dropped lightly on to the brick floor. The walls were strung with cobwebs, beaded with coal dust and dead flies. He took out the ball of explosive jelly, pressed most of it into a cavity between two bricks where the cement had powdered away. It would be wiser not to keep it all in his pocket in case anything went wrong and he was discovered.

He rolled the remainder of the putty into a ball the size of a marble, put this in his pocket. Then he went up a flight of gritty wooden stairs to the door, waited for a moment, and then pushed this open for half an inch.

He was in a corridor, the ceiling lined with lighting cables; old-fashioned pull wires led to bells on coiled leaf springs. He smelled garlic cooking, and radio music was playing. He had surfaced somewhere behind the kitchen.

He came out of the door, closed it gently behind him, put his torch in his pocket, took out a handkerchief, tied this round the lower part of his face. Then he combed his hair with a parting at the right hand instead of the left, so that if he were seen he would be more difficult to recognize afterwards.

He walked along the corridor, keeping close to the wall and came out in a hallway hung with candelabra and bright with gilt-framed mirrors. The safe would probably be in a study, but it would almost certainly be connected to some fairly sophisticated alarm system which would ring a bell or flash a light elsewhere.

He opened the door nearest to him. The room was in darkness, and smelled of stale cigar smoke and old leather: it might have been a stage-set for A London Club: Act Two, Scene Three, A club in St James's, three weeks later.

He flicked the light on and off quickly, just long enough to absorb a mental picture. An eighteenth-century pole ladder, covered with leather studded with brass-headed nails, lay against one wall of books, all bound in red and green leather, with their titles in gold. This was the library of someone who wanted to appear better read than he was. Antique dealers sold these books by the yard, or by the ton, and buyers had them bound to match the decorations. He would be unlikely to find a safe in this room.

The next door opened on to an empty dining-room, a third on to a room panelled with pale varnished wood with an air extractor fan in one corner; a spotlight in the ceiling was directed down to a plain desk. This was more like a room where work was done.

He went in, shut the door behind him, drew the curtains, and switched on the light. The wall safe was where he expected it would be, behind an oil painting to the right of the desk, but as he moved the painting, he saw, too late, that the hook on which it hung also moved slightly. This was obviously a switch that worked some hidden alarm. In his haste, he had given himself away before he started.

He felt panic and anger at his own stupidity rise like bile in his throat. He switched off the light, sprang up on the desk, pressed the tiny ball of explosive putty against the bulb. Then he jumped down and waited behind the door, right hand in his jacket pocket feeling the Smith and Wesson hard in his sweating palm.

Feet came running outside; the door opened; the light went on. A man glanced round the room, surprised to find it empty.

Parkington began to count, the putty should explode within five seconds under the heat of the bulb. He heard a faint rattle of cogs as the man spun the safe dials, then a heavy dry creak of hinges.

He held his hands over his ears as the whole room rocked with the bellow of the gelignite exploding.

Pictures smashed to the floor with a tinkle of splintering glass. He heard a gasp of fear and amazement, and jumped from behind the door. A man was standing in front of the open door of the safe holding some papers in one hand. His other hand was up in front, of his eyes; the explosion had momentarily blinded him.

Parkington hurled himself at him before he could recover, smashed his right fist into his face and, as he went down, brought up his knee. The blow hurt his knee; he did not know what it did to the other man's nose. Then he flicked on his torch, but the papers were strewn across the floor, and already other feet came drumming along the corridor, and he had no time to pick them up.

Men were shouting to each other in French; if he stayed where he was, he would be caught within seconds. The best way was to go out fighting. He ripped open the door, because he had more of a chance outside than in.

He started to run - and fell headlong, his revolver firing with the force of his fall.

He had forgotten that there might be other traps for the unwary. He had tripped across another hazard he should have anticipated - a thin copper wire stretched six inches above the floor between the door posts.

A boot came down like a steel stamping press on his right wrist as he lay. He heard the bone grate under the metal heel, and cried out with the shock and the pain. His fingers opened; another boot kicked away his revolver, and then smashed into his temple.

'Get up!' a voice ordered in French.

He crawled shakily to his knees. His handkerchief had fallen down round his neck. Expert hands frisked him, found his knife, his empty shoulder holster, then gripped him under his arms and levered him upright. They dragged him into the library. He heard the click of a lock behind him, as they went through into another room.

Love was standing there, back pressed flat against the wall, hands above his head. His face was grey and streaked with blood. His body drooped with fatigue.

A large fat man with expensive fillings in his teeth sat at ease in a chair, legs crossed, cigar in hand, facing them.

'We found him in the study, sir,' said one of the guards. 'He had attacked Pierre. The safe was open.'

'Has he got the papers?' asked Diaz, not even raising his voice, as though this type of incident was one of the hazards of his position, and indeed it probably was.

'He had no time, sir. They were on the floor. We picked them up.'

'Have you searched him?'

'He was armed with a knife, and a Smith and Wesson thirty-eight. We have them here, sir.'

'Who are you?' asked Diaz.

He looked at Parkington's face, trying to recognize it through the blood and the coal dust and the shining patina of sweat.

'Ah, yes,' he said at last. 'I have seen your photograph. You are the local representative of the Midland Widows Insurance Company. And, I believe, an English agent. You are registered as Mr Carter, but no doubt that is not your real name. You are also a friend of Dr Love here. And how did you get into my house?'

'Through the door.'

'Impossible,' retorted Diaz. 'All the outside doors have magnetic locks. They can only be opened from this desk. You are lying, Mr Carter. I do not like lies. Now, tell me the truth. What do you want here?'

'To know why a dead man was dumped in Wilmot's flat.'

'That was very regrettable,' agreed Diaz.

'It's more than that,' said Parkington. 'That man was Wilmot's brother-in-law.'

'So I understand,' said Diaz. 'But that doesn't tell me why you are here. So you must.'

Parkington glanced at Love. He was not sure how much Love might have told Diaz; how much more he had discovered to tell. Time's tide was running strongly against them, and silence would buy them nothing.

He said, 'I understand that Wilmot has been ordered to kill the Egyptian politician in Beirut tomorrow.'

'Really?' said Diaz. 'What's that to do with me?'

'You briefed him.'

'You must be mad,' said Diaz, smiling, showing off the gold in his teeth., 'I don't know what you're talking about.'

'You will tomorrow. You're being picked up by the Lebanese police in the early hours. Just in case.'

Diaz roared with laughter.

'Now I know you are mad,' he said. 'The chief of police here is one of my oldest friends. We were playing canasta here only last night. You are making this up, Englishman.'

He nodded imperceptibly to one of the men who stood holding Parkington's arms. The man let go his grip and brought the back of his hand across Parkington's face, so that his skull jarred back against the hessian-covered wall and he felt vomit bitter in his mouth. He staggered with the sudden, unexpected pain.

The man who had hit him was squat, with thick lips and mean pig-eyes set in dark brown flesh. Spittle had dried round his mouth in a white salty rim. He watched Parkington gloatingly, hoping he would move so that he could hit him again.

Parkington let his body relax. He hung his head to allow the blood in his brain to clear some of the pain and the dizziness.

'Stand up when you talk to me,' Diaz ordered him sharply. 'Put your hands above your head. I believe, in the old days of your so-called British Empire, that this was the way in which your people punished some of the more re-calcitrant natives. Up!'

His voice cracked like a whip.

Parkinson slowly brought up both hands. As he did so, he glanced across at Love, who had used the interest in Parkington's arrival to lower his own arms slightly, so that his elbows were down beneath the level of his shoulders. This allowed more blood to reach the starved and aching muscles — and made him more able to ward off any unexpected attack.

'Mr Diaz,' said Parkington, nodding towards Love. 'That man, that English doctor, knows the answers to all your problems.'

'I am sure he does,' agreed Diaz. 'But you will also help me, Mr Carter.'

He turned towards Love as he spoke, removed the wet, round end of his cigar from his mouth, so that a long thin silvery rope of saliva linked his blubber lips with the chewed tobacco leaf. As he glanced at Love, the others in the room followed their master's eyes with instinctive obedience.

In that instant, Parkington closed his own eyes and brought his wrists together so that the metal bracelets of his watch and identity disc clashed.

The room exploded in the sudden blue blaze of a magnesium flare.

Parkington dropped to his knees in case anyone fired, and as he went down he opened his eyes. The guards had been caught off balance, and were momentarily blinded by the unexpected flash. Parkington balled the fist of his right hand and drove in into the stomach of the guard who had hit him.

He heard his animal scream of pain, and, as the man sagged forward, knees folding, Parkington whipped the pistol from his hand. Then he brought up his knee into the groin of his companion, and rabbit-punched the back of his neck as he collapsed across a table.

Love, half-blinded, seized a chair and brought it down over Diaz's head. Bells were ringing somewhere, whether in his head or in the house, he did not know.

Diaz ducked, very smartly for so fat a man, and the chair hit him on the shoulder. His right hand scrabbled like a plump, five-fingered crab for press-buttons on his desk.

Love seized him by the tie, and, picking up a telephone with his other hand, smashed this into his face. Diaz slid down sideways on the carpet.

One guard was unconscious, the other was crawling about on hands and knees, groaning.

Love leant over Diaz's body, prudently, removed the automatic from his side pocket, ripped the telephone wires from the wall.

They started for the front door - and then remembered the electronic locks.

'Through the cellar!' shouted Parkington.

A cook, wearing a white stove-pipe hat, came running out of the kitchen, a large metal ladle in his hand. Love tripped him up as he went by, and threw a tureen of soup from a hot-plate over him. If Diaz wanted dinner that night, he'd have to make do with a cold first course.

They clattered down the stairs and into the cellar. Parkington flicked on the light, scrambled up the sloping wall, and pushed the manhole cover. It moved about half an inch and then stopped.

'Give us a hand,' he gasped. 'It's jammed.'

Love came up beside him. Pressing their backs against the sooty bricks to gain leverage, they flattened their hands under the cover, and pushed. It moved slightly, but then they were pressing against dead weight.

They looked at each other, faces streaked with sweat .and blood, eyes wild with the terrible realization of what had happened.

In the time that Parkington had been in the house, a car had parked with one wheel on the cover.

They were trapped in the cellar with no way out.

CHAPTER NINE

The green telephone began to ring on MacGillivray's desk before he could take off his coat. He heard Miss Jenkins pick it up, and then her calm voice, unruffled as a seabird's feathers, on the intercom.

'It's for you, Colonel.'

It always was for him, MacGillivray thought sourly. He was the man in the middle, between the workers in the field, as he liked to refer to his agents, using the old missionary analogy, and the head of the Service, Sir Robert L—. But Sir Robert was away in Bonn for a week, and so some of his calls were also coming through to MacGillivray's office.

He picked up the telephone, pushed over the scrambler button, and said, in his clipped, Scots way, 'MacGillivray here.'

A male voice, hushed as an undertaker's mute at a rich man's funeral, said, 'The Foreign Secretary to speak to you, sir. Are you secure?'

'Of course.'

What a bloody silly question to ask - and coming from the Foreign Office, whose record for security over the last twenty years, from Burgess and Maclean, on through Blake and Philby and all the rest, surely deserved mention in The Guinness Book of Records.

He listened to a click of indirect connexions, picking his teeth idly with a silver toothpick his wife had seen in Harrods and bought him as a present for the wedding anniversary he had forgotten.

He wasn't quite sure whether he should be pleased at her remembrance or sad that she must object so much to his cheroots that she thought he needed cleaner teeth. At least, he thought, cheroots were better than a pipe. He associated pipe-smokers with indecision and declension of. will. They puffed away importantly, marking time for other men to make up their minds, all the time exuding an adman's interpretation of maleness.

The Foreign Secretary's familiar voice sounded in his ear.

'Beirut,' said the Minister. 'I have been reading the signals, and this Egyptian visit looks very risky. Have any of your people managed to find the man Wilmot?'

Before he had become a politician, the Foreign Secretary had been a successful silk. Derogatory phrases, from years of referring in court to hostile witnesses, still clung to him like burrs: the man Wilmot; the alleged person; someone who was described as this or that, or who purported to be something else.

'We're very close, Minister,' said MacGillivray diplomatically.

'But have you got him?'

'We're in contact.'

'Well, don't lose contact. And have him out of Beirut by any means you can before tomorrow morning. You know what will happen if this visitor is shot?'

He'll either be bloody dead, thought MacGillivray sourly, or the man will miss. Either way, there will be one hell of a riot, and all kinds of people will seize the opportunity to smash shop windows and indulge in organized looting. The Americans and the British would conveniently be blamed, their Embassies would be stoned and their cars overturned. Meanwhile, the Russians would protest in the United Nations about imperialists and the provocation of peaceful nationalists. It had happened often enough before; he could not see why this time should be any different.

'I haven't been briefed on that, Minister,' he said.

'Well, I'll brief you now. This person Wilmot had a Jewish mother. Although he's not British, he has lived in this country since the war, which makes him as good as British, at least in foreign eyes.

'The Egyptian Minister, despite his public utterances, which are largely for local consumption, is one of the West's very few real friends in the Egyptian Government. He was educated in America – Boston - and he has an English wife, although he doesn't shout about it. We've a number of contacts going for us through him.

'If he, as an Arab, is killed by a very-nearly British half-Jew, then not only do we lose this most important contact with Egypt, at a time when we are trying to heal our differences, but a hell of a lot of other trouble is stirred up. And with all the Arab guerrillas already in Lebanon, with the Lebanese government struggling for survival, and the recent Israeli business - we'll, work it out for yourself.

'So far, the Lebanon has tried to keep some sort of uneasy neutrality between Israel and the Arabs, but it's like parking a petrol tanker between two forest fires. Things have nearly caught alight on a number of occasions. The petrol is already very warm. This time, the whole lot could go up.

'We've millions invested in the Middle East, on both sides - and so have the Americans. We simply can't afford to lose this Egyptian, either financially, politically, or - to use a word politicians don't usually employ - morally.'

'It's that important, then?'

'At least that important,' said the Foreign Secretary. 'I'll be at the House tonight for the Middle East debate. Then I'll be in my room there till about ten, or you can get me at home afterwards. The Prime Minister wants to know personally when Wilmot is found, and on his way out. Do I make myself absolutely clear?'

'Perfectly, Minister.'

MacGillivray replaced the telephone, pressed the buzzer for Miss Jenkins.

'Anything?' he asked as she appeared in the doorway.

'Nothing at all - either from Parkington or Love.'

He looked at his watch. Two-thirty. He had been out for a quick lunch at The Nag's Head, and had met an old friend from Army days in the bar, now in a job with an insurance company in the city; the quick lunch had grown progressively slower.

He glanced at the clock across the room, which gave the differences in hours in the main capitals of the world. Two-thirty in London; three-thirty in Beirut.

He lit a cheroot and sat back in his chair. He thought of one of his retired agents who used to reassure him comfortingly when things went wrong, 'It'll all be the same in a hundred years.'

You could argue one way or the other. Everything might be the same in a hundred years, or again it might not. But what happened in a hundred years' time was not what concerned him. It was what happened now, and in the years between now and then, that made MacGillivray feel his age.

Parkington and Love looked at each other, each seeing their own desperation mirrored in the other man's eyes.

'Some bloody car's parked on it,' said Parkington. 'We're stuck.'

'The front door,' suggested Love hopefully. Maybe the electronic locks were not switched on.

Parkington shook his head.

'Not a hope. And goodness knows how many men are up there now, waiting for us.'

They could hear feet running on the boards above their heads; shouts in French and German, the metallic click of a rifle bolt being slotted into place.

They searched frantically around the cellar for another way out. Its white-washed brick arches ran at right-angles to the road. In one corner stood three hardboard crates of Beaujolais; electric wires and water pipes lined the roof. There was no other way out.

Then Love saw the lump of grey putty like a fungoid growth in a crack in the wall.

'What's that?' he asked; anything rather than dwell on the immediate future.

'Plastic explosive. I'd forgotten about that,' replied Parkington excitedly.

He reached up and peeled off the gelignite, kneading it between his fingers to soften it. As he did so, he tapped the arched walls with the back of his other hand. One sounded hollow. He pressed the gelignite against this, but it would not stick to the old flaking whitewash; it was like rolling out dough on a floury table.

Love dragged two of the crates of wine across the floor, and rammed them against the wall, wedging the ball in between. To blow a hole effectively through the bricks, they needed some shield behind the gelignite. Otherwise, it would simply bounce back off the wall and explode in the cellar.

'How are you going to set it off?' he asked.

'I don't know yet,' grunted Parkington, dragging the third crate along to wedge it even more closely to the wall.

I'll tell you,' said Love. 'Gas-lighter. I saw one in the kitchen.'

He bounded up the stairs into the kitchen. The cook, his face burned and blotched with carrot slices and gobbets of green vegetables, threw a meat cleaver as he saw Love. The blade missed Love by inches; the cleaver dug, quivering, into the wood beside the door.

Love hit the man in the stomach and, as he doubled up, brought up his fist into his ruined face. This was no time for a more relaxed doctor-patient relationship.

Across the kitchen, all ceramic tiles and anodized aluminium, he saw the gas stove, with a red casserole still cooking on it. On the wall hung an electric gas-lighter - the type with a battery in the handle, and a long chromium tube with a tiny filament at its end.

He ran down into the cellar three steps at a time. Parking-ton took the lighter, bent the switch so that it stayed on, and then pushed the lighter, red-hot filament pointing downwards, so that it was about half an inch from the explosive.

'Get back into the far corner,' he told Love. 'Crouch down and face the wall. Cover your ears with the palms of your hand against the blast.'

'How long will it take?' asked Love, as Parkington came and knelt beside him as though in prayer.

'About three seconds. As soon as the jelly warms up.'

Love counted five before the earth shook, and the boom of the explosion blew his breath back down his throat. Despite his clutching hands, his ear-drums reverberated like tiny timpani.

Love shook the dust out of his hair and opened his eyes. A hole about three feet wide had appeared in the far wall, and through it he could see another cellar. Thirty-six bottles of Beaujolais had exploded in theirs. The walls and ceiling, and their clothes ran with red wine, like blood.

The sharp smell of the wine, the foul stench of a cracked sewer, and the heavy burnt-out fumes of the gelignite scored their nostrils. But, no matter, they were alive, and above their heads the running had stopped. The force of the explosion could have flung their pursuers off their feet.

They climbed through the hole, and into the other cellar, almost exactly similar except it contained two huge deep-freezes that hummed busily as though their white cases concealed captive swarms of bees. Love flicked on the light, and they ran up the stairs, and out through the kitchen into the hall. A large dog rushed at them from a side room. Love cuffed it, and the beast slipped on a loose Persian rug that slid across the white marble floor under its weight.

Then they were at the front door, wrenching away the safety chain, opening the lock, slamming the door shut behind them.

People came running from both sides of the street towards the house, brought out by the boom of the explosion. A woman stood screaming at an upstairs window, her voice a huge round hole in her face, like an opera singer gone mad on high C. The pavement under their feet was sprinkled with broken glass like sharp, frosted confetti.

The crowd saw Love and Parkington, covered in wine-soaked dust, and ran towards them, but this was not the moment for explanations.

Parkington pointed back dramatically to Diaz's house.

'In there!' he shouted in Arabic. 'It's murder! They've gone mad! Get the police!'

Excitement mated with rumour, and spread like forest flames. A taxi had just dropped a young man and a girl four, doors up the road; its sign 'Libre' glowed above the roof. Love and Parkington dived inside the back door.

'Avenue de Paris,' said Parkington, as he slammed the door behind him. 'And quickly.'

'What number?' asked the man, accelerating away wildly, as though he was a late Le Mans starter and had only just remembered.

'I've changed my mind,' Parkington told him. 'The airport.'

It would be useless to go back to their hotel. Either Diaz's men or the police would be there within minutes; and which would prove their most dangerous pursuers?

'You're not flying out?' asked Love.

Parkington shook his head. He looked pale. But then the ethereal glimmer of the swan-necked sodium lights above the Avenue de Paris made even the flowers in the central strip between the dual carriageways seem sickly and waxen.

'I've changed my mind again,' Parkington said suddenly, leaning forward. 'Drop us here.'

'As you say, monsieur.'

The driver slowed, stopped.

'That will be four pounds,' he said.

Parkington gave him a five-pound note, waved away the change, watched until the taxi was out of sight, and then they ploughed back along the road they had come.

'An all-night cinema,' he explained. 'We can hole up there for a while. Decide what we're going to do.'

They went into the first cinema they came to, a 1930s building revamped with a mass of neons and frosted glass at the foyer windows. A Western was showing; American with French subtitles. The crack-crack of revolver shots from the wide screen sounded uncomfortably close to Love as he bought his ticket.

Parkington followed him in, three minutes later. They met in the men's cloakroom and took seats together in the back row. The cinema was half empty; most of the audience seemed asleep. Those who were not lying back, eyes closed, and mouths open, were huddled up close, lips locked on each others' mouths, oblivious to the action on the screen and to everything else.

Love tipped forward his seat and sat down thankfully. The hands of the wall clock pointed to 11.30. It had been about the longest day he could remember, and it was not finished yet.

'Well, we're out,' he said. 'Thanks for arriving at the right moment.'

'Any time,' said Parkington magnanimously.

He lit a cheroot, and then suddenly stubbed it out, and stretched in his seat, head on the back of the chair, eyes closed.

Love glanced at him. Strenuous action affected people in different ways. Some were almost immediately overcome by the reaction, and had to rest for an hour or two. Others, like himself, were spurred on. by the sudden rush of adrenalin through the blood. Action was like wine or sex; the more you had, the more you wanted - and the greater your capacity.

The film ended, lights went up, and dark-skinned usherettes moved down the aisles, selling ice-cream, and drinks sealed in plastic packets. Love bought two orange drinks, and handed one to Parkington, but he had fallen asleep. He nudged him awake. The lids of his eyes raised slightly, and even in the warm amber glow of the house lights, Love could see he still looked unnaturally pale.

'A drink,' he said softly.

Parkington raised his head slowly and focused his eyes.

'I could do with that,' he agreed, and held out a hand.

His voice was only a whisper, unlike his usual deep-throated rasp. Love tore off the corner of the plastic packet, and stuck in the straw, but Parkington seemed unable to hold it. His hand trembled and the packet tipped. Yellow, cold liquid, speckled with shreds of orange pulp, dribbled out down his suit.

'What's wrong?' asked Love, and even as he asked he knew the answer.

You're hurt?'

Parkington nodded.

'A bit. In the guts. That explosion.'

His voice was even fainter now, and perspiration varnished his forehead. His suit was soaked with wine, his shirt stained red with it. Sweat arid cement dust had matted his hair like dusty thatch.

'Which side?' Love asked him.

'Left.'

Love opened his jacket, then his shirt; put his hand in gently, watching Parkington wince as he touched the hot flesh.

'You've either busted a rib,' he said. 'Or it's your ulcer.'

'Is that the only choice you offer me?' asked Parkington weakly.

'Maybe not. How's the pain?'

'I've known worse.'

'You'll certainly know a lot worse, if we don't get you somewhere with this. I'm going to call an ambulance.'

'No. It's too risky. I'll be all right in a bit. Then I can shack up in the hotel.'

He tried to stir himself out of his seat, but sank back wearily, his face creased with pain.

'It's riskier staying here,' Love told him. 'I'll get you to hospital. You'll be safe there. I'll see if the manager here has a phone.'

He waited until the lights went out, and the advertisements began to flicker on the screen, then he stood up. As he did so, he remembered his own appearance: he must look about as vile as Parkington.

He went into the men's cloakroom. His face and hair were also matted with white concrete dust, streaked with sweat and reddened with wine, his suit sodden and creased and foul. He looked as though he had survived an earthquake, but only by a small margin. It was amazing that no one had remarked on their appearance as they came into the cinema.

Or perhaps someone had?

The Lebanese were a polite people. Maybe the police were already on their way, or had actually arrived in the cinema and were waiting for the right moment to seize them?

He stood in the cloakroom, at the centre of walls of mirrors, irresolute. Then he washed his face, soaked his hair in the basin, and scrubbed away the worst of the dirt. He should change his clothes, but how and where? He towelled himself dry, thinking over the problem. As he combed his hair, a man came in, humming to himself. He had thick black hair and sideboards, and wore rings on all the fingers of his left hand. He bent down, glanced at himself in the mirror, preened his hair, first on the left temple, then on the right, fluffing out the oily curls a little more with his hand, then moved to the urinal.

Suddenly, he glanced at Love, and turned with a half-smothered exclamation. What a rough-looking man, he thought. In that filthy suit, soaked surely with blood. His eyes opened like camera irises, and then closed suddenly as Love hit him.

'Sorry, stranger,' said Love, and he was.

But he was sorrier still for Parkington and for himself. Maybe the man had his name inside his jacket and he could write and explain and send him a cheque. But first he had to survive before he could send anything.

He ripped off the man's jacket, then his trousers, and bundled him into the nearest lavatory cubicle, pulled the door shut.

Then he took off his own suit, tore out the inside of his jacket pocket on which he had written the number from Herbert Ellis' head, emptied his pockets and threw his suit on top of the man.

The suit was not a good fit, but then Love wasn't entered for a Tailor and Cutter award; it was clean and pressed and that was enough. He sauntered out as casually as he could and knocked on the door of the manager's office.

The manager was a fat Arab, wearing a white dinner jacket with a purple cummerbund, and a purple complexion to match it. He sat behind his desk, pecking at his teeth with a gold pick, examining a large folder of publicity stills for next week's films.

'Excuse me,' said Love in French, 'but a friend of mine has had a heart attack. Can you please call an ambulance from the American hospital?'

'He's American?' asked the manager resignedly, looking up, putting away his toothpick.

'English.'

'Is he conscious?'

The manager was thinking of the damage that vomit or blood or bile could do to his seats, and whether he'd have to telephone the projection room to stop the film, while they put on the house lights to see how best to remove this wretched man. If he wanted to be ill, why had he to be ill in his cinema?

Love read his thoughts from the expression on his face.

'It's urgent,' he said. 'I'm a doctor. I know.'

'But, of course,' said the manager. For clients, everything they wanted was always urgent.

He picked up the telephone, dialled a number, spoke in Arabic.

'Only minutes,' he told Love, 'and they will be here. Where is your friend sitting?'

'Back of the stalls,' said Love. 'But don't put the lights up. We're quite near the aisle. I can get him out to the ambulance.'

'Take me to him,' said the manager.

They went into the cinema. The Englishman looked very ill to the manager; it would be extremely bad publicity for his cinema if he died there.

Love put his hands under Parkington's armpits, and half-lifted him out into the aisle. The manager picked up his feet, and together they carried him through the swing-doors, under the turning fans, to the manager's office.

The manager looked in amazement at Parkington's filthy appearance.

'Is that blood?' he asked in horror, indicating his reddened suit. Love nodded.

'Please don't speak more than you have to. It disturbs him.'

It also disturbed Love, for the longer they talked, the greater the risk that the unfortunate man in the cloakroom would recover, or that someone would find him and immediately report his odd discovery to the manager.

Parkington lay on the carpet, groaning slightly. The telephone rang once, like a sharp explosion in the tiny office, and they both jumped. The manager answered it in a whisper, eyes roaming round the room, looking anywhere but at the figure on the floor.

'Who is it?' asked Love. 'The ambulance?' The man shook his head.

'The police,' he said. 'Wanted to know if two people had been in the cinema who looked as though they'd been in an accident.'

He glanced suddenly at Parkington, then back at Love. Love said easily, 'You'd almost think my friend here was one of the two.'

'Yes,' agreed the manager. ^You would.'

Love wasn't sure whether he was suspicious, or whether, like most people, he simply could not imagine himself being caught up in anything that smacked of action. He lived his lift at second hand, watching shadow adventures, practised and rehearsed to perfection, illuminating a screen that went blank after every performance. That reality could even remotely resemble this magic-box world of light and shade was beyond the limited spectrum of his experience; at least, Love hoped it was, and that it stayed there. The manager cleared his throat, about to speak, but the rising whine of the ambulance siren robbed his tongue of words.

Three ambulance attendants in grey uniforms with Sam Browne belts, and Red Crescent arm bands, came running up the stairs in step, carrying a folded stretcher.

'In here,' called Love.

They knelt down by Parkington's side; opened the stretcher frame; jabbered away in Arabic to each other.

'They want to know if you're with him?' the manager said.

'At the same hotel,' said Love. 'I'll see him to hospital.'

They had Parkington on the stretcher by now, held down by one strap high across his chest, another just below his knees.

'I'm sorry to have inconvenienced you like this,' Love told the manager, and he was. The manager glanced down at the stain that Parkington's filthy suit had made on the carpet, and was about to reply, when the telephone rang again. He put out his hand to pick up the receiver. Love nodded to the stretcher-bearers. This was the time to be away; that call could also be from the police with perhaps a more specific description of the two wanted men.

The ambulance was waiting, half up on the pavement, back doors already opened, blue light revolving above the roof, driver standing by to help steer the stretcher into its runners.

'The American hospital,' Love told him. 'I'll ride with him.'

He climbed up, sat on the black leather folding seat by the side of the stretcher. One bearer came with him; the other two went in the front of the ambulance. As they set off, Parkington opened his eyes.

'That hippie,' he said faintly. 'Did you find anything?'

'A number,' said Love. 'On his scalp. Under his hair.'

'I've a book of stamps in my pocket,' said Parkington. 'Write it on the cover.'

Love did so, then turned to the ambulance man who sat, sucking a sweet, looking at nothing.

'Do you speak English?' Love asked him in French.

The man shook his head glumly.

'Would the figures mean anything to MacGillivray?' Love asked Parkington.

'God knows. I can't get through to him now, anyway.'

'Is there anyone here who could?'

'Yes,' said Parkington. 'A man who owns a toy shop in the Rue Massive. A hospital for dolls, he calls it. Give him the number, too. He'll get it back to London. If it means anything, they can cable you here.'

'Is there a password?'

'Deep in the heart of Texas,' said Parkington. 'He'll answer with another line from the song. Trust him.'

'I'll have to,' said Love. 'There's no one else.'

'Listen,' said Parkington, raising himself up painfully on the stretcher. 'Stop that bugger Wilmot from doing anything silly tomorrow. Kill him if you have to. It's that important. And don't look so squeamish, Doctor. You must have killed off many of your patients. Only thing is, this man's not paying you a fee.'

'That's where you're wrong,' said Love. 'He's promised me an enormous fee. Which I want him to live to pay.'

'He will so long as you stay with him. Drop off at the hospital. Don't frig about with these idiots here, otherwise you'll be hours filling in forms for nothing. When they open the door, just scarper.

'And another thing. Here's my cigarette case. No commercial value, as they say. But a lot of sentimental value. I'm afraid someone will pinch it in hospital. Keep it for me, will you?'

'Surely.'

Love slipped the case in his back trouser pocket, buttoned down the flap, wondering who had given it to Parkington, and when, and where she was now.

The ambulance slowed, stopped. Bolts slid open on the rear door. Love jumped into the road as the orderlies ran out the stretcher. As they turned up the steps of the casualty entrance, he moved behind the ambulance, and then crossed the road and dodged into an alleyway that came out into the Place des Martyrs.

He hailed a passing cab, told the driver, 'The Rue Massive.'

This was no more than two hundred yards long, crammed with houses, all squeezed in tightly together, ground floors converted into unusual and unexpected shops, the sort that made him wonder how the owners earned a living, or whether all the shops were simply covers for other more lucrative if illicit activities.

One window, decorated in purple, with unlit candles in imitation silver sconces, dealt entirely with mourning materials. The window piece was an open coffin, upholstered in white nylon, containing an effigy of a corpse, hands crossed, a white fluorescent cross flickering at its head.

The next shop was hung with eighteenth-century French political prints, with balloons coming from the mouths of enormously gross characters. Two gigantic men rode a dejected, skinny horse, 'La Belle France'.

The third shop was a horse butcher, steel shutters down over the window, and a plaster horse-head stuck above the door. Next to this, was The Dolls' Hospital. A small window was hung with masks, and dolls in pierrot costumes. A giant red cross and red crescent painted on the glass showed even those who could not read that here was a hospital of some kind.

The door, with a large pane of green-painted glass edged with gold, had two bell buttons at one side. Love had forgotten to ask Parkington the name of the man. The first button had a card, 'M. Brigonet', pinned to it; the next, just 'Hopital de Poupees. He pressed this. Nothing happened. He did not even hear a bell ring. Perhaps the man was out? Perhaps he had never been there.

Love beat on the glass with his fist, and the door rattled on its loose lock. Finally, he heard shuffling along the passage, the click of a bolt, the rattle of a chain.

The door opened a few inches.

An old man, very small, with a large head streaked with thin tufty hair, looked out at him. He wore a pair of blue denim trousers and sandals, a shabby sweat-shirt.

'Oui?' he asked.

'The Dolls' Hospital?' asked Love in English.

'Who else?' asked the man.

'I was told I might find you either here or deep in the heart of Texas,' said Love, with a half-embarrassed smile.

The other man regarded him for a moment, eyes like almond stones, showing no flicker of interest.

'The stars at night are big and bright,' he agreed. 'Come in.'

He slipped the chain, then locked and re-chained the door behind him when Love was inside.

'Who are you?' he asked, peering at him in the dim light. The green glass filtered the rays of a street lamp outside; it was like meeting someone underneath the sea.

'Can I speak here?' asked Love.

They were in a narrow corridor; brown walls and a naked electric bulb hanging from a flex in the ceiling. The floor was covered with brown lino, worn thin as the old man's hair; he could see the grey, dusty, hollowed boards through holes a foot across.

'In the shop,' said the man. 'Follow me.'

He pushed open a door at the back of the shop, switched on a light. The walls were hung with dolls' bodies and legs and arms, like a do-it-yourself baby-making factory. Scalps had flaxen hair, pinned up alongside tiny dresses, pants, trousers, shoes. On a table lay a mass of dolls' waxy faces, all with unnaturally pink cheeks and long-lashed blue eyes. The internal mechanism of one doll, to make it cry and urinate and squeal, was spread out on a sheet of newspaper; plastic tubes, a rubber bladder, a clockwork motor actuated by a swinging weight.

'Now,' said the man.

Although he was so light, he had a hard tenseness about him, like a fine Toledo blade. In this Middle Eastern world of wax dolls, each cast in the unlikely image of an Anglo-Saxon child, he dealt in the trade of death.

'I'm a doctor,' said Love, and gave his name.

'A friend of mine, Parkington, over here as Carter, is injured. He's in the American Hospital. He asked me to contact you.'

'Why?'

'There's a number I found written on the scalp of a dead man. He wants to get it back to London.'

'Where in London? You speak in riddles.'

Love looked at him sharply. Was he in the wrong place altogether? Was there, perhaps, some other dolls' hospital. But surely there couldn't be - not in this short street? And after all, the old man had replied to the password as Parkington had told him he would.

Puzzlement showed in his face. The other man smiled. 'Give me two names,' he said. 'We may yet understand each other.'

Douglas MacGillivray. Sensoby and Ransom. An office in Covent Garden.'

'Where's the number?'

Love pulled the frayed piece of cloth from his pocket, read the figures aloud.

'Where will you be?' asked the old man, as he wrote it down on a sheet of headed notepaper.

'Uncontactable.'

The old man showed neither interest nor surprise; maybe he had other callers who also did not leave their addresses.

'Anything else?' he asked.

'Yes,' said Love.

'What?'

The man's voice was sharp as a dagger point.

'Have you any contacts with the local police - the secret police or security people - I don't know what their, exact title would be?'

'Why do you ask?'

'Because I know something they ought to know. But I don't know how to get the information to them.'

'My wife's cousin is their Director of Operations. What do you wish to tell them?'

'That an attempt's going to be made tomorrow morning to kill the Egyptian who's coming here.'

'How do you know?'

'Never mind. But I do. It will be made on his way from the airport, in Beirut. Can you ask your wife's cousin to warn the guards or something?'

'I will do what I can. But there are only so many policemen in the whole force. Time is very short. He may not be able to investigate a rumour.'

'This isn't a rumour. It's a fact.'

The old man said nothing. He edged Love towards the door.

Love held out his hand; the man did not take it. He said, 'Goodbye, Doctor.'

Then he shut the door behind him. Love heard the bolt and the chain rattle into place, and his feet shuffle away up the hall.

He looked at his watch. It was half past five. Had he been foolish to try to pass on a warning to someone in authority? If he had, it was too late to worry about that now. It seemed too late to worry about anything.

He felt suddenly almost unbearably weary. So much had happened, and nothing had been achieved. He'd been running like hell ever since he arrived, simply to stay in the same place. He needed something to eat, a rest, time to shake his thoughts into some sort of order.

He walked slowly along the street. In doorways, beggars, cocoons in filthy rags or shreds of sheets, lay curled up like embryos or the unburied dead.

A cafe was open. Some taxis were pulled up outside it, lights out, while the drivers ate supper - or was it breakfast? Love sat on one of the wide-slatted chairs under a flapping canvas awning that advertised a local beer. A waiter, who had not stood close to a razor for some days, came out, carrying a towel over his arm and a grubby menu.

Love ordered a double cognac, a jug of coffee, a three-egg omelette. This proved unexpectedly good, and after the cognac he ordered another, and felt peace begin to slide through his veins.

He lay back in the hard chair, feet stretched out, eyes closed, somewhere between sleep and wakefulness, trying to work out what he should do.

CHAPTER TEN

He must have dozed, because he was suddenly alert, tired-ness gone, all senses sharpened by the approach of danger.

A small Simca had stopped farther up the street. One man sat at the wheel, two others were out beside it, fiddling with a street door.

They jumped back inside the car, which shot past him in third gear, accelerating all the way. He recognized Diaz's secretary as the driver.

Then the cafe rocked, as though hit by a giant's fist.

Orange tongues of flame poured from the door along the street, and the dawn sky was suddenly peppered with tiny bodies, arms, legs, faces. The two men had blown up The Dolls' Hospital.

Love heard someone screaming in mortal pain. The screams dwindled to a bubbling, tortured moan, and then sank to silence.

So maybe the ambulance man had understood English, after all? Maybe they were all closer to him than he imagined? Windows were opening, tousled heads peering out in terror and alarm. Somewhere a child began to cry and a whistle blew. Love stood up. The waiter came running out, horror on his bristled face.

'The terrorists!' he cried. 'The second time this week!'

Love paid him, and hurried down the street, before any-one could make it a third time.

The man from whom he had taken the suit would have told the police how he had been robbed, so he had to assume that the police would have his description as a wanted man. He could not risk returning to the hotel. But Diaz's men would be combing the roads for him - so where could he go?

The British Embassy? He imagined the reception he would receive there, beating at the baroque front door at that hour asking for the Ambassador or the First Secretary, the doorman reasonably thinking him to be a drunken British tourist out of money, or out of luck. He could not go there - not, at least, until office hours.

He glanced at his watch. Seven o'clock. He must have been asleep for more than an hour.

There was really only one place in Beirut where no pursuer would expect him to be: on top of the skyscraper where Wilmot was to shoot the Egyptian.

Presumably, the arrangements for Wilmot's departure would stand, and where one man could escape, another could go along with him. That was Love's only way out.

The streets were filling now with cars, and people walking to work. He walked on, across squares and down ever-widening avenues lined with palms, until he came to the sea, and then he recognized some landmarks; a yellow block of flats, a clock tower with red-tiled roof.

He drank two cups of Turkish coffee in an open-air cafe, bought a morning newspaper, to use as a shield for his face if he needed to stay concealed, and headed towards the sky-scraper.

He saw a chemist's shop open, went in and bought a tin tube of benzedrine tablets. He could dose himself if he felt too tired; the drug should give him enough false energy to last for three or four more active hours.

The roads were now packed with people. Lines of spectators were forming on every pavement. Little children ran in and out between the legs of the grown-ups; stray dogs barked in an ecstasy of excitement.

Bored troops, wearing shabby uniforms, with unpolished brass-work on their belts and dull toe-caps to their boots, stood at regular intervals along the road, facing the crowd, with rifles and bayonets. As Love passed one of the loud-speakers suspended from a lamp-post, martial music began to play. Little children beat time to it, waving paper Egyptian and Lebanese flags.

He felt an almost overwhelming weight of approaching doom that he was powerless to prevent.

He leaned wearily against a wall, the early morning sun warming his face like a burning glass. How different he would feel if he had spent the night in bed, then risen to a cool shower, half a pint of iced orange juice, and two lightly poached eggs! Never again would he take for granted such simple comforts.

He looked again at his watch; ten to eight. It had taken him longer to reach the sea than he had imagined. He was not used to walking; he drove too much. The next generation would be in danger of only having residual legs, like the feet of a coelacanth.

The skyscraper he sought soared splendidly up to the cobalt sky; ropes and gantries swung from the upper storeys. The windows each had a cross whitewashed on them to show that they were glazed. They looked out blankly, a hundred dead eyes in a huge steel and concrete skull.

Some of the lower floor windows had been opened, and groups of people were already inside the empty rooms, and stood peering out, framed by the windows, chattering excitedly. He wondered grimly what they would be chattering about in another ten minutes. The back door of the skyscraper was wedged open by a piece of wood, just as Mac-Gregor had said it would be. This was cheering; maybe he was not quite alone.

A concrete mixer panted asthmatically to one side. Two workmen in black dungarees and peaked caps shovelled sand into a metal wheelbarrow. They paid no notice to Love; he walked past them, up the steps and into the back entrance hall.

The same coils of black plastic hose, the same planks tied with string, the same cement burst out of grey paper bags; nothing had changed. He walked up the stairs to the lift on the first floor. Workmen had been busy here, too. Two huge concrete mixers were churning their giant drums of grey gritty cement and stones. A pulley had been set up through an open window, with a swinging yellow bucket to another part of the building across the back courtyard. There was more activity than he had expected or imagined. He pressed the lift button and went up to the sixteenth floor.

He opened the trellis gate, picked up a wedge of wood from the junk that littered the floor, jammed it under the gate, then gave the handle a sharp tug to make sure it was firmly fixed. If anyone noticed that the gate was held open, they would assume that a workman had done it to allow himself to wheel a barrow in and out more easily.

Love smoothed back his hair with both his hands, rubbed the stubble on his chin, and walked slowly up the flight of steps to the top floor. He came out of the door on to the roof, screwing up his eyes against the blaze of sun, reflected from a thousand white walls and the shimmering sea.

The city lay spread out beneath him. White yachts speckled the bay, decked with flags in honour of the visit. A ship's siren was snoring somewhere, and motor horns blared like distant trumpets.

Miles away, an airplane was climbing slowly down the sky, pulling a white wraith behind it. This could be the Egyptian plane arriving. How ironic, Love thought, that he had flown so far, to receive such a welcome, with all the ceremonial trappings of a guard of honour, bands, and outriders - simply to be shot by a man of whom he had never heard, who did not even know his name.

Love looked down at the street beneath him. Flags fluttered in the gentle wind, and a buzz of conversation came up like a swarm of innumerable bees. Otherwise, the street seemed unusually quiet.

All cars and other vehicles had been banned from it. One policeman on a white horse was riding pompously along, waving the crowd back with a long stick. As soon as he had gone, they crept out nearer to the road again. The soldiers leaned on their rifles and shifted their weight from one foot to the other.

Love checked his watch; five minutes to eight. He walked carefully round the side of the wooden hut on the roof. Everything was as it had been yesterday - with one difference.

A man lay full-length on the ground, rifle aimed down at the street, butt tucked into his right shoulder, legs splayed out, feet wide apart, inner edges of his shoes on the ground in the classic position of taking aim.

Love called gently.

'Wilmot!'

The man turned round.

'You!' he said in amazement. 'Why are you here, Doctor?'

'To stop you killing yourself.'

'I'm not going to kill myself, Doctor. Only some bastard in a car who deserves to die, anyway.'

'You'll never get away with it. I've been through the city. It's swarming with troops and police. They'll be on to you as soon as you fire.'

'You were coming back yesterday,' said Wilmot accusingly, not answering Love directly.

His face was grey and pudgy. He was no longer the alert, rather sharp-eyed person he had been on the previous day. His eyes now appeared dull and yellowish. Stubble grew like grey dust on his chin and his upper lip. He turned the rifle over on its side.

'I did come back,' Love told him. 'But you weren't in your room. Some other people were waiting for me. They took me off to see Diaz. They gave me a rough time.'

'Diaz? Who's Diaz?' asked Wilmot without much interest.

'I don't know,' said Love. 'But he's up to his neck in this, whoever he is.'

Then Love remembered, with a spear-thrust of horror, that MacGregor had given him the instructions about the priest's robes, the police car, the Rapide waiting at the airport. So how was Wilmot here at all?

'Who gave you the gun?' he asked him, his throat suddenly dry as the baking concrete roof.

'I don't know his name. He called at the hotel with it, all folded up in brown paper. And an alarm wrist watch and a bag of clothes for me to wear. Said he was from the cleaner's. I couldn't be bothered with them.'

Wilmot jerked his head towards an airline bag beside him. The whole business seemed of no interest, no consequence, no importance to him.

Love knelt down and shook his shoulder. Wilmot's head rolled easily, like the head of a rag doll. Love put out his right hand and, with his thumb and forefinger, he opened one of Wilmot's eyelids. The pupil did not focus. The man was drugged, half stoned. And how could he find an anti-dote when he did not know the drug?

Love glanced at his watch. Two minutes to go. He knelt down beside Wilmot.

'You've got to get out of here,' he told him, speaking slowly, as though to a child. 'Both of us have - before you shoot. The whole thing's a bloody trap. Don't you see that?'

He shook him again. Wilmot's mouth sagged open; a thin dribble of saliva leaked out and down his chin.

'No. I don't. It's a business deal, Doctor. Profit and loss. I can cope.'

'Give me the rifle,' said Love. 'You're drugged.'

'No.'.

Love grabbed the rifle suddenly, and Wilmot lunged at him angrily, but without any real impetus or strength; he was like a blindfolded man struggling in deep sleep.

Love rolled him to one side, and as he still grappled with him, trying to claw at his throat, Love hit him on the jaw. Wilmot fell back, arms outstretched.

At that moment the alarm buzzed in his wrist watch. The target was due to arrive.

Love slammed back the bolt. Even if he were caught, surely it would be a strong point in his favour that the rifle had not been fired? But the bolt slid for barely an inch. A metal bar had been welded behind its head. It was impossible to expel the cartridge. The only way the bullet could leave the breech was out of the end of the barrel.

He examined the action more closely. A second tube had been welded beneath the telescopic sight, a tube with a small ferrous rod about two inches long protruding from its forward end, and a metal lever from the rear. This was connected by a link to a bar just in front of the trigger, and at right angles to it, like a metal trigger finger.

It only took Love a moment to realize that this was an electronic device to fire the rifle by remote control. He turned over the rifle, examined the silencer hood. It was a useless empty dummy, adapted from a toy rifle, in matt black plastic.

The desperation of the situation scored his mind like etching acid.

The real killing would be done down in the street by experts with silenced automatics, or compressed-air guns firing cyanide darts.

But the scapegoat would be whoever held this rifle - which would be fired by someone maybe a mile away - whether Wilmot took aim or not, whether he was holding it; whether he was even there.

Then, under cover of the rush to reach the skyscraper when this unsilenced shot was heard, the real assassins could melt expertly away. And what policeman would search elsewhere for a killer when a man with a bag of disguises was hiding on a rooftop, holding a rifle that had just been fired?

Love's realization of their danger momentarily over-whelmed him, as icy water chills a diver until he can strike out.

Down in the streets, the cheering grew suddenly louder, like the bursting of a giant dam of sound. The smooth vertical walls of the tall buildings, the acres of polished glass panes, amplified the cheers, the wailing of sirens, the boom of the recorded bands, deafening Love at the vortex of this volume.

Round the corner of the intersection came four motorcyclists with headlights blazing, then two black cars, then the white Cadillac, its hood up, windows closed against the dazzling sun.

Love flung the rifle away from him. It slid over the concrete, striking . sparks. The cross-lever moved, the trigger jerked, the rifle fired. Above the roar of the crowds, the crack of the shot sounded sharp and unmistakable as a whip lash. The bullet scored the concrete; the rifle pivoted on its bolt.

Love threw himself flat, and peered down through the hole between the cement sacks. The first car in the convoy had already stopped, one front wheel on the pavement. The second was stopped behind it. Its rear doors were open, and men were diving out, hands going to shoulder holsters.

A police motor-cycle lay over on its side, rear wheel still spinning like a chromium-spoked Catherine wheel, blue light flashing from the handle bars. Other motor-cycles were up on their stands, and the riders were running back towards the Cadillac, revolvers drawn, blowing their whistles.

The Cadillac had also stopped, and its horn was blaring continuously. The doors were open, and the driver and a guard who had been sitting with him leaned over from the front seats into the rear of the car.

A man lay across the fawn Bedford cord back seat, head down, arms outflung in a frighteningly lifeless pose. He wore a khaki uniform and black glasses. His cap, heavily braided with gold, had fallen off, and lay upside down on the thick fawn carpet. On both pavements, crowds were swarming angrily towards the car through the sweating line of soldiers, who clubbed them back desperately with rifle butts.

Behind the Cadillac two other cars had arrived, and men from them were running towards it. One carried a briefcase; probably a secretary or a doctor, thought Love, but from the angle at which the Egyptian lay, he did not need to be by his side to feel that they were running in vain.

Well, he had tried to prevent this, and he had failed. Reaction and the bitterness of defeat gripped his stomach.

The real killers no doubt had already dismantled and discarded their guns, or palmed them into someone else's pocket in the crowd, and were moving expertly out of danger.

Now the whole, senseless whirligig of violence was due to start; riots, demonstrations, arson, more murders, maybe even war.

Love lay face down on the hot concrete, eyes closed as though he could shut out the horrible prospect, but the sun shone red as blood on the lids.

He opened his eyes and peered down at the street. A policeman was scanning the tops of the buildings, shading his binoculars against the fierce blaze of the sun.

He saw Love move, and pointed, and then shouted and blew his whistle, and other men in the crowd looked up and pointed, and then they all started to run towards the skyscraper, shouting to each other, so that soon a vast crowd of soldiers and civilians were pouring towards the main doors.

They had barely seconds to escape. Love slid back farther, rolled clear, shook Wilmot. His head lolled and sagged like a scarecrow. He moaned slightly. The drug had now run its course; the spring of action was unwinding. Love shook him like a sack of straw.

'Where am I?' Wilmot asked him weakly.

'In bloody great trouble. Get up and run!'

He dragged Wilmot on to his knees and hands, but he sagged down again on the rough concrete like a sleeper overcome by the unbearable burden of slumber.

Love took out one of the tablets he had bought at the chemist's shop and rammed it into Wilmot's mouth, moving his jaw to make him swallow it. He chewed mechanically. The benzedrine poured through Wilmot's blood with every sluggish beat of his drugged heart. Then his eyelids fluttered, his eyes opened and narrowed. He was coming round.

The drug would give him at least three hours of energy, and if they could not escape in that time, they would never escape at all.

'Now!' said Love, pumping Wilmot's arm to increase the blood circulation, and so speed up the benzedrine's travel round his body. 'Follow me.'

They clattered down the flight of stairs, slipping on the cement dust, missing steps, cursing, holding out their hands to steady themselves against the rough, plastered walls. Love kicked away the chock of wood under the lift door, pressed the Down button. The lift did not move.

He ripped open the door.

'The stairs!' he shouted.

On the landing of the eleventh floor, Love saw two chunks of newly sawn wood, threw one to Wilmot, kept the other in his hand as a club.

The loudspeakers had been silenced, and, deeper than the

sirens, like the thunder of an unseen sea, Love heard the angry shouting of the mob, repeating slogans, with police whistles blowing shrilly above their growing roar.

Love's flesh crawled at the thought of what would happen if they could not reach MacGregor's car before the mob reached them. Something must have gone wrong with his arrangements for diversionary thunder-flashes, and the lift had also jammed - or maybe the current had been cut off. But they would be all right in the car. Who would think of searching for an assassin in a police car?

They reached the second floor, with its unusually wide landing, where an anodized metal balustrade overlooked the entrance hall. Over this he could see the crowd pouring in through the front doors of the building. Maybe they had not thought of the rear entrance? Maybe they did not even know it existed? They would discover it within minutes, maybe less, but this could just give Love and Wilmot time to escape.

Then Wilmot tripped and fell, sprawling face down on the stairs, moaning in the unexpected pain as his jaw rasped along the concrete steps. He lay for a second, sobbing for breath. Love dragged him to his feet, and propped him up against the wall. The cement mixers were still churning. The bucket swung to and fro in the light breeze.

'I can't go on,' gasped Wilmot. 'I can't.'

'You've got to.'

There was only one flight more of stairs and they would be out at the back entrance, and in MacGregor's car. Safety lay literally only yards away. To delay another moment was to be overwhelmed by the mob.

He grabbed Wilmot's arm with his left hand and the back of his coat with his right, and tried to propel him along. Wilmot stumbled, and they both almost fell, Wilmot crying out as his twisted ankle unexpectedly took their combined weight.

The mob now filled the entrance hall, only the thickness of the floor away. It seemed incredible to Love that they had not seen them - simply because no one had looked up. But now Wilmot's scream, echoing back from the bare concrete walls, reverberated like the cry of a wounded animal.

He saw faces looking up at them, eyes met his eyes; fear and horror grew like a tree in his stomach. Immediately, the mob churned, like a human whirlpool, and swarmed up the stairs' towards them, grabbing pieces of wood, tearing up loose or broken slabs of concrete, to use as weapons.

For a fraction of a second, an instant carved from eternity, danger numbed Love's brain.

There was no hope now of any easy escape. They would have to fight every foot of the way. And what chance had two, armed with wooden sticks, against two hundred blocking the staircase?

He lobbed his stick at the face of the nearest man, about twenty feet away. He fell, and others dropped with him in a milling, angry, screaming heap near the top of the stairs.

Their shouts shattered Love's inaction.

'The mixer!' he shouted to Wilmot, and pointed to the thundering drums of liquid concrete. He seized the spoked wheel by the side of the machine nearest to him. For a second, it jammed and then spun easily.

Like a giant cannon at the siege of Jerusalem, the huge iron snout of the mixer tipped and, when Love slammed home the release lever, voided its tons of stones.

Churned to a thick, grey, gobbety mass, they poured down the stairs over the heads and bodies of the mob, burning their eyes, filling their open mouths, choking them, so that they fell- back, slithering and screaming, fighting for a foothold on the slippery steps.

As they struggled, Wilmot reached the other mixer, which

spewed out its cement. Pouring over the heads of the men struggling on the stairs, it streamed beyond them down to the first landing, a wide grey slippery unclimbable cascade.

'Now!' shouted Love, and seized Wilmot's arm.

It was impossible for them to go down the stairs past this seething glutinous mass, just as it was impossible, at that moment for their pursuers to climb and reach them. Their only chance lay in the overhead pulley. Love grabbed Wilmot round the waist, and with a leap he gripped the rim of the yellow bucket above their heads with his other hand.

It swung to one side like a huge inverted cathedral bell.

Love jumped up on the other side to balance it and heaved on the control rope. They hung, panting, facing each other across the swaying rim. Then the ratchet slipped, wheels turned, and slowly the bucket moved out through the open window, away from the building, out over the sunlit emptiness of the rear courtyard.

Love waited until they were only six feet from the ground, and pulled the knotted control rope. The bucket stopped with a jerk, and swung crazily from side to side.

Love jumped down, helped Wilmot to drop, and tore the sparking-plug lead from the donkey engine that drove the pulley, in case other people in the skyscraper had the idea of using the bucket to follow them.

Then they ran, three-legged, Wilmot holding on to Love's arm, sobbing with every step he took, till they came into the back hall, among the piles of wood, the drums of adhesive, the flapping polythene covers over the bronze sculptures. The workmen had abandoned their barrows at the first sound of shouting; the hall was empty.

So was the street, except for the rows of cars parked on both sides.

Where was the police car?

Love closed his eyes and opened them again suddenly in case he was suffering from momentary blindness. He wasn't. The car simply was not there. He leaned wearily against the wall for a second, trying to shake fatigue from his brain.

Perhaps it had been delayed by the traffic Possibly the police had sealed all streets as soon as the shooting started? Maybe it was still jammed in some unknown road, nose to tail with dozens of others? Any of these might be the answer: the point was academic. The car was still not where it should have been.

'We'll have to run for it,' he told Wilmot.

'I can't,' groaned Wilmot. 'My ankle.'

'There's just no other way.'

They set off, keeping in the shadows of the high buildings. Wilmot limped along beside Love, half running, half walking. As they passed each parked car, Love glanced in, hoping to find one with the key left in an ignition lock; anything to help them escape more quickly from this section of the city.

An empty Chrysler taxi pulled out of a side road, mounted the pavement ahead of them on two. wheels, and stopped. The driver cut his engine, climbed out and ran back along the road, anxious to have a closer view of whatever was happening.

Love peeped in through the nearside window. The key was in the lock, a little disc of St Christopher, and a tiny photograph of a child in a plastic cover, hanging from it on a silver chain.

'In there,' he ordered Wilmot, who crawled thankfully through the back door, and collapsed across the seat.

Love jumped in behind the wheel, turned the key. The engine fired. He jammed the gear in second, and they were off.

A light gleamed bluely on the dashboard. He wondered what it was, and then remembered the 'Libre' sign on the roof. He reached over to the meter and threw the switch. The light went out. He might be any taxi driver with any client.

But which way was the airport? He blundered to the end of the road, grating the gears. The brakes had four inches of travel in the pedal; the steering seemed connected to the front wheels by sponge. The whole car was so badly maintained he felt they were riding on square wheels.

He turned left into the first main road and followed the signs. A police car and an ambulance raced against him, headlights flashing, sirens blaring. He pulled into the right to give them as much room as possible, and then sped on, over the first intersection where traffic lights flashed perpetually at amber, up the main Corniche Chauran.

To their left, buildings rose in a solid wall of sun-bleached sandstone; old houses wore terracotta roofs, like giant summer hats.

To the right, lay the Grotto of the Pigeons, a wide bay ringed with reddish cliffs, the sea blue as liquid cobalt. Cars and yellow buses, with a red stripe round the centre, were all cruising along the Corniche calmly enough, drivers in shirtsleeves and sunglasses. No police cars were in sight, no road blocks or police checks had been set up, so maybe news of the assassination had not yet spread this far; But it would, and within minutes, at the very most

They had only four or five miles to go to reach the airport. Love had memorized the Rapide's number, and imagined the pilot already strapped in his seat, sun glasses and earphones on, oil warm in the engines, propellers lazily beating the burnished morning air; everything ready for their arrival. And within minutes they would be airborne, on their way to Cyprus.

The thought of deliverance poured sweet relief through his body. He glanced in the rear-view mirror at Wilmot.

'Only a few minutes now,' he said.

'Thanks,' said Wilmot. 'I don't know what you injected me with, but I feel about a hundred years younger. If it wasn't for this bloody ankle, I'd be perfect. I feel as thick as an elephant's hide.

Reckon I'd been drugged?'

'Possibly,' said Love, 'but you'd find that hard to prove. Especially in a Lebanese court.'

'What about the fellow I was to shoot? Did he get off?'

'No,' said Love.

'But I didn't shoot him,' protested Wilmot. 'I know. Nor did I. But someone did. And hit him. I saw his body sprawled across the seat. Whoever organized it just wanted you as a convenient scapegoat to hang the murder on. And they damned nearly had you, mate.'

'But why me?' asked Wilmot, perplexed. 'I just don't understand it. I came out here to get away from trouble.'

'But you forgot the world is round. You ran so far away you nearly met yourself coming back.'

Wilmot said nothing. He massaged his ankle carefully.

'Up on the roof,' Love went on, 'I asked if you knew a man named Diaz. You said you didn't. Do you remember him now your mind's a bit clearer?'

'No. Never heard of him.'

'I wish I hadn't,' said Love. 'For, as I told you, when I came to see you in your hotel, two of his villains took me off to meet him. He seemed to be keeping a watch on your place. Any idea why, if you don't know him?'

'What did he look like?'

'Middle-aged. Fat. Dark skin. I only saw him sitting down.'

'Could be almost anyone in Beirut,' said Wilmot reasonably enough.

'Well, he happens to be Diaz,' said Love. 'And he's missing the tip of his right index finger.'

'Ah,' said Wilmot, now showing interest for the first time. 'I know who that sounds like. Massine.'

'Who's Massine?'

'Same line of business as me. Property. Mainly holiday stuff. Has a whole interlocking empire of flats, whore-houses, casinos, the lot. He hoped to get the concession for the North African deal. But I beat him to it.'

Wilmot smiled, savouring the sweetness of victory.

'Did you get it signed?' asked Love.

'No. Only a verbal agreement, but the Egyptian Minister's having the deeds drawn up. It's only a formality now.'

'What's his name?' asked Love.

'Ahmed Hussein.'

'You mean he was having the deeds drawn up.'

'What do you mean - was?'

'He's the bloke who's dead in the Cadillac. The late Minister of Culture and Development. I'd say that Diaz, or Massine, or whoever that character calls himself, has got your little deal sewn up now with his successor. And with one big difference. He has the concession. Not you.'

'My God,' Wilmot said softly. 'Hussein used to have another title - Minister of Lands. And his is such a common name I never imagined he was the same man.'

He seemed to shrink with the realization. He sat, desperately turning over permutations of the situation in his mind, trying to find earlier parallels when he had won against even worse odds.

Love glanced again in the mirror. A grey Pontiac was following them, half a dozen cars behind, weaving in and out of traffic as they moved, always keeping pace. He dropped down a gear and pushed the accelerator down into the rubber mat on the floor. The old Chrysler leapt forward, bucking on its worn springs.

He could only manage about fifty-five, top whack, for the engine was probably governed for taxi work, and the mileometer had been two or three times round the clock. He felt in his back pocket for a Gitane, instead found Parkington's cigarette case. He sighed. He only smoked French cigarettes. This just wasn't his day.

The other car kept up with them easily, neither increasing nor decreasing the distance between them. The signs for the airport appeared, with the ironic message, 'Thank you for your visit. Bon voyage.'

Love turned off the main road, following the arrows showing the outline of an airplane, then swerved down the long wide track with cedars on either side, towards the sandstone airport building. He drove into the main car park, as MacGregor had shown him - was it only hours or a whole lifetime before?

The Pontiac followed him in, and slowed almost to a stop. Of course, it could be someone else in a hurry for a departing plane.

Love accelerated up past the long lines of empty cars, bright as coloured beads in the sun, until he saw the welcome tail-fins of the private airplanes in the air-park. Freedom was now only seconds away. He swung into a spare slot between two other cars, cut his engine and jumped out.

He was sorry about the taxi driver losing his cab, but he would find it again soon enough; and life was full of sorrows much larger than this.

Wilmot limped after him.

'This way,' shouted Love.

He ran down the wide tarmac track painted with parallel white lines, and vaulted the two-rail metal fence at die end. Wilmot climbed over more slowly and painfully.

Three private airplanes faced them : a silver and blue Cessna, a silver Piper, and one he did not recognize, all empty, their propeller blades neatly parallel with the ground, chocks wedged under wheels, weighted ropes holding down their wings.

But where the hell was the air attaché's Rapide?

Horror and disbelief spread through Love's body, like poison after breakfast with the Borgias. Heat beat down on them relentlessly. The sun blazed back from the white runway, so that his eyes ached, and he could feel a thin trickle of sweat between his shoulder blades. His mouth was dry as the inside of a flour mill.

'What's wrong?' asked Wilmot.

'The plane's not here, that's what.'

Everything fell into place now, but much too late to be of any use to him. Wilmot was expendable; that had been obvious for some time. But now the full impact of the realization, and the intricate planning behind it, hit him a hammer-blow.

If Wilmot, in his drugged state, managed to escape from the skyscraper alone, he would have faced his second hurdle; no car waited for him at the back door.

If he had somehow commandeered another car, it would only take him to the end of his road at the airport, for the escape plane was not there, either.

Possibly that particular plane did belong to the air attaché at the British Embassy. Probably it had flown in from Cyprus, and maybe it was back there now, but it had never been intended to spirit Wilmot away, as MacGregor had assured him, any more than the dummy silencer could muffle the shot from the FN rifle.

They had only one chance left. They might conceivably be able to board an airliner to Cyprus, Amman, Cairo, London — anywhere out of Beirut.

'Follow me,' he shouted to Wilmot.

They ran back between the rows of cars, under the roasting sun, and dodged into a side entrance of the airport. The main hall was crammed with people, the sort of angry, impatient, frustrated scene that never appears on any airline advert. Loudspeakers crackled in Arabic and French and English. Mountains of luggage were stacked on trolleys, but no one was waiting at any of the rows of airline ticket offices.

The wire grilles were down oh the counters, and clerks stood talking behind them in hushed groups.

Love saw the BOAC sign, and ran to the weighing-in booth.

'Have you a plane out anywhere"? he asked. 'It's vitally important. I'm a doctor.'

He almost caught himself using the cliché that so irritated him in others - 'It's a matter of life and death,' and this time, ironically, it was. His own life; maybe even his own death.

'I'm sorry, sir,' the' booking clerk explained gravely, with the air of a man who has said the same words too often that day, 'But all planes are grounded. Nothing is leaving.'

'Why? Is there a strike?'

'It's much worse than that, sir. An assassination. An Egyptian Minister has been murdered in Beirut.'

'But that's nothing to do with me,' said Love, not entirely accurately. 'I just have to get out.'

'So must all these other people, sir. They've all got onward connections, holidays booked, business trips waiting. But there's nothing we can do. It's a police order. No plane leaves the airport until the assassin has been found.'

'Do they know who he is?'

'According to the radio, they've a pretty good idea. They've issued a description, anyway. Six foot tall, dark hair, grey suit, wide staring eyes.'

'So we're all stuck until they find him?'

'I'm sorry to say, yes, sir.'

'How long do you think it will be until something does leave?'

'It's impossible to say. We're trying to book hotel rooms in Beirut for our own passengers. There's never been anything like this.'

'I'm sure,' said Love with feeling.

He turned to Wilmot.

'You heard?'

Wilmot nodded.

'Right,' said Love. 'Back to that car.'

'Where are we going, then?'

'Anywhere, so long as it's out of Lebanon. We can't get a boat, so our only other chances are Israel or Syria. Syria is a police state, so we'll never get in. If we did manage to, then we'd never get out. That leaves us with Israel.'

'I've no visa for Israel,' said Wilmot.

'Nor have I,' said Love. 'Let's cross that frontier when we come to it.'

The car that had followed them in was waiting outside the departure bay, three men inside, all wearing light suits and black sun glasses. The driver reversed and turned and followed them back patiently to their own car.

Love climbed into the taxi as though he hadn't noticed them, and started the engine. The Pontiac stopped behind them, across their exit, blocking it.

Doors opened. The three men climbed out slowly, deliberately, as though they had all the time in the world, and not enough to do in it.

Love glanced around quickly. He was hemmed in on all sides; by an old Packard on the left, a Ford on the right, and, in front of him, a blue Mini.

'We want a word with you,' the first man said in English. He was heavily built, with a lined, leathery face. Love wound down the window.

'I'm a bit deaf,' he explained mildly.

The man pushed his head inside the car.

'We want to speak to you,' he said more loudly. His breath was heavy with garlic.

'Why? Who are you?'

'The Security Department.'

Love glanced at the two companions behind him. Despite the dark glasses, he recognized one of them: MacGregor.

'My God,' said Wilmot in a hollow voice, as though he was really trying to contact his maker by long distance.

'Say that again,' Love asked the man. 'I can't quite hear you.'

This time, the man put his head right into the car.

'Security Department,' he bellowed.

'No need to shout,' said Love, and seized his tie. He jerked down with all his strength. The man's face hit the steering wheel. Love rabbit-punched him across the back of the neck, and then flung him away from him. He pivoted on his heels and collapsed between the two cars, the back of his head beating the door of the Packard like a bone gong.

The other two men were still behind the car, but as their companion fell, they leaped to one side.

Love saw the blue glint of an automatic, and jammed the gear into reverse.

He accelerated back wildly, spinning the wheel as he did so, crushing one man against the Ford on his right. Then he dropped into first gear and barged the Mini in front. The driver had left it with the handbrake on, but not in gear. The little car squealed forward, its locked rear tyres laying two strips of black rubber on the hot tarmac.

Then Love was out and away, accelerating through the silent car park. No one was about; no one had seen them.

'You bloody fool!' shouted Wilmot. 'If those were police, we'll never get away.'

'They weren't, and we will.'

'How?'

'Because we have to. Those were Diaz's men. One of them was MacGregor. If we're caught by the real police, then we'll go down for shooting that Egyptian we didn't shoot. If Diaz's men get us, we'll just go down, period.

'Also, your wife is paying my expenses to bring you back, and you're also paying me to do the same thing. Remember? I've too much tied up in you, Wilmot, not to get you away. My mother was Scots. I like to show a profit.'

'I like to stay alive,' retorted Wilmot.

Love swung left at the end of the airport approach road, and out on the main twin-track highway, with the red desert on either side, raw as ochre paint. The hills shimmered in the distance, brooding like the spine of some enormous sleeping animal.

Love felt down in the door pocket. Nothing but a few sweet papers and a tyre lever, a taxi-driver's insurance, in case a customer decided not to pay. He opened the lid of the dashboard cubby-hole; it contained a small bottle of bitter lemon. He passed this back to Wilmot.

'Take half,' he said. 'I don't know when we'll get any more.'

Wilmot gulped it down, and handed the bottle back to Love. He drank it in two swallows, and immediately sweat beaded his forehead.

They had probably fifty or sixty miles to go to reach the frontier. No doubt their description was already out, but if they stopped a mile or two before the border and abandoned the car, it should not be impossible to walk across after dark without being seen.

The road suddenly dwindled into a single-track highway, and there were no more houses. The giant hoardings that advertised unlikely airlines, air-conditioned hotels with swimming pools, transistor radios, Japanese cameras, and a lot of other things that Love didn't want, fell away with the houses, and they were out with nothing on either side but the flat earth and a string of telegraph poles carrying wires along which their descriptions were probably already being flashed.

He glanced at the instruments. The petrol gauge registered full, and the oil pressure warning lamp was out, so they should have no mechanical problems.

He wondered what was happening back in the city; whether Diaz's men had given the police the description of their car. It was the only car he had, like the only life he had, and he meant to stick to them both for as long as he needed them.

The road began to climb slowly, almost imperceptibly, so that Love only realized they were climbing quite steeply when the engine began to knock in protest on the cheap petrol. The wind from the sea was slightly cooler now, and as they climbed, he could see the incredibly beautiful promontory on which Beirut was based, stretching out its hand into the blue Mediterranean.

The air was empty of all planes. None could be coming in to the airport, either; the city was sealed off, but so far they had escaped the sealing process.

He wondered about Parkington back in the hospital, and how he was faring; about the old man in the dolls' hospital; about Mrs Wilmot. He also wondered about himself. What would his patients think, if they knew how their doctor was really spending his holiday, driving a stolen car to cross a frontier illegally, facing certain arrest and probably death if he were caught?

The road now began to climb more steeply, and the Z-bends had white arrows painted on the rock-face to mark the sharpness of their curves.

The only other vehicles were brightly painted private taxis, carrying tourists on day trips to Byblos or Baalbek, and a handful of huge lorries. Their polished aluminium bodies gleamed bright in the sun, carrying heaven knew what, drivers stripped to the waist behind their blue-tinted windscreens, radio aerials gay with tiny plastic pennants.

They were running into the trees now. Forests of green cedars, the national tree and symbol of Lebanon, stretched away on either side of the road, feathery, dark, cool and mysterious. They covered the hills like thick green hair, standing so close together it seemed impossible for any animal to move between the trunks.

Love glanced at his watch. Five past nine. A long day stretched ahead, the elasticity of time making the minutes move slowly. They would not dare to attempt the frontier crossing before darkness, and this was nearly twelve hours away, as the clock measured time, and twelve centuries by his own feelings.

Now that the immediate danger seemed to be receding, the reaction of the past few hours made him feel chill and tired. He could not remember when he had last eaten or slept properly. He seemed to have been living in the same socks since his arrival; but at least he was living in them, and not dead in them, like the Egyptian in the Cadillac, or the hippie in the morgue.

Milestones flashed past. Love dozed, and then shook himself awake, as he entered a left-hand bend. He tore at the wheel and the bald tyres squealed, and the engine spluttered as though it were tired, like the driver. Then it picked up and spluttered again, and died.

Love flicked the gear into neutral and coasted to the right of the road, stopping on the sandstone strip that bordered the tarmac. He twisted the ignition key. The starter spun the engine, but it did not fire.

'What's wrong?' asked Wilmot nervously.

Love shrugged. He jumped out, opened the bonnet. The old side-valve engine shimmered in its own fierce heat; oil leaks were coated with red dust; the battery had corks stuck in the fillers. He rummaged in the tool box. It contained a jack, a pair of pliers, a filthy rag, and half a pint of oil in a glass bottle.

He put the pliers around the nut holding the petrol feed to the carburettor, loosened it slightly, pressed the starter solenoid. The engine turned, but no petrol came through.

'We're out of juice,' said Love flatly.

'We can't be,' said Wilmot. 'The bloody gauge says full.'

'Then it's lying,' said Love. 'We should have checked.'

'So what do we do now? Walk to the border?'

'Dump the car first. Every policeman in the country will be after it if we leave it here. We might as well send them a telegram saying where we are.'

'My God,' said Wilmot hoarsely.

Now that the noose of danger seemed to be tightening about them again, Love's fatigue momentarily left him; adrenalin can be a stronger stimulant than alcohol.

Wilmot climbed out and stood by the side of the car. His face was grey. He looked like a man carved from driftwood; the stubble on his chin showed white, and he seemed to have shrunk in adversity. His shoulders slumped down in weariness and dejection. His lips were rimmed with blue. He had lost his deal; now he could lose his liberty, even his life.

Love leaned into the driver's seat, released the handbrake. The car rolled backwards, gathered speed, scraped against the side of the rock-face, striking sparks, and hit one of the marker posts on the corner. Then it went off the road, crashing down, with a great splintering of wood, into the cedar forest.

Branches waved furiously and the smell of new-split wood sharpened the air, and some birds squawked in terror; and then they heard nothing but the wind in the rustling leaves.

The car had not gone as far off the road as Love, would have liked, but there was nothing he could do about that now. In fact, there seemed very little he could do about anything.

He turned to Wilmot.

'How much money have you on you?'

Wilmot unbuttoned the back pocket of his trousers, took out a thin sweat-soaked wallet, counted out fifty Lebanese pound notes.

'I've about the same,' said Love. 'First thing is to get off this road. We can keep fairly near it, but under cover. Maybe we'll find another car we can pinch, or we can thumb a lift in a lorry, though I think that's pretty risky. Most of these trucks have radios, and I'm sure Diaz has put out a pretty good description of us - if the police don't know it already.'

'So what do we do?' asked Wilmot dully, as though he did not greatly care, as though he accepted that nothing they could do would help them much, as though defeat should already be conceded. If all the gods were against you, who could be on your side?

'We start marching,' said Love as forcefully as he could, and led the way through the soft, feathered undergrowth into the dark, cool greenness of the forest.

CHAPTER ELEVEN

It was eleven o'clock in MacGillivray's office, and he sat watching the clock on the wall - and the ones on either side of it that offered him the equivalent time in New York, San Francisco, Singapore and Sydney. Not that this mattered greatly; MacGillivray was not at that moment much concerned with what might or might not be happening in these faraway cities. He was concerned with something much nearer home.

He sat at his desk, elbows on the black blotting pad, tips of his fingers spread spatulate together, wishing that the day was either younger or older.

Eleven o'clock in the morning always seemed to him to be the worst hour of every working day. It was just too late to look back on decisions he had made on arrival; just too early to look forward to the relief of lunchtime, and a couple of club-sized gin-and-bitter-lemons in the East India and Sports before his usual lunch of cold roast beef, green salad, and sweet mango chutney.

Today, eleven o'clock seemed even worse than usual. He impressed his fingers, and smoothed out the flimsy on which the cable from the dolls' hospital in Beirut had been decoded.

The number 134262426 meant nothing to him, but then there was no reason why it should, and yet every reason why it must.

It could mean anything or it could mean nothing: the number of a patent specification; a secret bank deposit; an insurance policy; a private code that might never be broken, because no one held the key except two married lovers he would never meet. It could be a car registration number in a foreign country, a telephone exchange, the prefix for a cable address, the serial number of a contract or specification.

His staff had already tried every kind of permutation. They had fed the number into the computer in the basement of the Ministry of Defence in Whitehall and had searched the files and cross-references of agents and traitors, known or suspected, looking for some clue from their birth-dates, even their telephone and National Insurance numbers.

They had tried the number on telephone exchanges throughout the British Isles, put it back to front, squared it, cubed it - but still it meant nothing more than nine isolated digits on an overseas telegram form.

The more MacGillivray looked at the number, the more he felt personally convinced that it was some form of amateur code. Official codes tended to break down into blocks of five or six figures to make their cracking a more difficult task. Amateurs usually stayed with simpler transpositions of figures and letters of the alphabet.

He pressed a button on the desk, and Miss Jenkins came in, wearing her regulation office clothes, tweed skirt and white buttoned blouse. Sometimes he wondered whether she owned any other clothes, but this was not the time to ask.

'Your coffee is just coming,' she began.

'Never mind that,' replied MacGillivray ungraciously. 'It's this bloody number.'

'I've got some news for you about that,' said Miss Jenkins. He looked at her more closely.

'Good news?' he asked.

'News,' she said noncommittally. 'I think it's a radio call sign.'

'Is it now? What makes you think that?'

'The young man who went to see Mrs Wilmot from Inspector Mason was on the telephone about his expenses - who he was to charge them to — our department or his. I told him, his. And I asked him about her house and so on — I have a brother, a retired bank manager, who lives near there, and he's always interested in hearing about beautifully renovated old houses.

'The young man told me all about it. He said the only thing that spoiled the look of the place was a lot of TV aerials on the roof of the lodge.'

'Ah,' said MacGillivray appreciatively. 'Only they weren't TV aerials, but aerials for something else, eh?'

'Yes. Nothing sinister, though — simply an amateur radio enthusiast who lives in the lodge. He'd asked one or two people in the local pub. So we checked with the Radio Society of Great Britain, and the number does work out.'

'How?'

'Apparently England is covered by the letter M, which could refer to the first figures, thirteen. The second figure after this refers to the present series of licences. The last six numbers are like car registration numbers — they refer to individual licence holders. Thus, twenty-six could be the last letter in the alphabet - Z. Twenty-four could be X.'

'Well?' prompted MacGillivray, not caring a damn about the mechanics of the thing, only anxious to come up with a solution. He scribbled out the nine figures on a piece of paper, and wrote under them the letters they could represent.

'So who holds 134262426 or M4ZXZ?'.

'A retired naval petty officer, a Mr Snelling, formerly a radio operator.'

'Who presumably lives in the lodge of Esdaile House, Bishop's Combe?'

'Yes.'

Miss Jenkins paused, savouring her moment of triumph. She looks almost human, thought MacGillivray, almost flesh and blood, instead of being a sexless typing machine with a flair for filing and making strong black coffee.

'Good for you,' said MacGillivray, and he meant it. 'Anything known about Snelling?'

'Nothing hostile. He did twenty years in the Navy. Retired eight years ago. Ran a wireless shop for a time, but went bust. Took a job at Esdaile House as a chauffeur and general handyman about eighteen months ago.'

So why the hell should his call sign be found written on the scalp of the brother of his employer's wife? There was only one way to find out; to ask the wife, and to keep on asking until she told the truth, willingly if possible, or if not, to force it out of her as he would squeeze toothpaste from a tube.

MacGillivray stood up.

'I may be back this afternoon, or I may not,' he told Miss Jenkins enigmatically. 'You'll know where I am - the insurance office - but don't ring me unless it's absolutely vital.'

He took down his old deerstalker hat from its peg, the tweedy symbol of the estate in Scotland he would like to own, and never would. As the laird, treading the purple hills, watching stags bound away, crossing burns clear as gin where they twinkled over dark brown peat, he went down the back stairs into grey reality: Covent Garden, with the air sour with stale fruit, and caught a cruising cab to an office in Finsbury Square.

A number of brass plates were screwed to the door of a first-floor office in a sham Gothic building, showing that this address was also the registered office of a surprising number of companies, which ranged from Beechwood Nominees Ltd, through Quendon Estates (1952) Ltd, to Assessor's Office, Midland Widows Life Insurance Company, Ltd.

He put a curiously shaped key into the lock, turned it three times, opened the door, then locked it carefully behind him.

The room inside was fusty and rather small, with two desks and swivel chairs, and a leather armchair in one corner. He took down a calendar advertising Quendon Estates from the wall, replaced it with one advertising Midland Widows Insurance, which he took out of a cupboard. He thought it looked very impressive; it mentioned their assets in millions.

He hung his hat and coat on the rack, sat down, picked up the telephone, dialled a number.

When a woman's voice answered, he pushed over a switch beneath the desk that started the hidden wire recorder.

'Am I speaking to Mrs Caroline Wilmot?' he asked.

'Yes. Who is that?'

'My name is Brooks,' said MacGillivray, his voice rich and mellow, like dark brown fruit cake soaked in port. 'I'm the claims manager of the Midland Widows. I understand our representative had a most helpful talk with you.'

'Well, he came to see me,' she allowed. 'About my brother. What do you want?'

'It's very difficult to explain over the telephone, Mrs Wilmot,' he said hesitantly, 'but a rather unusual complication has arisen with regard to this policy.'

'How unusual?' she asked. 'Don't you want to pay out?'

'Please don't misunderstand me, Mrs Wilmot,' MacGillivray said quickly. 'I do assure you the Midland Widows is always most anxious to honour every obligation. This is simply a question of the currency in which the policy was drawn. I must say we've not had one drawn in Moroccan currency before.'

'Well, what about it?' asked Mrs. Wilmot. 'There's always a first time. Can't you pay out in sterling or dollars?'

'That's what I was coming to, Mrs Wilmot. Is there any chance of your being in London today, or could I come down to Somerset to see you?'

'I could come up,' she said, rather unwillingly. 'There's a quick train from Taunton. But is it very important? I'm rather involved with things here.'

'It is really important, Mrs Wilmot,' MacGillivray assured her earnestly, and it was, although not for any reason that he hoped she could imagine. 'I wouldn't ask you to do this otherwise. I'll send a car to Paddington for you if you'll tell me what you will be wearing so that the driver can recognize you.'

'Oh, I suppose, a grey coat, blue shoes and blue handbag. I'll have lunch on the train. I should arrive about two-fifteen.'

'I look forward very much to meeting you, and I'm sure we can settle this up very quickly. It's so much easier, face to face, than by telephone or letter.'

He replaced the receiver, looked up a train timetable from the drawer of his desk, then dialled Inspector Mason.

'Mrs Wilmot,' he told him. 'She'll be arriving at two-fifteen in London from Taunton. Wearing a grey coat, blue shoes and blue handbag. Send a car with a chauffeur to pick her up. But see she's followed on the train in case she talks to anyone on the way up - or anyone tries anything. If there's any trouble, whip 'em all in. Not that I think she'll get involved.'

'Will do,' replied Mason.

MacGillivray sat back in his chair for a moment, then stood up, and opened the windows. The room felt altogether too dusty to be the office of an insurance executive; last time he had used it he was supposed to be a mortgage broker with Beechwood Nominees. He rather liked that name; he had once looked at a house called Beechwood.

He pulled out the drawer of a filing cabinet marked 'Midland Widows Claims', sprayed the air with a pine-scented aerosol, scattered a few papers headed Midland Widows Life Insurance Company Ltd - Departmental Memo — across his desk. Then he telephoned Miss Jenkins to be there by two o'clock, and checked the time with his own watch.

It was eleven-thirty; only half an hour after the worst hour of the morning, and quite a lot was happening. Perhaps the best really was yet to be?

The Lebanese doctor was a small round man with very black hair and a lot of it, except right on top of his head, where baldness had made a landing patch for flies.

'You lead a very hard life, Mr Carter,' he told Parkington, with perhaps a little envy.

'I do. But that's the way I'm made. And you've only got one life, Doctor. You might as well live it. No one else can do that for you.'

'Quite so. I've heard that view expressed before by many people. But you personally can also live it for just a little longer - perhaps a lot longer, Mr Carter - if you don't drink quite so much. If you eat more regular meals. If you slow down the pace of all your activities.'

'I've heard that, too, often enough,' said Parkington. 'But I prefer to burn-out rather than die out. And that's what's happening to me here, doctor. I want out of this hospital today. There's nothing wrong with me a few drinks won't cure.'

'I would not advise you to leave for at least two or three days, Mr Carter,' said the doctor seriously. 'The man who is his own doctor has a fool for his patient, you know. Here, you are on a light diet. With rest, you give that ulcer a chance to heal.'

'It can heal somewhere else,' said Parkington. 'What happens if I get up now?'

'Maybe you'll re-open the haemorrhage. Have you had haemorrhages before with this ulcer?'

'Frequently,' said Parkington. 'I'm so used to them, I'd miss them if they weren't there. What I want from you, Doctor, is an assurance that I won't drop dead if I get up now and go back to work.'

'I can give no one that assurance, Mr Carter. None of us say when we'll be born, and only a few of us can say when we'll die.'

'So I'll take the risk of dying another day. But, with your permission, Doctor, I'll die out of here, in my own time.'

The doctor passed on to the man in the next bed, shaking his head. What an extraordinary philosophy, he thought. And then he wondered if it were quite so reprehensible as he had been brought up to believe. After all, if some people didn't follow it, there would be a lot less work for him.

Parkington waited until the doctor had left the ward, and then he carefully slid his feet out of bed, on to the polished, brown-tiled floor. He tested his weight, walked a few careful paces. He could still feel the hard focus of pain above his stomach, as though he'd swallowed a red-hot coal that burned with every breath. But a burst ulcer was, so far as he was concerned, a great deal less serious than a broken rib.

He stood up gingerly, flexed his muscles, winced as the pain bored deeper into his body. It was madness to go on as he was doing. He knew that, but then his was a mad business, in a mad world. He could either go on or he could give up.

If he'd had time, maybe he would have stayed in bed, and endured the milk diet, and maybe he would have cured his ulcer; but there was no time. Right now, time was vastly more important than money; it could be life. His own, someone else's; maybe a lot of other people's.

He sat down on the edge of the bed, ran his fingers through his hair.

A nurse came in.,

'Why, Mr Carter,' she said, 'you can't get up yet.'

'It's all right,' Parkington assured her. 'The doctor said I was fine. I just have to nip out this afternoon for a business thing. Be back in an hour or so. If you can just tell me where my clothes are - so I don't have to disturb you when I go?'

'If you're sure it's all right?' the nurse said doubtfully.

'I'm perfectly sure,' he said, so confidently that he almost believed it himself. 'After all, I'm the only one affected.'

'Your clothes are in the next room, then. There's a cup-board with your name on it. Your shoes are underneath your suit. Everything else is on a shelf. And come back soon. You don't want to overtire yourself.'

'Thank you, nurse,' said Parkington, and meant it. 'I'll be back.'

If he was not back here, he knew he would probably be in some other part of some other hospital, but in a less aseptic room, where the sheets were rubber and no one had any need to speak in hushed whispers; in fact, no one spoke at all, for they were dead. That room would be the mortuary.

'Mrs Wilmot to see you, sir,' announced Miss Jenkins primly, and opened the door. She went back to her outer room, checked that the hidden recorder was set at the right speed, and sat down at her desk to monitor the conversation.

Mrs Wilmot came into MacGillivray's office and the tiny room was immediately filled with the scent of crushed flowers. Very richly crushed, too, thought MacGillivray, and by Schiaparelli or Lanvin. He appreciated these things, especially when he did not have to pay for them; indeed, only when this was so. She wore three ropes of pearls and a Kutchinsky bracelet that must have cost all that MacGillivray earned in a year, and probably a lot more.

He gave a little sigh, for he had nothing else to give, and to sigh cost him nothing. Even the rich have their problems, he allowed. But then, so did the poor, and it must be very pleasant to be able to spend so much money without missing it; even more pleasant to have a husband who'd spend it for you, on you.

'Mr Brooks?' asked Caroline Wilmot.

'Please sit down,' said MacGillivray, holding out his hand.

She sat in the only easy chair, leaning back, crossing her legs easily.

'Our car picked you up all right?' he asked, holding a gold-capped pen between both hands as though he wanted to break it.

'Yes,' she said. 'It was kind of you to send it. Now, what's this trouble about my brother's policy?'

MacGillivray put down his pen and leaned forward on his desk, elbows widespread, fingers together under his chin, looking at her. He said nothing. The clock on the wall ticked away. He gave it a minute before he spoke.

'Well?' she said, puzzled. A frown ploughed faint furrows between her eyes.

'It's a rather complicated problem, Mrs Wilmot,' MacGillivray said at last, speaking slowly, weighing out each word as though it cost him money.

'It's not particularly your brother who concerns me now, because, unfortunately, that poor young man is dead. I'm worried about your husband, Mrs Wilmot.'

'John?' she asked, puzzled, the frown deepening. She ran the tip of her tongue over her dry lips; MacGillivray wished she was running it over his.

'I understood you wanted to see me about the policy on my brother's life? How is my husband involved?'

'I don't know,' said MacGillivray, 'but I hope that you can help us.'

'What's all this got to do with an insurance claim? You said there was some trouble about paying out in Moroccan currency. My husband's not in Morocco.'

'I think that before we go any further, Mrs Wilmot, I should make something clear to you. I'm not really an insurance man. I'm a member of the Security Department. So is the young man who came to see you.'

'There is no insurance claim pending under the Midland

Widows Company, but it was absolutely imperative that we saw you, and at the time this seemed the easiest way to do so without causing you undue anxiety.'

'I just don't understand,' protested Mrs Wilmot. 'Someone comes to me in Somerset and tells me I'm named in an insurance my brother took out on his life. You phone me, and ask me up to see you on the same matter. Now you tell me you've got nothing to do with it. I don't like the sound of all this at all. I'm going to see my lawyer.'

'Speak to him by all means. Use this telephone. But before you do so, here's proof I'm who I say I am.'

MacGillivray showed her his Foreign Office and Ministry of Defence passes, slipped the plastic cards back in his pocket. He pushed the receiver towards her. She put out a hand towards it and then drew back.

'How can I believe you?' she asked. 'Those passes may be as false as the name on your door - as everything else about you seems to be.'

'Sometimes I wish they were,' said MacGillivray. 'At times like these, especially, when it's very painful to say what I'm going to say. But before you call your lawyer, let me tell you a little more, so you will be in a position to brief him more thoroughly. First, have you seen the papers today, Mrs Wilmot?'

She shook her head

'No. I had a book. I read that on the train.'

'Have you heard any news on the radio?'

'No. Why?'

MacGillivray opened the desk drawer, took out that morning's late edition of a newspaper, pushed it across the desk top to her.

The main story carried the headline : 'Egyptian Minister shot in Beirut; Middle East at flashpoint.'

Mrs Wilmot read on, her lips moving, her face a mask of amazement. 'The entire Lebanese Army and police force were alerted this morning, when the Egyptian Minister of Culture and Development, Ahmed Hussein, was shot dead less than an hour after arriving here for a state visit.

'A sniper, hidden on a skyscraper rooftop, shot him as he rode in a state procession. The line of cars had slowed to walking pace, to turn from Rue Royale into Avenue du Pont when the assassination occurred. The marksman had, literally, a sitting and almost stationary target.

'Immediately, all main streets, Beirut airport and the docks were sealed off and all frontiers closed.

'Shops were shuttered and blinds lowered, both as a mark of respect and in fear of reprisals by mobs of Arabs and gangs of students who surged through the streets, tearing up paving stones, overturning cars, and daubing buildings with slogans.

'Wild rumours circulated that a Briton named as John Esdaile was involved.

'A British Embassy spokesman denied this.

' "There is no British subject of that name in Beirut, either as a resident or a visitor," he said categorically.

'Some political observers believe that this allegation is simply a means of involving the West, to find an excuse for anti-Western demonstrations, never far in the background in this divided city. Certainly, as soon as it was made, mobs gathered outside the British and American Embassies, chanting, waving placards carrying slogans, apparently printed in advance and in English and French : "Down with imperialists", "Freedom for the refugees", "Death to Nixon".'

Mrs Wilmot let the paper drop on the green leather desk. Her hands were trembling: the Kutchinsky bracelet rustled its delicate gold pieces in sympathy.

'My God,' she said softly. 'Is that true?'

'What is truth?' asked MacGillivray rhetorically, quoting Pilate. 'It's what the paper says, and they have a man on the spot. But what's happening there now, I've, no idea. All telephone and radio links with Lebanon have been cut. There is strict censorship on all Press messages. I've been on to Reuters, and their last message came out yesterday morning about ten o'clock.

'Our Embassy still has its own radio, of course, but the situation is too confused for any proper assessment to be made. No one can get into the country, and until they find this Mr Esdaile - if there is such a man - I shouldn't think anyone will be allowed out.'

'There is such a man,' said Mrs Wilmot. 'He's my husband.'

Her face was as pale as the newspaper.

'I know,' said MacGillivray. 'And do you also know, Mrs Wilmot, that when your brother's body was examined, under his rather long hair, someone had written a number?'

'No,' she said, hardly taking in what he said, her mind thousands of miles away. 'I didn't know.'

'That number was a coded version of the radio call sign of your chauffeur, Mr Snelling. Do you still want to call your lawyer?'

She shook her head, almost imperceptibly, as though she was suddenly incapable of movement.

'What do you want me to do?' she asked, and her voice was faint as the echo of a whisper.

'Have a cup of tea first,' said MacGillivray, watching her shrewdly, hoping she would not break down before she told him what he needed to hear. He hated to see a woman cry; it made make-up run, and invariably their handkerchiefs turned out to be useless squares of gossamer, and if he lent them one of his, then his wife saw mascara and lipstick stains and asked jagged questions. After all, what reasonable excuse could a fruit importer provide for a handkerchief reddened by another woman's lipstick? He pressed a button beneath his desk.

'Do you think John is dead?' she asked him dully.

'I just don't know,' said MacGillivray. 'Lebanon can be a difficult country to get out of if the Lebanese want to keep you there. And, whether your husband is guilty or not guilty, you must accept the fact that the authorities there will desperately want a scapegoat — any scapegoat.

'After all, it's a very serious blow for Arab friendship if your first important Arab visitor in years - and a guest of state - is shot dead on arrival. The fact that your husband's been named so soon doesn't look too healthy. We can only hope.'

Miss Jenkins knocked discreetly at the door, then carried in a tray, with a white china teapot, stamped with the Civil Service cipher, cups and saucers of rather thick china, a bowl of wrapped sugar cubes, a small plate of biscuits. She put the tray down on the desk, poured out two cups of tea, added the milk, left the room.

'I've been a bloody fool,' said Mrs Wilmot bitterly, her eyes dark and unhappy. 'First, my brother. And now — John.'

'We're all bloody fools at one time or another,' MacGillivray reminded her gently. 'Now, suppose you drink that cup of tea, and tell me exactly why you were so foolish?'

Love wiped his forehead and the back of his neck with a soaking handkerchief. He felt like a refugee from a Turkish bath. His body streamed with sweat, his shirt hung clammily to his back like a second nylon skin.

Wilmot leaned wearily against a tree, his weight on his good leg. He had thrown away his tie, and his shirt was open down to his belt. Underneath it, the skin of his chest was wrinkled and pale, as though it had never seen the sun.

'Are you sure we're going in the right direction?' he asked apprehensively.

'I'm sure of nothing,' Love told him. 'We're going by the sun, for we've no other means. I can't use my watch as a compass because it's stopped. But our general direction's OK.

After all, the border runs for many miles. We must hit it eventually.'

'When is eventually?' asked Wilmot petulantly. 'I can't stand this heat. I feel so bloody ill. Out of breath. Sick. And this ankle's giving me hell.'

He had aged years since they left the car, only hours ago. The skin on his face hung loose as a leather handbag; his eyes were pouchy and his lips drawn back, exposing his gums. He was exhausted, and when he spoke he had to stop walking, for he lacked strength to walk and talk at the same time.

'It's better than inside a Lebanese jail,' Love pointed out.

'How do we know we won't end up there?'

'We don't,' said Love. 'That's why we've got to keep marching.'

The forest stretched dark and, hot, almost airless, seemingly endless, in every direction. Love had hoped to stay within a few hundred yards of the road so that, by catching sight of passing vehicles, or even the occasional flash of sunshine on their windscreen, he could keep on course. But they had been forced to make a long detour around a deep copse, and in so doing he had lost the road.

The trees filtered all traffic sounds, so there was no means of telling how far from the road they were. The only sounds were an occasional surprised crash of wings in branches as some bird took flight, whackering its way up the sky; or when a little animal, startled by their stumbling progress, fled away with a dry cracking of tiny twigs.

The air seemed full of buzzing insects that settled on their sweating flesh, at the roots of their damp hair, and stung the edges of their eyes. As fast as they wiped them away, others returned.

Love had only a hazy idea how far away the frontier lay, and no idea at all how far the forest stretched. It could be for a few hundred yards or for fifty miles, but so long as they kept going in a south-westerly direction, he calculated that they were bound to reach the border. The only problems were how long this would take — and whether they could physically walk it in their condition.

Every now and then they reached a clearing, and the sky burned burnished blue above their heads as he checked his direction. The sun seemed to be moving at a different angle to the one Love thought it should keep, and the dread grew that maybe they were walking in a wide circle, and would finally come out on the road near where their car had run out of petrol.

They came to a stream that tinkled down over mossy rocks, glittering with silver veins from quartz deposits, and sank their mouths gratefully into the cold water, and splashed their faces and soaked their wrists.

The more they drank, the more sweat poured from their hot tired bodies. They lay for a moment beside the stream, oblivious of the flies and the sweat and the discomfort, feeling their hearts pounding like pistons against the dried moss on the bank.

Wilmot asked lifelessly, 'When we do reach the border, how do we cross it?'

'I don't know,' said Love. 'But it shouldn't be difficult. In places, it's, probably only a wire we can get under after dark. The hard thing's going to be getting there.'

They lay on in silence for a moment, and the flies buzzed about them, savouring the saltiness of their sweat.

'Funny thing, Doctor,' said Wilmot at last, thinking aloud. 'I've always read money's useless if you're on a desert island - or somewhere like this. And it's true. I've probably enough money to buy anything I want and anyone I want. But there's not enough money in all the world to buy our way out of this bloody forest.'

'We'll make it,' Love assured him. He sensed the note of rising panic in Wilmot's voice, and wondered whether he should give him a second benzedrine pill, whether he needed one himself.

'You may make it,' corrected Wilmot. 'I don't think I will.'

'You'll feel better when it's cooler.'

But would it ever be cooler? When night fell, unless they could find their way back to the road, they would not be able to see their way, and would be forced to take shelter in a tree.

Love stood up, pulled Wilmot wearily to his feet beside him, and they set off again, the smooth soles of their thin city shoes slipping on the moss and the rocks.

Suddenly, ahead of them, as they climbed, Love heard a rising whine of gears. He paused. Fifty yards away, through gaps between the trees, he could see a lorry and a trailer, all dusty aluminium, grinding their slow way up the hill road.

They were much nearer to it than he had imagined. They were not keeping in a straight line, but, as he had feared, they were turning in a circle. Wilmot looked at him, and Love could see his own despair mirrored in his dull, hopeless eyes. They had marched for hours, or so it seemed, and for all the distance they had covered, they might as well have stayed where they were.

It would be better to try and hitch a lift, to offer a lorry driver all the money they had between them to carry them fifty miles on, instead of this dragging, slow trek through these infernal forests, going nowhere, killing themselves in the heat while they did so.

Wilmot followed him painfully through the trees, until they both saw a white milestone by the side of the road, near the parallel blue lines of rubber left by countless lorry tyres.

They heard another lorry coming up the hill, and Wilmot started forward to wave to the driver; but Love, a few yards behind him, saw the lorry before he did and called softly, 'Comeback!'

They both dropped on their stomachs in the undergrowth, and watched. The lorry was a shabby open Studebaker, probably left over from the Second World War, painted khaki, and full of troops. They sat in the back in two rows, facing each other, their rifles between their knees, muzzles pointing up in the air.

The lorry stopped about two hundred yards beyond them, and the troops swung down the tailboard and climbed out, the studs in their boots ringing on the hard, hot road.

Love and Wilmot crawled back into the forest as quickly as they could. They heard the soldiers calling to each other in Arabic, and laughing and crashing their way noisily through the undergrowth on the far side of the road.

They were still safe, but for how long? Someone must have given their description, or maybe their car had been discovered. The searchers were far too close for safety.

'We'll have to keep away from the road until it's dark,' Love told Wilmot.

He nodded. He seemed beyond speech. Could he survive, holed up under some tree, for at least ten more hours, without food, and then set out in the evening on a forced march to the frontier? Love felt doubtful, but they had no other choice. Wilmot's face was red with exertion. It must have been years since he had known any hard exercise. The unhealthy blue tinge had deepened around his lips.

Wearily, they plunged back into the forest. Although they had drunk pints from the stream, their mouths were already parched, but they had to go on, because to stay where they were meant capture, and capture could mean death. It would be infinitely easier for the soldiers to report that* two suspected assassins were shot while resisting arrest, than to set in motion all the cumbrous machinery of a rigged trial charged with only one aim - to find them guilty.

They climbed a small knoll, because it seemed safer to be above the level ground, and sank down beneath the bole of a tree. The rough, serrated bark was encrusted with huge fungoid growths like mushrooms, soft and white and fleshy. They smelled faintly sour and rancid.

Love had no idea where he was, or what time it was. The sun had hung like a burning glass above their heads for so long he did not know whether it was still morning, or afternoon. They seemed beyond time and its measurement, in a humid world of heat and thirst and weariness.

Then suddenly, they heard shouts and the stutter of a sub-machine gun, and a great thrashing of wings as dozens of pigeons soared up out of the forest across the road.

They started up, looking at each other in alarm, listening, heads on one side. Had that simply been a trigger-happy soldier, or had he fired because he thought he saw a human target?

As they listened, another truck arrived, a smaller one, it seemed to Love, judging from the sound of its engine. Doors clanged, and then they heard the faint, excited barking and whining of dogs. If the soldiers brought the dogs over to their side of the road, nothing could stop their discovery.

Wilmot sagged back against the tree again, as though too weary either to stand or lie down. His shoes were cracked, trousers torn with thorns, his face lacerated by branches, his eyes bloodshot. Love saw he was in poor shape to move; maybe it would be safer to stay where they were in the hope that the dogs moved elsewhere? One dry branch breaking could give away their position.

'We'll rest,' Love told him. 'For as long as you like. We'll go on when it's cooler.'

'What about when it's dark?' asked Wilmot fretfully, eyes closed, lips barely moving. 'How can we go then? We won't be able to see our way.'

'It'll be harder for them to find us then, too,' said Love. 'I reckon the troops will call off the hunt when it's dark'

'We'll never make the border, Doctor.'

'Of course we will. We have to.'

'You speak for yourself. I know I won't. I don't even know if I want to. Not now.'

'You've got to. Otherwise you're stuck here in this bloody forest.'

'What is there for me back home?' Wilmot asked him. 'I've been on the run for so long, Doctor. Too long. First, from income tax. From racketeers who wanted to cash in on my business. Then, from a Board of Trade investigation. Maybe, if I'm honest, most of all from myself, and what I've made of my life.'

'But you've got everything to live for,' Love told him. 'You're rich. A lovely wife. A pretty daughter. You're a story book success.'

'That's the trouble. It's all fairy story stuff. It's not real, any of it, except the money. My wife doesn't love me. She loves what I represent, what I can buy for her. She loves the yacht at Antibes. That house in Somerset. The flat in Eaton Place. But not me.

'Have you ever known what it is to be in love with someone yourself, but aware that so far as she's concerned you're just a provider, someone who picks up the bills, who turns a gentlemanly blind eye to all her boy friends?'

'No,' said Love, thinking of the young man in the Alfa that Mrs Hunter had told him about. 'That's why I'm still a bachelor.'

'And maybe you're the wise one. I've been thinking, out here in this forest. What do I go back to? Questions in Parliament about how I made my money? Arguing with lawyers to get British nationality - which I don't particularly want? Thousands of pounds in fees for accountants, solicitors, counsel, all parasites on my back? And what does it really all add up to in the end? To be in a bed with a much younger woman, who's only a legalized whore, selling herself for a gold bracelet here, a necklace there, a new dress later on.

'Haven't you finished yet? I want to go to sleep.'

'I'm through with all that, Doctor. Finished with it. I'm not going back to that life. Not ever.'

Wilmot's speech slurred as though he had been drinking, but all he had drunk was water from the stream.

'You're dramatizing things,' Love told him sharply. 'Let's get out of this damned forest, first. You'll be better over the border.'

Wilmot did not reply. He sat down clumsily as though on rubber legs, and lay back against the tree, his eyes shut. Suddenly and unexpectedly, he began to snore loudly. Love shook him awake, the noise could give away their position. Wilmot half struggled up, and then sank back again.

He was hopelessly out of condition, of course. Any sort of exertion would tire him, and this sustained effort, coming on top of the disappointment at losing his deal, plus their desperate danger of discovery, had drained him of all vitality. He'd be better after a sleep.

Love thought he might doze for half an hour himself, but he had no means of measuring how long this would last, and sleep was a luxury he could not yet afford. He moved away from the tree and lay down on his stomach, elbows out, one hand on top of the other, supporting his chin, so that he could scan the approaches to the hill in case any soldiers picked up their trail.

Love must have dozed unknowingly, for a faint crackle of twigs brought him instantly awake. He had a headache, his mouth was dry, his neck cricked and his knee-caps had bored blunt holes in the ground. Otherwise, he felt fine.

A file of soldiers was moving carelessly across a clearing about a hundred yards to his right. He could see their uniforms, a darker, deeper green, against the leaves. They were not laughing and talking now. Maybe they were tired, too. They carried sub-machine guns of a type and make he did not know. Somehow, they had the relaxed look of troops going off duty.

He turned round towards Wilmot, hoping he did not wake up or call out, or snore. Wilmot lay exactly as he had lain when Love had left him.

Love watched until the last of the soldiers had crossed his field of vision. They seemed to be going back to the road, without any attempt at silence. The sound of the crashing twigs and branches grew fainter, and then he heard a whistle and an engine starting, and dogs barking. Maybe they were being moved on by truck to search another area - or to be called off for the night?

He turned back to Wilmot, shook his right shoulder.

Wilmot's hat rolled off; the black leather band inside was shiny with sweat, that had plastered his hair to his forehead. A little saliva had drooled out of the right side of his mouth and trickled down over his lapel. He looked like a tramp, asleep on a summer afternoon after an unaccustomed bottle of beer.

Love shook him again, and his head lolled like a marionette. He put out his hand to feel his pulse, and then raised Wilmot's right eyelid. The pupil was wide and blank, like a camera iris held open, seeing nothing. He let Wilmot's wrist drop, and his damp hand fell like a bag of bones to his thigh. His lips were blue; flies buzzed unchecked around his mouth, caked with dry saliva, and at his nose.

He was quite dead.

Had he suffered a heart attack? Or was it simply a mental inability to run any farther, because, deep down, he knew he had nowhere to run to, and far worse, no one? Perhaps it was not Wilmot's body that had died first, but his spirit.

Love thought suddenly and inconsequentially of the wording of death certificates he had so often signed for other people :

'Other significant conditions contributing to the death, but not related to the disease or condition causing it.'

He would probably never be asked to sign Wilmot's death certificate, but, if he were, what could he honestly put against this question?

A struggle to survive that had proved too strong for survival? A fight to prove himself in an alien land? Or lonely years with a woman who did not love him, wondering how she had spent the time when she was late home, whether he could believe her reasons for her trips to town? Not that any of it mattered now. Death paid all debts; only the living could be called upon to pay for their mistakes. Sometimes, their repayments lasted all their lives.

Love bent down, took out Wilmot's wallet, a couple of letters from an inner pocket, a fountain pen, a handful of notes and small change, and buttoned them in his own breast pocket. Then he replaced Wilmot's hat, and pulled it down over his dead, sweat-streaked face.

He had no idea how long Wilmot would lie there, or whether the soldiers would discover him in the morning, but there was no need to leave his name and address for them. Within a day, if he were not discovered, his body would be unrecognizable.

It was colder now, and the sweat had dried on Love's shirt, stiffening it like starch. He shivered with distaste and fatigue. He felt as he did when he brought a baby into the world, only to see the child die within minutes. More than an acute sense of failure, it was a feeling of almost personal loss. If he had acted differently, would Wilmot have lived?

He had not known Wilmot well, and he had not particularly liked him, but he had recognized a rare spirit; one of that handful of men in every generation who can focus their talents and abilities and energies on one target, like the sun through a magnifying glass, and burn on through all setbacks to what they imagined they wanted.

But what, in the last analysis, did anyone want? Was it to be rich like Wilmot, and yet, paradoxically, to be virtually an exile, and attempt to buy that most unbuyable thing, love? To be, ironically, at the same time the envy of those who knew nothing about him, and the pity of the few who realized the truth?

Life itself was as inconclusive as these questions without answers. There were no happy endings, for there were no endings: old problems and flashes of happiness were continually being rekindled against new backgrounds, for new generations.

Love stood up. Ants were already crawling over the backs of Wilmot's hands; soon they would begin to devour the waxy flesh. He could not approve of a lot that Wilmot had done, but he admired the courage and singleness of purpose that had made him do it - even if this meant ending his life years before his time, in an unknown Lebanese forest, fleeing from men who had never seen him.

Love walked away slowly, buttoning his jacket and turning up his coat collar against the evening mosquitoes. He would have to find somewhere to lie-up for the night, or at least until the moon rose, for he could not possibly walk in complete darkness without a landmark to guide him.

He tried to think ahead, what he would do when he crossed the border, not if he crossed.

He would head for that refuge of all broken-down, impecunious British travellers in foreign lands, the nearest Consulate. He did not imagine that anyone there would be wildly pleased to see him, but he would quote MacGillivray's name, and give them his address, and then, possibly with another passport, he might be helped to catch a plane home.

He was walking more slowly now, and stumbling occasionally. He stopped and leaned against a tree, feeling his heart flutter with hunger and weariness like an imprisoned bird. The troops would probably be called off when darkness came. He might be able to keep marching then if he could stay near the road within sight of headlights, for they would almost certainly expect him to hide for the night, as he had imagined himself that he would have to do.

He walked on through a clump of trees and, to his surprise, saw he was within twenty yards of the road. It stretched dull grey into the deepening evening mist. He stood, watching it. There was no sign or sight of anyone.

A bird of some kind hopped out of the grass on the other side of the road, looked carefully to left and right, and then flew down on to the oil-stained surface. A hedgehog had been run over and it lay, burst red intestines against brownish, spikey fur. The bird pecked greedily at the beast's entrails.

Nothing else, and no one else.

Love felt safer, and started to walk again, keeping the road on his left. The undergrowth seemed thicker now, and he tripped once or twice, and crawled to his feet again. And all the time the light was failing until, quite sharply, the short twilight dwindled and Love was walking in deepening darkness.

Once, a car came past, going up the hill, travelling slowly. Its headlamps touched the trees with amber, and he waited until its tail lights had died with the noise of its engine, and then he went on.

He came to a Z-bend and halted, glad of any excuse to rest. It was just light enough for him to see that the hill fell away to the right in an almost perpendicular precipice. Far beneath him, the tops of the cedar trees were laced with shreds of pale mist. He had either to go down this cliff in the dark, and climb up on the other side, or he had to cross the road, and risk being seen.

Love lay down among the ferns and dusty bracken, watching the road for any movement. He felt too tired, and it was now too dark, to risk climbing down the rocks and up again. On the other hand, the road was empty, and therefore relatively safe. He'd run across it and, once round the curve, he could take to the forest again.

Then he must have dozed, because he was suddenly aware of the coldness of the night, and the fact that the moon was riding high and full, and the road gleamed under it like a long strip of pewter.

His joints had stiffened, his throat felt rough as a rasp, and, as he moved, he shivered. He stood up slowly, stretched himself, dusted down his ruined clothes, and walked out on to the road.

His heels rang like the taps of a steel drum band on its hard metal surface, echoing from the rock wall. He crossed quickly in half a dozen paces, flattened himself in the welcome shadow of the rocks, and listened. Cliffs soared up almost vertically on his left, the rock and earth still faintly warm to his hands. On the right, he could see nothing but a row of white stones that marked the rim of the road like huge teeth, and then the silent darkness of the drop beyond them.

He began to walk.

His shoes slipped on the loose gravel at the side of the road, and he paused, holding his breath in case someone challenged him, but he could hear nothing but his own blood beating in his ears. He walked on more cautiously. Another few hundred yards, and he should be clear of the corkscrew corners and able to sink back into the cover and silence of the forest.

Then, in the distance, far away behind him, like the faint hum of an approaching bee, he heard an engine: a vehicle of some kind was coming up the hill.

It was probably still several miles away, but he would have to hurry, or it might overtake him before he could leave the road, and foot travellers would be so rare as to invite suspicion, even if this were an ordinary lorry and not an Army. truck.

Love began to run, shambling up the hill, his heart pounding within him. The road turned and bent, each corner leading to another. He had imagined there was only one bend; there seemed to be dozens.

The noise was nearer now. He heard it change tone as the driver dropped down a gear. The smooth, sheer wall of rock on his left gave him nowhere to hide; he slowed to a walk, believing that someone walking must appear less suspicious than a man on the run at night.

With luck, the car or whatever it was would pass him; the driver might even stop and offer him a lift. He was imagining trouble where no trouble existed. Don't cross your bridges until you come to them - and, even then, do your best to find another way over the river.

Now Love could see the glow of yellow headlights, reflected from the rocks, throwing his own shadow ahead of him, faintly at first, and then more deeply, as the car came nearer. One last curve of the road and he would be able to dash for the forest, for the precipice had dwindled to a gentle slope, and he could see the dim outline of trees a hundred yards ahead of him - but could he make that hundred yards?

Love increased the length of his stride, trying to walk as fast as he could without appearing to hurry. Ninety yards. Eighty-five. No more than seventy, surely? Perhaps even sixty. The lights were brighter behind him now, yellow and unwinking, but he would make it; he had to.

He came round the last corner of the hill, and the whole road ahead of him exploded into one immense concentrated incandescent blaze, bright as the sun.

He put up his right hand to shield his eyes, blinded and numb with shock, and leaned against the cliffside, feeling it rough and warm through his thin suit.

His heart thundered like a cannon. He had walked straight into a trap His pursuers must have calculated that he would have to cross the road eventually, for he could not risk climbing down the cliff in the dark. And as soon as they heard his feet on the road, they had known he was finished.

They had swiftly set up their searchlight, and no doubt radioed down to the driver of this car waiting at the bottom of the hill for their message. The driver was steering him into captivity, as gently and inexorably as a sheep is guided into a pen.

From the unseen darkness behind the blinding light, Love heard the hard metallic rattle of rifle bolts. Someone shouted a command in a language he did not understand, and hobnailed boots tramped on the tarmac.

The car was close behind him now, and he could smell its hot engine, and the fumes from its exhaust blown in on the wind.

He started to walk, because he could not stand for ever. The car followed him at a walking pace. He was only feet from the searchlight, feeling the raw white heat of its beam on his face, when, through the darkness behind him, he heard a voice he remembered so well.

'You silly bugger,' said Parkington genially. 'Why don't you come inside? I'll give you a lift.'

CHAPTER TWELVE

It was Sir Robert L—'s first day back in the office after his visit to Bonn, and he was not in a particularly good temper.

There was no reason why he should be. For a start, the A30 up from Salisbury had been unexpectedly busy, and even his Bentley Continental had been unable to overtake the long lines of tankers running together in that particularly narrow stretch of the old Roman road between Stock-bridge and the southern end of the Basingstoke by-pass.

Consequently, he had hit all the early morning commuter traffic outside London, and it was nearly ten o'clock when, feeling rather frayed around the edges, he had reached the sanctuary of his office in Whitehall.

Its three telephones - one green to the Foreign Office; red, the direct line to the Prime Minister's personal office, and the third connecting him with his adjutant - had been ringing almost incessantly, with people asking questions to which he could provide no instant answers.

And, as the head of the Secret Intelligence Service, it was his job to have ready answers (or so various Ministers kept telling him) so that they could deal with their persecutors in Parliament in a casual/reassuring/patronizing way, according to their temperament, their guile, and the validity of the questions concerned.

Also, the Bonn visit had been neither a complete success, nor a complete failure. He had given some points, and he had gained some in return. It was too early to say whether he had won much or lost more, or whether he had just been running very hard to keep running on the spot. And at his age, he didn't want to run at all, either mentally or physically.

His buzzer hummed on his desk.

'Come in,' he said briefly, not wishing to see anyone, but hopeful that perhaps someone might have at least a few answers to his problems.

His adjutant, a one-armed colonel, came in rather diffidently from his outer office.

'That Beirut business, sir,' he began.

'What about it?' asked Sir Robert, neither committing himself by the question to any policy, or to any admission that he knew what had happened in Beirut, or greatly cared, if he did know. By such outward calmness he had successfully concealed serious inner doubts and misgivings all his adult life; there was no need to change now.

'Foreign Minister's PPS has been on the blower, sir. He wants to know how much part we really had in it. Or was it a CIA job? Or just something the newspaper people on the spot have blown up on a day when not much was happening?'

'Well, the newspapers certainly made a meal of it,' agreed Sir Robert, spreading out the clippings under his beautifully manicured, spatulate fingers. This gave him the opportunity to glance at them, to absorb the nub of their news.

He read one headline aloud as though he knew it off by heart, but, in fact, he had only seen it seconds before the colonel came into the room.

'"SECRET AGENT BODY-SWITCH SAVES EGYPTIAN LEADER'S LIFE: MID-EAST TEMPERS COOL AFTER BEIRUT PLOT FAILS."'

He read on.

'"Almost certain civil war between pro-Arab and pro-Israel factions in Beirut was averted this morning by an amazing coup, believed to have been inspired by a British secret agent.

'"All Beirut was gay with flags, and crowds crammed the streets, to celebrate the state visit of Dr Ahmed Hussein, Egypt's Minister of Culture and Development - and top Egyptian politician to visit Lebanon for several years.

' "Lebanese Secret Police, acting, it is said, on a tip from British Intelligence sources, persuaded Dr Hussein not to travel on the route originally planned, because an assassination attempt was feared.

' "Instead, the 48-years old, balding, portly Minister was hustled into an ambulance with black glass windows, and driven in secret to the Prime Minister's office in the Great Seraglio where the Lebanese President and members of the Diplomatic Corps waited to receive him.

' "The original convoy of cars, with police outriders, took the advertised route. But instead of Dr Ahmed Hussein in the back seat of his Cadillac phaeton, a tailor's dummy dressed in Army uniform, took his place.

"'As the entourage turned the sharp corner from Rue Royale into Avenue du Pont, slowing almost to walking pace for the right-angle turn,' gunmen - believed to be hidden on top of an overlooking skyscraper - pumped bullets through the plate-glass windows.

' "At that precise moment, as the dummy slumped for-ward, the real Egyptian Minister was being introduced to the Lebanese Cabinet half a mile away.

' "Prompt action by Lebanese police and troops in sealing off the capital, the airport, and all frontier crossings into neighbouring countries, means - so informed sources tell me - that the hired would-be assassins cannot escape."'

Sir Robert paused.

'I wouldn't put it as high as that,' he said mildly, looking up. 'For my money, they'll be over the border long since, or off in a speedboat to a submarine. But it makes good reading, I don't deny that. And it's certainly in our favour, for a changed

'But is it true, sir?' asked the colonel anxiously. He had his pension to consider, and his only daughter was getting married on

Saturday and so he had a lot of expense. Any failure that might affect him was a worry. 'That's what the Foreign Secretary wants to know. He's got to answer two questions on it in the House this evening.'

'What is truth?' asked Sir Robert grandly. 'It probably contains grains of truth. Frankly, if I were an Egyptian Minister visiting Lebanon, I would certainly prefer to travel in an ambulance alive, rather than in some state procession as a sitting target.'

'Tell him it's true in substance. Even the greatest lie usually has a grain of truth somewhere. Like the bit of grit inside an oyster that makes the pearl.'

'Very good, sir,' said the colonel, telling himself that Sir Robert was a foxy old bastard, but a clever one. He withdrew to draft his memo.

Sir Robert sat back in his chair. He felt more relaxed now. He had shown himself to be in command of events without really doing anything, or knowing anything more about them than what he could read in a daily newspaper. MacGillivray would fill him in on the details. After all, he had been away for nearly a week. Thank God for MacGillivray. He pressed a switch.

Miss Jenkins answered.

'The Colonel,' said Sir Robert briefly; he hated speaking to subordinates.

'He's not in his office, sir.'

'Well, where is he?'

Surely he could not be ill or on leave? He'd just had leave; he was always having leave, trudging like a damn fool round Scotland looking for his ideal house.

'He's at Claridges, sir.'

'Claridges? What's happening there?'

Could it be something he was missing? Some diplomatic invitation he had received and never acknowledged? His mind backtracked with the speed of an instant survival kit.

'He's with Mrs Wilmot, sir. In her suite. Shall I connect you?'

'Mrs Wilmot?'

He repeated the name slowly to give the impression he knew all about her. But who the hell could she be? Must be someone involved with something that had happened when he was away.

'No. Ask him to ring me when he gets back. I don't want to speak to him on an open line.'

Sir Robert replaced the receiver, lit a cheroot, and looked out beyond the Adam fireplace, through the double-glazed windows towards Trafalgar Square, where the pigeons strutted about, puff-chested, around Landseer's lions, as though they owned the freehold.

How fine to be a pigeon, he thought, with nothing worse to face than the problem of enough crusts to eat, a ledge to shelter on a rainy night.

Then he thought of his farm in Wiltshire; his Bentley; that Rousseau painting he'd bought at Sotheby's only last week, and the approaching rosy glow of congratulations on his department's coup, about which he had known nothing, still knew nothing, and probably would never know much, but which, after all, would reflect favourably to his credit because he was head man. Probably, on balance, being Sir Robert L— was better than being a pigeon; not much, may-be, but possibly a little, just a little.

Two miles west, across London, in an equally soundproofed room, but one rather more elegantly furnished, MacGillivray sat in an expensive replica Louis XIV chair, balancing a delicate Spode cup of black coffee on the arm.

Mrs Wilmot, in a trouser suit that had cost more than twice his monthly salary, sat opposite him, smoking a cigarette decorated with her initials. A little gold tray on the ormolu table by her side was filled with cigarette stubs wearing red ends to match her lipstick. She looked pale, and fiddled nervously with her necklace.

'I asked you to stay in London, Mrs Wilmot,' said MacGillivray slowly, like an auctioneer beginning to warm-up to a long speech, 'simply because it is much easier to say some things face to face. Unter vier augen, as the Germans say, between four eyes. Or, as the Americans like to put it, rather more crudely, eyeball to eyeball. You've heard the news from Lebanon?'

'You mean, that my husband didn't kill that Egyptian after all?' she asked. Her eyebrows were two question marks in an unlined alabaster forehead on which Time had yet to write his name. But he would, thought MacGillivray, he would. And the signature might start at that meeting.

'That, and a bit more that you won't read in the papers,' he went on. 'We have our own sources of information, Mrs Wilmot. After all, it is our business.'

'Tell me,' she said. 'Tell me everything.'

'I can't do that,' he said, 'because I don't know everything. You know more about some aspects of the business than I do, obviously.

'In my line of country, we piece little things together, like you might do with a broken Willow Pattern plate. There may be some bits missing in the end, but the general picture's there. First, Mrs Wilmot, a few questions that may seem a little personal - maybe a lot personal - but which I must get out of the way.'

He paused like an actor for a cue. She gave it to him.

'Go on,' she said.

'You are having an affair with a younger man, Mrs Wilmot, aren't you? I understand his first name is David, and he has an Alfa Romeo sports car?' -

'Go on,' she repeated, her face showing neither admission nor denial. How the hell could he know about David? Or did everyone know - did John know?

'You feel a little mean about this, but not too mean. Because, let's be realistic, you thought your husband might be having the odd little affair himself. And, of course, he was twenty years older than you.'

'Was?' she repeated quickly. "What do you mean, was?'

'What I say, Mrs Wilmot. Was. I'm sorry to have to tell you that your husband had a heart attack in Lebanon. He is dead.'

'How can you possibly know?'

'On the very best authority. From his doctor — and yours, I believe. Jason Love. An old friend of mine, too, as it happens. Dr Love was with him. He's still out there. But he leaves for France tomorrow. St Raphael. He's sending back your husband's papers, his watch, a few other personal things he had on him.'

'You're making this up,' said Mrs Wilmot. Her voice wound itself up a couple of keys. Her face, for the first time, looked strained and tired, as she would be in twenty years' time, when her looks were leaving her, when her younger lover had fled elsewhere, when even the Alfa was old.

'You're making it up. You want to trap me into saying something, into making some admission. Isn't that what you're after?'

Her voice sounded harsh and shrill as a circular saw. MacGillivray hoped she was not going to become hysterical. He took a sip of coffee. It had grown cold, and the grounds tasted bitter on his tongue. He did not even bother to answer her. He went on:

'You were having this affair, and someone - you thought your husband - put a private eye on you to follow you. There were infra-red photographs, accounts of lunches in the country, hotel rooms booked for an afternoon. A familiar pattern, Mrs Wilmot. I can give you dates and places, if you want them?'

She shook her head almost imperceptibly. The past was all past now; the present seemed terrible enough.

'But it wasn't your husband who did this. It was one of his competitors. In fact, his only real competitor. A man named Massine, who is also known as Diaz.

'Diaz, as you came to know him, met you in London - by chance, as you thought at first - but in fact he'd had you followed into a restaurant where you were going to lunch with David, simply so that he could appear to bump into you.

'You'd met him once before with your husband, so you did know each other by sight. He made a deal with you, Mrs Wilmot. For his own reasons, which he didn't specify at that time, he wanted your husband in Beirut. He said there was a political campaign here against him. He would be safe there. He asked for your help to get him out there. He made out he was your husband's friend - then, at least.'

MacGillivray paused. She jumped into the pause like a swimmer into a heated pool.

'I wanted to help John,' she said. 'I really did. You must believe me.'

'I believe you,' said MacGillivray in a level voice. 'But when you are as old as I am, Mrs Wilmot, when you've been in my line of country as long as I have, you begin to recognize that, to different people, truth is like plasticine. We all bend it into shapes to suit ourselves. I believe you, Mrs Wilmot, but maybe others would have their doubts. But let me go on.

'Anonymous phone calls and letters now began to arrive, but your husband ignored them. Then they got under his skin, and finally, you persuaded him to go to Lebanon. Maybe you didn't realize that Diaz was behind all the letters and the calls. Or maybe you did, and you just ignored it.

'He thought you were helping him. Perhaps you were. You were also helping yourself, because Diaz made it clear that he knew a great deal about your extra-marital activities. Two serious affairs, and the occasional brief liaison, as when you travelled alone to Venice last spring, and then that time in Cyprus when you met a handsome airline pilot.

'I know that this is a permissive age, but would your husband permit this, Mrs Wilmot? You thought not. And who else would keep you in the way he could keep you? Certainly not David. So you did what Diaz asked, and your husband was finally persuaded to go. He discussed it with Dr Jackson, who thought a change would do him good. Doctors always say that - especially if their patients' wives put the idea into their heads first.

'When you went out to Beirut with your daughter to see your husband, he told you about this deal he was anxious to tie up - for the North African coast. He was very keen on this. It would be the crowning achievement for someone who had started with nothing, and who'd lost both his parents when he was a boy.

'He told you he'd been promised this deal by Ahmed Hussein, who was then Minister for Land. When you came back, Diaz wanted to know how your husband was. To try and buy him off your back, you told him about this deal.

'Then you realized he was also in the running for the deal, and desperate to get the concession. By telling him about your husband's lead, you had signed your husband's death warrant. You might not love the man - you probably didn't - but you still had some shreds of loyalty.

'So you tried to warn him. You'd even be willing to tell him about your lovers — well, one of them — because now you realized you were dealing with real danger, mortal danger. But, of course, you couldn't get in touch with him. Diaz saw to that. He had the ingenious idea of giving two of his men forged papers and passing them off as police officers. A shrewd move psychologically, for your husband was not a British subject, and had this fear of being deported.

'Your husband did what they told him - so you couldn't phone him. And he wouldn't answer your letters or telegrams. You were afraid to fly out there yourself in case you were followed as you probably would have been.

'Your only hope was to get someone else to go out for you. You've a girl friend who's an air hostess on the Moroccan run. And your brother was in Morocco, coming back on the hippie road from the Himalayas. He'd always been abroad since your marriage, so he'd never even met your husband.

'So you asked this stewardess friend to see your brother and persuade him to go to Beirut instead of you.

'That young man was too far stoned to remember any message, and it was too risky to give him a letter to carry. So when he was in a coma, she wrote a number on his scalp under his hair. Your husband would recognize it.

'He knew nothing about radio himself, but his chauffeur knew a lot. It was his hobby, and this was his call sign. Your husband could radio him direct. You could then get a message through to him that would be virtually impossible for anyone to pick up, simply because they wouldn't know it was being sent. Isn't that what you told me in the Midland Widows office, more or less?'

'Yes.'

'Your stewardess friend is a well-read girl. She knew the story of the slave in one of the Greek and Persian wars thousands of years ago who carried a message in the same way.

'She sent a telegram to your husband on her own initiative, hinting he should cut the visitor's hair, but he never received it.'

'How do you know?' Mrs Wilmot asked.

'Again, on the best authority. His doctor. Your doctor. Diaz's men picked up your brother on arrival at the flat. They'd probably got his name from a contact in Immigration at the airport. I don't expect they meant to kill him, but years of mainlining didn't leave him a lot of resistance.

'While all this was happening, as a second string, you persuaded, Dr Love to take a holiday in Beirut with five hundred pounds expenses - a lot of money to him, not so very much to you. Right?'

'So far.'

'There's not a lot more,' said MacGillivray. 'We had a tip that this Egyptian was going to get bumped off. And we had a man out there who knows Love. They worked together.

'Your husband was to have been the fall-guy, the scape-goat. He was drugged, given a rifle, posted on top of a sky-scraper, and told when to shoot. He believed he was doing this on behalf of the British Secret Service, God help us, and as a result, he'd be allowed back to Britain, and given British nationality.

'It was all lies, of course, but the sort of lies he'd believe, because he wanted to believe them - just as the poor, lonely, rich bastard wanted to believe the lies you told him, that you loved him. We all believe what we want to believe, Mrs Wilmot, and sometimes it's fatal.

'Anyhow, Dr Love went up there on the roof with him. They managed to get away.'

'Then how did John die?' she asked. 'And where?'

'In a forest about twenty miles out of Beirut. He and Love were trying to reach the border, but your husband wasn't as well a man as he seemed.

'All those deals without backing when he was beginning. Then the worry of millions of borrowed capital - buying things with money he didn't have, selling things he only owned on option.

'He had to pay a price for that. The bill came in out there in the forest. His heart was already affected. He just couldn't make the distance.'

'Did he ever find out about—' she paused for a moment, and swallowed. 'About - David?'

'No,' said MacGillivray. 'He never did, not so far as I know. Nor about any of the others. He may have suspected. I don't know. But most men like to trust someone. He chose to trust you. Is that important now?'

She shrugged.

'If anyone had to tell him, I would rather it had been me,' she said.

MacGillivray nodded, and poured himself another cup of coffee. Odd, the quirks a belated conscience takes, he thought, but now Wilmot would never know and he would never worry. Confessions were only important in this world, not in the next; if there was a next.

'That's it, then,' he said. 'Case closed.'

And it was; so far as they were concerned.

'What about Dr Love?' she asked. 'And your man out there? Did they come through?'

MacGillivray glanced at his watch.

'Yes,' he said. 'At this exact moment they should be in Cyprus.'

Actually, they were still in the RAF VC10 several thousand feet above Limassol, waiting for Control to give the pilot the all clear to come in.

They sat side by side in the grey canvas seats, strapped in, feet out, heads back. Far beneath them, the feathery trees of the Cyprus foothills stretched out along white beaches towards the even whiter rim of surf.

They each held a glass in their right hand.

Love took a sip of his whisky, and then turned to Parking-ton.

'But how the hell did you know I was up in that forest?' he asked.

Parkington took out his cigarette case, opened it, removed a cigarette, tapped it on the side, handed the case to Love.

'Thanks, but I don't smoke them,' said Love.'

'Only my own.'

'I know that,' said Parkington. 'Just wanted you to look at the case. That told me.'

'How?'

'When I was in the ambulance, I gave you this cigarette case - I said to stop anyone whipping it from me in hospital. But that wasn't the main reason. It's got a bleeper inside the lid.

'I've another case in my back pocket that can pick up the signals from this.

'Once I'd discharged myself from hospital, I committed the unforgiveable sin in our business. I contacted our man in British Embassy - the man who never exists - who's either a passport control officer, a fifth secretary, the assistant trade commissioner, or maybe the lavatory attendant. He's the man we only call on when everything else has gone wrong, when there's no one left. The ultimate long stop.

'Our man in the doll's hospital had already got through to the Lebanese your news about the projected killing of Ahmed Hussein. Our Embassy boyo amplified this, and the Lebanese agreed to switch their route and put a dummy in the car.'

'Did they pick up the real gunmen in the crowd?'

Parkington poured himself another whisky from the bottle on the floor beside him.

'Be your age, Doctor,' he said. 'How could they in all that mob? But they were worried about your safety - so they gave me a car. The troops were out after you, not to kill you, but to rescue you, you stupid bugger.'

'My best friend should have told me,' said Love. 'It would have saved a hell of a lot of effort. Might even have saved old Wilmot's life.'

'Can't have everything,' said Parkington, lighting a cigarette. 'Maybe old Wilmot wasn't so keen on coming back. Would you be - even with all that money? A bad heart, your wife having it off with other men half your age? All that adds up to a great big nothing for any rich husband to come home to.'

'You may be right,' said Love, remembering Wilmot's views on the subject. 'But it's still better than being dead. What about Diaz, then? What happens to him?'

Parkington shrugged.

'What can happen to him? He'll survive. He'll peel off a few thousand in bribes, one way and the other, to keep a jump ahead of the Lebanese law, which possibly isn't the most active in the world. But no one will really have anything on him. He's too smart.

'The Diazes of this world, my good doctor, are always too smart - for a time. But the wheel turns, you know. He can't win every battle. The Communists won't be too happy with the way things have gone, either. He'll get his, one day. They'll see to that, if no one else does. Maybe he's got his now. Maybe he's got pox, for all you know.'

'It's a beautiful thought,' said Love, thinking it. 'So who has the development concession?'

'Who indeed? Probably someone we've never heard of. Certainly not Wilmot, who's dead. Obviously not Diaz, because the wrong man's still in power. It's back to square one over that little lot.'

'So what have we achieved?' asked Love.

'You tell me,' said Parkington, stubbing out his cigarette as the 'No Smoking' sign came up. 'I often wonder, in these things. We take one step forward, two steps back, and a jump to the side.

'Diaz hasn't won, Wilmot hasn't won. So who's lost? Not you - or me. You've had your five hundred quid from Wilmot's wife, but you've lost your bigger fee from Wilmot. I've got a burst ulcer, but I'm still alive.

'Sir Robert will bask in the credit for something he didn't even know was happening. The Egyptian still lives - probably keeping up his strength to meet another bullet somewhere else. We've all won a little and we've all lost a little.

We're just really running on the spot. And that's my message in this particular unhappy year of Our Lord.'

The plane was coming down fast now, and Love braced himself against the first bump of the tyres on the sun-dried tarmac.

'That's life,' he said. 'It's like tennis - when there's no score. Love-all.'

'Or words to that effect,' agreed Parkington, and said them.

Beirut, Lebanon; Swallowcliffe, Wilts.

ABOUT THE AUTHOR

James Leasor

James Leasor was one of the bestselling British authors of the second half of the 20th Century. He wrote over 50 books including a rich variety of thrillers, historical novels and biographies.

His works included the critically acclaimed The Red Fort, the story of the Indian Mutiny of 1957, The Marine from Mandalay, Boarding Party (made into the film The Sea Wolves starring Gregory Peck, David Niven and Roger Moore), The Plague and the Fire, and The One that Got Away (made into a film starring Hardy Kruger). He also wrote Passport to Oblivion (which sold over 4 million copies around the World and was filmed as Where the Spies Are, starring David Niven), the first of nine novels featuring Dr Jason Love, a Cord car owning Somerset GP called to aid Her Majesty's Secret Service in foreign countries, and another bestselling series about the Far Eastern merchant Robert Gunn in the 19th century. There were also sagas set in Africa and Asia, written under the pseudonym Andrew MacAllan, and tales narrated by an unnamed vintage car dealer in Belgravia, who drives a Jaguar SS100.

www.jamesleasor.com Follow on Twitter: @jamesleasor

BOOKS IN THIS SERIES

Dr Jason Love
The West Country doctor, vintage car expert - particularly the pre-War American classic, the Cord - and part time secret agent.

One of the best-selling thriller series from the 1960s through to the 1990s. Published in 19 languages.

Described by the Sunday Times as the "Heir Apparent to the golden throne of Bond"

Passport To Oblivion

Passport to Oblivion is the first case book of Dr. Jason Love . . . country doctor turned secret agent. Multi-million selling, published in 19 languages around the world and filmed as Where the Spies Are starring David Niven.

Passport To Peril

Passport to Peril is Dr Jason Love's second brilliant case history in suspense. An adventure that sweeps from the gentle snows of Switzerland to the freezing peaks of the Himalayas, and ends in a blizzard of violence, hate, and lust on the roof of the world. Guns, girls and gadgets all play there part as the Somerset doctor, old car expert and amateur secret agent uncovers a mystery involving the Chinese intelligence service and a global blackmail ring.

'A runaway success story'
Daily Mirror

Passport In Suspense

West German submarine 'Seehund' is hijacked during N.A.T.O. manoeuvres in the North Sea. Neo-Nazis want it for a daring operation; seeking out pockets of escaped war criminals in South America, they promise the elderly men free trips home under new identities if they will detonate three atomic devices at carefully positioned points on the sea bed. The subsequent chain reaction will then drastically affect the world's climate, turning both Britain and America into arctic wastelands.

Holidaying in the Bahamas, Dr. Jason Love witnesses at close range the shooting of a beautiful brunette in a speedboat. She had been mistaken for Israeli spy Shamara, assigned to investigate millionaire Paul V. Steyr. Blind and insane, Steyr is the mastermind behind the terrible neo-Nazi plot. Only Love, teamed with Shamara, can stop him...

'The action is supersonic throughout.'
The Guardian

'A superb example of modern thriller writing at its best'
Sunday Express

Passport For A Pilgrim

Dr Love's fourth supersonic adventure.

Dr Jason Love is going to attend a medical conference in Damascus and one of his patients asks him to find out how his daughter died in a car accident on the outskirts of Syria's capital. But all is not as it seems. Fulfilling a simple favour turns into a nightmare for the Somerset doctor, turned part-time secret agent…

'Super suspense and, as usual, Love finds a way.'
Daily Express

'Bullets buzz like a beehive kicked by Bobby Charlton'
Sunday Mirror

'Action is driven along at a furious pace from the moment the doctor sets foot in Damascus.. a quite ferocious climax. Unputdownable.'
Sheffield Morning Telegraph

'Thriller rating: High'
The Sun

A Week Of Love

Seven short stories featuring Dr Jason Love, the country doctor, old car lover and sometime spy in which he solves cases in Giglio off Italy, Praia da Luz in Portugal, Amsterdam, the Highlands, Spain, England and at home in Stogumber in Somerset. Travelling in his famous supercharged Cord again and again battles a range of villains in his efforts to crack a myriad of mysteries.

Love And The Land Beyond

On vacation in the Algarve, with his precious Cord car, the country doctor, and occasional spy, Jason Love, accepts an invitation from a rich friend of a friend. This leads to a web of double-cross, murder and mystery, connecting deaths in Oregon and Portugal, in a race to secure smuggled vital secret formulas, against East Germans and the Mob.

Frozen Assets

Dr Jason Love, a West Country physician, is regarded as one of the world's experts on the pre-World War II American Cord car. With its long, coffin-nosed bonnet with two stainless steel exhaust pipes protruding on either side, its steeply raked split windscreen, front wheel drive, retractable headlights and integral construction, it is not so much a car as a personal statement. When an insurance company is asked to insure for 10 million pounds a Cord Roadster in Pakistan, it asks Dr Love to fly out and check why the car is worth so much.

What appears to be a routine trip becomes a nightmare.

The discovery of the body of an early traveller - preserved for centuries in an Afghanistan glacier — leads to a hunt to uncover deposits of rhodium, one of the world's rarest minerals. Its discovery could revolutionize Afghanistan's economic future — but can Love get there before the Russians?

'Splendid sit-up-all-night-to-finish fun' Sunday Telegraph

Love Down Under

Before Jason Love - the West Country doctor with a passion for the 1930s American Cord car flies out to visit Charles Robinson, a fellow Cord enthusiast, in Cairns, Australia, someone in his Wiltshire village entrusts him with a straightforward mission: to find the Before Jason Love - the West Country doctor with a passion for the 1930s American truth behind a relation's mysterious drowning accident off Cairns.
But when he arrives down under, the simple enquiry rapidly leads to other, more disturbing questions: what is the fearful secret hidden in Robinson's past that has terrified him for years, and who are the shadowy figures he dreads will find him? Who is

the man with metal hands who can see as well in darkness as by day, and why should a total stranger attempt to murder Dr Love on the top of Ayers Rock?

Jason Love, in his latest and most baffling case, must battle to find the answers to these and other questions as the wheels of suspense and surprise spin as fast as the tyres on his supercharged Cord.

'A mixture of Ambler, a touch of Graham Greene, mixed well with the elixir of Bond and Walter Mitty'
Los Angeles Times

BOOKS BY THIS AUTHOR

Follow The Drum

'Once in a while, a book comes along that grabs you by the throat, shakes you, and won't let go until you have read through to the last page.' - Hal Burton, Newsday

'Follow the Drum is superb reading entertainment' - Best Sellers India, in the mid-nineteenth century, was virtually run by a British commercial concern, the Honourable East India Company, whose directors would pay tribute to one Indian ruler and then depose another in their efforts to maintain their balance sheet of power and profit. But great changes were already casting shadows across the land, and when a stupid order was given to Indian troops to use cartridges greased with cow fat and pig lard (one animal sacred to the Hindus and the other abhorrent to Moslems) there was mutiny. The lives of millions were changed for ever including Arabella MacDonald, daughter of an English regular officer, and Richard Lang, an idealistic nineteen-year-old who began 1857 as a boy and ended it a man.

Mandarin-Gold

It was the year of 1833 when Robert Gunn arrived on the China coast. Only the feeblest of defenses now protected the vast and proud Chinese Empire from the ravenous greed of Western traders, and their opening wedge for conquest was the sale of forbidden opium to the native masses.

This was the path that Robert Gunn chose to follow... a path that led him through a maze of violence and intrigue, lust and treachery, to a height of power beyond most men's dreams — and to the ultimate depths of personal corruption.

Here is a magnificent novel of an age of plunder — and of a fearless freebooter who raped an empire.

'Highly absorbing account of the corruption of an individual during a particularly sordid era of British imperial history,' The Sunday Times

Ntr: Nothing To Report

"Superbly authentic atmosphere, taut narration. Mr Leasor would have delighted Kipling." - The Observer

"The most clinically accurate description of India and Burma about the time of the Kohima breakthrough I have yet seen." - Daily Telegraph

"Mr. Leasor brings to 'Nothing to Report' a journalist's straightforwardness, and an on-the-spot sureness about how frightened men behave, that are both refreshing and effective." - Spectator

In the early spring of 1944, when the British fortunes of war in the East were low, the Japanese invaded India.

Viewed against some other catastrophes of the war, this was only a minor invasion; an intrusion of some 20 miles or so on the North-East frontier. But, at the time, it was considered very important indeed. Political discontent was rife in India and there was constant fear that the British would withdraw as they had already done in Malaya and Burma. If this invasion were not checked and the Japs flung back there might be revolution in India.

The story concerns a draft that was sent to help repel the invasion. An odd lot, that draft, and not quite sure what it was all about. The author tells of men in adversity, some shrewd, some cynical, some loved and others lonely. In the end they sent back the message N T R—Nothing to Report. The reason behind this, illustrating all the futility of war and its consequences, is related in this moving and realistic novel.

The One That Got Away

'A good story, crisply told' – New York Times

Franz von Werra was the only German prisoner of war to escape and return to Germany after being captured by the Allies. An incredibly charismatic, inventive and self-confident man, he was a Luftwaffe ace shot down in the Battle of Britain. The One that Got Away tells the full and exciting story of his two daring escapes in England and his third and successful escape: a leap from the window of a prisoners' train in Canada. Enduring snow and frostbite, he crossed into the then neutral United States. James Leasor's book is based on von Werra's own dictated account of his adventure, coupled with first-hand accounts from many of those involved, and makes for a compelling read. First published in 1953 it was probably the first book about WWII that gave an objective and fair view to both sides, and as such, was an immediate sensation. It was filmed in 1956 with Hardy Kruger starring as von Werra.

The Millionth Chance: The Story Of The R. 101

'Mr Leasor's account of a tragedy that ought not to have happened, is full and moving.' The Times

The R101 airship was thought to be the model for the future, an amazing design that was 'as safe as houses...except for the millionth chance'. On the night of 4 October 1930 that chance in a million came up however.
James Leasor brilliantly reconstructs the conception and crash of this huge ship of the air with compassion for the forty-seven

dead, including a cabinet minister – and only six survivors. One of the biggest disasters of British aviation history, which marked the end of commercial airships as a serious form of transport, this book also reads as a textbook of how state attempts to manage commercial ventures so often end in a disaster of one kind or another.

Printed in Great Britain
by Amazon